Praise for Nico Walker's

CHERRY

"[Walker] writes dialogue so musical and realistic you'll hear it in the air around you."
—*The New York Times Book Review*

"*Cherry*'s descriptions of Army life are as acerbic and unsparing—and often darkly hilarious—as the boot-camp scenes from *Full Metal Jacket*." —Mother Jones

"Heavily indebted to the profane blood, guts, bullets, and opiate-strewn absurdities dreamed up by Thomas McGuane, Larry Brown, and Barry Hannah, *Cherry* tells a story that feels infinitely more real, and undeniably tougher than the rest." —The A.V. Club

"Epic and exhilarating. . . . A remarkable accomplishment."
—*Harper's Magazine*

"Harrowing. . . . Propulsive. Fiction of late has rarely felt as bracing and lived-in as does Walker's *Cherry*. . . . The narrator is a generous, wry guide as he conducts this tour through hell." —*Los Angeles Review of Books*

NICO WALKER

CHERRY

Nico Walker is originally from Cleveland.
Cherry is his debut novel.

CHERRY

NICO WALKER
CHERRY

VINTAGE BOOKS
A Division of Penguin Random House LLC
New York

FIRST VINTAGE BOOKS MOVIE TIE-IN EDITION, MARCH 2021

Copyright © 2018 by Nicholas Walker

The Library of Congress has cataloged the Knopf edition as follows:
Name: Walker, Nico, author.
Title: Cherry : a novel / Nico Walker.
Description: First edition. | New York : Alfred A. Knopf, 2018.
Identifiers: LCCN 2017056634 (print) | 2017061588 (ebook)
Subjects: LCSH: Veterans—Fiction. | Drug addicts—Fiction. | Bank robberies—Fiction. | Identity (Psychology)—Fiction. | Iraq War, 2003–2011—Fiction. | BISAC: FICTION / Literary. | FICTION / Crime. | FICTION / War & Military. | GSAFD: Black humor (Literature). | Love stories.
Classification: LCC PS3623.A359552 C54 2018 | DDC 813/.6—dc23
LC record available at https://lccn.loc.gov/2017056634

VINTAGE MTI ISBN: 978-0-593-31548-4
VINTAGE BOOKS TRADE PAPERBACK ISBN: 978-0-525-43593-8
EBOOK ISBN: 978-0-525-52014-6

Author photograph courtesy of the author
Book design by Iris Weinstein

www.vintagebooks.com

Printed in the United States of America
10 9 8 7 6 5 4 3 2 1

Such use these times have got, that none must beg, but those
that have young limbs to lavish fast.

—THOMAS NASHE, *SUMMER'S LAST WILL AND TESTAMENT*

And it feels like the whole wide world is raining down on you.

—TOBY KEITH, "COURTESY OF THE RED, WHITE AND BLUE"

CONTENTS

AUTHOR'S NOTE

This book is a work of fiction.
These things didn't ever happen.
These people didn't ever exist.

CHERRY

PROLOGUE

Emily's gone to take a shower. The room's half-dark and I'm getting dressed, looking for a shirt with no blood on it, not having any luck. The pants are fucked too—cigarette burns in the crotches. All heroin chic, like I were famous already.

I go downstairs. Livinia pissed in the living room. There's a lake of piss. I say, "Livinia, goddamn," yet low enough that she won't hear me. She's a good dog; just we've been some fucks about house-training her.

I get the paper towels and a bottle of spray. There's a pack of Pall Malls on the kitchen counter. I shake one loose and light it on the stove. I check the rigs in the cupboard. The rigs in the cupboard are all blood-used and crooked, like instruments of torture. And there are two lengths of nylon in the cupboard, and a box of Q-tips and a digital scale, two spoons with old cottons in them. The needles on the rigs are dull, but they'll have to do. Emily has to be at school by ten, and it'll be a close-run thing. There won't be time to buy new rigs till afterward. It's twenty to nine but I think we'll make it. Black should be on time today, and he'll have something for us, so I'm not worried. I soak the piss up with the paper towels. I wipe the spot down with disinfectant, throw the used paper towels away.

Black pulls up in the driveway, and I let him in the side door. He hands me a .45 caliber pistol wrapped in a blue rag; and I say, "Let me hold another gram."

He says okay. "This'll make it seven twenty," he says.

"No problem."

I get the scale for him, and he sets to weighing out a gram. I say, "It was three light yesterday."

He knows. But he doesn't say anything. That's how they do it: they short you, they know they shorted you, and then they act like you're the one who's fucked up.

"Remember I called you about it?"

He remembers. But he's got to make things stupid because he's a dope boy.

I say, "C'mon. Don't be fucked up. You said I owe you money for it like it was right. And it isn't like I'm not gonna have you together real soon."

He says okay.

I go to the stairs and call up to Emily. "Hey, sweetheart. Black's here. Come down and do some of this dope with me."

She says she'll be down in a second.

I split the heroin up and set out some clean spoons: one for me, one for my best girl. I fill a glass with water and draw some out with a rig. I press the water out hard to break up any blood clots in the needle. I draw some more water out and add the water to the spoon. I hear Emily on the stairs, and I stir the heroin up with the water and go over to the stove. Emily says hi to Black. Black says hi. I say to Emily, "That's you over there on the counter."

She says, "Thank you, baby."

I turn the burner on low and cook the shot on the flame till the shot starts to hiss a little; then I take it off. Emily's rolled up a bit of cotton for me. She knows I'm in a hurry. Her hair is still wet. I take the cotton and drop it into the spoon. The cotton turns dark and swells. I draw the shot through the cotton and flick the air out of the rig. What's left in the rig looks pretty dark.

She says, "Are you doing all yours right now?"

"Uh-huh."

"Are you sure that's wise, baby?"

"It'll be alright. If I can't get more real soon then I don't see as it'll matter."

It hurts a little extra when the needle's dull like this. It can make it hard to hit a vein. But I hit a vein no problem, and this is a good omen. It's going to be a lucky day.

I shoot it.

The taste comes on first; then the rush starts. And it's all about right, the warmth bleeding down through me. Till the taste comes on stronger than usual, so strong it's sickening. And I figure it out: how I was always dead, my ears ringing.

I'M ON the kitchen floor and my balls are cold.

Emily's over me: "Come on."

I lift my head. I look at Emily. I look at Black. Black is backed against the counter. I want to laugh in his face, but I can't.

Emily's hands are cold. "Talk to me!"

My pants are undone and there are ice cubes in my underwear.

"Did you put ice cubes in my underwear?"

"I thought you were going to die," she says.

"The day's still young."

And I see she's about to cry. I say, "I'm sorry. I was only kidding. It was good of you to do that. There's no reason for you to be embarrassed. You did a good job."

"You fucking piece of shit!"

"Goddamn, lady. What do you want from me?"

I get up off the floor and I go to the sink and start digging the ice cubes out of my underwear. My cock can be seen; it's cold, not making a good show of it.

"If I'd have known this was gonna happen I'd have cut my pubic hair."

Black exits the kitchen.

"Are you okay?"

"I'm fine. Do yours, babe. We're gonna have to get you to school and it's almost nine."

I pick the ice trays up from off the floor. There are three different kinds of ice trays: green, blue, and white. I fill them all up in the sink and put them back in the freezer.

I FEEL bad about the dog sometimes. We had said, We'll get a dog and we won't be dope fiends anymore. So we got the dog. But we stayed dope fiends. And now we're dope fiends with a dog.

BLACK IS in the living room. I draw a picture for him: "This is Lancashire, this is Hampshire, this is Coventry. I'll park here, up past the stop sign, up past where it's one-way. You pick me up and take me over to Lancashire. Stop a couple buildings back from the corner and let me out. Then drive to the parking lot behind this storefront. Wait for me there. I'll be in and out real quick and I'll come around through here. Then all you'll have to do is drive me up to where I parked and let me out and that'll be that. We'll meet back here, split the money up, yada yada yada. Sounds good?"

"Yeah. Sounds good."

"So you're up for it then?"

"Yeah."

"Alright. Just give me a second and we'll go. Emily has to teach a class at ten."

She's in the kitchen, feeling better now.

I say, "I'm heading out. I'll be back in a minute."

She says, "Be careful."

I say I'll be careful.

WE LIVE on a street of red and white houses, where we don't belong, Emily and I. But we're happy enough, though we're often sad because we feel like we're losing everything.

Sometimes she gets to carrying on real loud and screaming at me about shit like I can help it; and I have to say to her, "What the fuck is wrong with you? Are you fucking crazy? Why are you making all this noise like you're being murdered? Are you being murdered? Am I murdering you? The neighbors will think I'm murdering you. And they'll call the fucking police. And the police'll come over here, and they'll see me, and they'll say, 'This guy looks like the one's been doing all these *fucking* robberies.' And then I'll go to fucking *prison*, and you'll feel terrible."

And sometimes she says she's sorry. Or sometimes she doesn't say anything. Or sometimes she punches me in the neck. And I'll say, "Ah, shit! Baby, why'd you punch me in the neck?"

And she'll run upstairs and lock herself in the bathroom and not come out for hours while I'm downstairs crying my eyes out over her. I love her so much it feels like dying every time she does that. She's a beauty and I tell her so all the time. I think she'd do anything for me.

I GET in the car and back out into the street. I'm behind Black at the light. I don't especially like Black because he's always on some bullshit. Still he's alright as far as dope boys go. All his brothers are in jail.

The arrow's green and Black makes a left. I follow him and pass him going up Cedar. The morning is overcast, but it's bright nonetheless—a bright overcast morning! In just-spring! And maybe it will stay this way forever. It would be nice, but it's a childish thing to wish for.

I go past South Taylor, past the pharmacy, past the abandoned KFC, past the Wendy's, past the high school, past the movies, past Lee Road, another pharmacy, more houses, and I'm twenty-five years old and I don't understand what it is that people do. It's as if all this were built on nothing, and nothing were holding this together. And then I hear people talk, and that just makes things worse.

I didn't make the light at Meadowbrook. I turn right at Coventry and follow it down to Hampshire and turn left. Here the street signs are painted to look like they've been tie-dyed. I used to live here before they did that. Then I couldn't anymore. It was like finding out you'd had some shit on your face the whole time you'd been talking.

I go up Hampshire where it's one-way and the brick apartment buildings on either side. Some of the apartments have balconies. And the trees are nice. I don't understand them either but I like them. I think I'd like them all. It'd have to be a pretty fucked-up tree in order for me not to like it.

The lane is two-ways with houses on either side after the stop. Some of the houses are duplexes, some are single-family homes, and they all look nice, and there are more trees, and bigger ones. I turn around in the street and park at the curb. Black pulls up and I get into his car. He cuts over and turns left onto Lancashire. He drives down and stops a little ways back from the corner. There is nothing more left to do now.

SOMEWHERE ALONG the way I got into this, and it's become a habit with me. One thing leads to another, leads to another. Things get better, they get worse. Then one day you're all the way thrown out, before you ever knew it was that serious. And you might be crazy, and you might have a gun, but even then it's usually no big deal.

I have the door open and the car chimes. "I'll be quick, so you might as well start now. You know where you're going, right?"

"Yeah."

"Just make the first left three times and you can't go wrong."

"Yeah."

"Are you sure you want to do this? Because you don't look like you do. It isn't too late to change your mind."

"I'm good."

"Okay. I'll meet you in the parking lot in about two minutes, give or take. Please be there."

He says, "I got this."
"Too easy, right?"
"Too easy."

I'M ON the sidewalk. I'm an Indians hat and a red scarf. I'm a blue hoodie and a white button-down shirt, some jeans, white Adidas, nothing out of the ordinary. The gun is in my waist. I pull the scarf up before I go by the ATMs, and the scarf covers the lower half of my face. It's a little late for it to do any good; I've been at this awhile now, and it's no secret what my face looks like. And here's a guy walking out and I'm at the door going in and I'm not worried. I'm through the door, and I have the gun out so everybody can see: "NO ALARMS. I'M A WANTED MAN. THEY'LL KILL ME."

I'm only kidding around. And I think everybody knows as much. But this is nevertheless a holdup, and I'll need some money before I'll leave.

I walk to the counter, with the gun down now so it's pointed at the floor. There's no sense in making a big deal out of this. One thing about holding up banks is you're mostly robbing women, so you don't ever want to be rude. About 80% of the time, so long as you're not rude, the women don't mind when you hold up the bank; probably it breaks up the monotony for them. Of course there are exceptions; about 20% have a bad outlook. Like there was one lady, looked like Janet Reno, wouldn't come off a cent more than $1800; she'd have seen everybody dead before she'd have come off another cent. She actually thought the bank was right. But this was a fanatic. Usually the tellers are pretty cool: you give them a note or tell them you're there to do a robbery, and they go in the cash drawers and lay the money on the counter, and you take it and you leave and that's all there is to it. Really it's very civilized. It's like a quiet joke you've shared with them. I say *joke* because in my case I don't imagine there was ever one to believe I'd do anything serious if push came to shove, though I do make it a point to try and at least look a little deranged because I don't want anyone getting in trouble on account of me. I have a lot of sadness in the face to make up for, so I have to make faces like I'm crazy or else people will think I'm a pussy. The risk you run is that sometimes people think you're a crazy pussy. But I have to do what I can; otherwise her manager might say to her, "Why'd you give that pussy the money? You're fired!" And she goes home and tells the kids there isn't going to be any Christmas.

It doesn't matter. Here is a teller. I say to her, "It's nothing personal."

And do you know we recognize each other! There was another robbery, on the West Side, Lakewood, maybe a month ago (the days run together). I robbed the other teller, but she was there too. It was funny how it happened. The other teller laid $1400 on the counter and said it was all she had. I remember the lie in her voice and thinking, This poor woman thinks I'm retarded. But then what did I care? She was pretty and it wasn't like I wanted everything, I only ever wanted what was enough for now.

So now I'm robbing this teller and we've recognized each other and it isn't a big deal. I don't think she's against me. I think maybe we're the same age. She's pale as I am. And her hair is dark. Her eyes are blue with flecks of gold in them, and I could be in love with her if things had been different. And then maybe we are somewhere.

I say, "I'm sorry."

"That's okay."

"What's your name?"

"Vanessa."

"I'm sorry, Vanessa."

"What's your name?"

"You're funny, Vanessa."

She empties out the cash drawers quickly, which is good as I'm not trying to hang out—there's a police station not a quarter mile from here. I take the stacks of money off the counter and shove them into my pockets. It looked alright: it doesn't matter, it isn't ever very much. It's like smash and grab, like hit and run: the important thing is to get away.

The important thing is to run fast.

I slam through the doors going out and round the corner, go past the ATMs. But I don't run back up the street; I turn and run behind the bank, past the dumpster, past the place where I used to live upstairs, then down the steps in back of the almost vegetarian restaurant, to the chain-link fence. And the parking lot is there, but I don't see Black. And I'm not at all surprised as this is typical fucking dope boy behavior.

The important thing is don't run.

My car is a block away and I think I can make it. So this isn't the end of the world. The parking lot's three sides where it's walls and the walls full of windows looking down on me. I take my hat off and put the gun in my hat. The gun's heavy on account of it's full of bullets. It's full of bullets because I can't imagine it being anything else. It's really too heavy to go carrying in a hat, but this arrangement will have to work as I have a ways to go and I don't want the gun trying to de-pants me in the getaway.

I walk down more steps that go into the parking lot, carrying my hat, with the gun in my hat, with my hat in my left hand. There's no one else in the parking lot when I cross it. The gun in my hat still isn't well hidden. I take my scarf off while I'm walking and I ball it up some and place it on top of the gun in my hat and it's a little better. Still there's the money sticking out of my pockets; I'll need to be careful that none falls out. I go left when I get to the sidewalk, and I'm walking up Hampshire. They'll be coming up Mayfield, and if they catch me I'm fucked.

Sometimes I wonder if youth wasn't wasted on me. It's not

that I'm dumb to the beauty of things. I take all the beautiful things to heart, and they fuck my heart till I about die from it. So it isn't that. It's just that something in me's always drawn me away, and it's the singular part of me, and I can't explain it.

There's nobody out here except me and one other guy; he's on the same sidewalk as I am, coming toward me from the other end of the block. We will meet eventually. I see he's dressed like an old-timer, and that's good: if he's old then I doubt he gives a fuck about what I'm up to. The important thing is don't act like you robbed a bank.

Act like you have places to go and people to see.

Act like you love the police.

Act like you never did drugs.

Act like you love America so much it's retarded.

But don't act like you robbed a bank.

And don't run.

The important thing is don't run.

The sirens coming up Mayfield now, and the grass is like a teenage girl. And the stoops!—the stoops are fucking wondrous! There's a fuckload of starlings gone to war over a big wet juicy bag of garbage—look at them go! The big swinging dick starling's got all the other starlings scared. He'll be the one who gets the choicest garbage!

This is the beauty of things fucking my heart. I wish I could lie down in the grass and chill for a while, but of course this is impossible, the gun in my hat could be a little obvious, the money sticking out of all my pockets too. And the sirens telling everyone I'm a fucking scumbag. I bet they hope I'll try something so they can drink my blood and tell their women about it.

I say good morning to the old-timer. He says good morning. And if he suspects me of wrongdoing, he is good enough not to mention it. We go about our business.

I'm three quarters there now.

So maybe I get away.
And here come the sirens.
Here come their fucking gangsters.
The sirens screaming now, now turning.
And I feel peaceful.

PART ONE

WHEN LIFE
WAS JUST BEGINNING,
I SAW YOU

You don't know how afraid I was you'd go away and leave me.
And now I'll tell you what happened at the zoo.

—EDWARD ALBEE, *THE ZOO STORY*

CHAPTER ONE

Emily used to wear a white ribbon around her throat and talk in breaths and murmurs, being nice, as she was, in a way so as you didn't know if she were a slut or just real down-to-earth. And from the start I was dying to find out, but I thought I had a girlfriend and I was shy.

We were 18. We met at school. She worried about money and I smoked $7 worth of cigarettes every day. She said she liked my sweater, said that's what she had noticed first, why she had wanted to talk to me. A grey cardigan—wool, three buttons, from the Gap—she called it an old sad bastard sweater. Which was fine.

She liked Modest Mouse and she played *Night on the Sun* for me. She had me read two plays by Edward Albee. I thought Albee was a kinky fucker. And I wondered about her. Her eyes—green—were bright, merciful, sometimes given to melancholy, not entirely guileless. And I'd listen to her tell me about the abandoned factories and the cemetery where she'd grown up, the places where she'd skinned her knees. And her voice took me over.

This is how you find the one to break your heart.

IN THOSE days I didn't know anything, I was going through a blotters phase, and Madison Kowalski thought I was a bitch. I did it to myself, but she was still a cunt for it since she was supposed to be my girl. And she gave head to Mark Fuller in the Woodmere Olive Garden parking lot. It fucked me up when I found out, but I forgave her.

"Because I love you," I said.

"I love you as well," she said.

Mark Fuller was good at lacrosse, that's what he was known for. And he had hair highlights. Maybe I should have had hair highlights too, but I didn't. And there were other girls who wanted to be with Mark Fuller, so he could afford to force Madison Kowalski's head down on his dick till she choked on it. That's why she said to me, "I appreciate that you don't force my head down."

And it fucked me up when I thought about it, but I thought about it anyway. I often fucked myself up thinking, like how I used to think you were always supposed to be in love with the girl. I'd got a lot of bad advice. It was 2003. All indications were that things were coming to an end.

MADISON HAD gone out of town for school, gone to New Jersey, to Rutgers. I didn't know why she had chosen the school she had; I didn't follow schools. But she was smart or she had got good grades anyway. With me it was different. I stayed on in the suburbs east of Cleveland, Ohio, where I had lived since I was 10. I was attending one of the local universities, the one with the Jesuits and a lot of kids who were fucks, a good school. I shouldn't have been there. Just my folks had enough money so that it was expected. It wasn't like we were especially fancy people or I was a legacy or whatever you're guessing at, more like with them it was one of those vicarious sorts of things that can set a kid up for failure, how they were saying they'd have liked to have gone to college and fucked around reading about Sir Francis Bacon and all that shit so why wasn't I happy? I didn't know. All I'd figured was the world was wrong and I was in it. So I went to school because people'd said go to school. Which was a mistake. Still you don't ever get to choose.

I sold drugs but it wasn't like I was bad or anything. I wasn't bothering anybody; I didn't even eat meat. I had a job at the shoe store. Another mistake I made. No interest whatsoever in shoes. I was marked for failure. But allow that I had tried. I went to work most days, in the afternoons, when I could have been doing better things, such as anything (we are talking $6 an hour). I had a well-cultivated sense of shame, what kept me going; didn't ever call in sick.

I went to classes in the mornings, sometimes missed classes. It was my shame again; my shame would keep me out of classes sometimes. I didn't ever miss English though. Emily was in my English class. The class was shit, but I always went because Emily'd be there. And we'd sit next to one another; that's how we first got to talking.

She was from Elba, New York, which was the same lake as Cleveland, the same kind of town, only a little shittier. She was impressed that I had a job at the shoe store, impressed that I sold drugs. She said she'd been educated by nuns and hadn't ever gone to school with boys. She made it seem as if she knew nothing of boys to speak of. Turned out this wasn't so much true, but it's whatever. She was good and I liked her. I liked her better than I liked Madison Kowalski. But I was still fucked up about Madison. I even showed Emily a picture of her.

"That's Madison," I said.

She said, "She's so pretty."

Madison was pretty.

THERE ARE countless women in the world. At times it's more than I can bear to think about: that there should be so many and they all start out the way they do, with all the brightness and their own invisible worlds and secret languages and what else they have, and that we ruin everything. And I have been mangled by vicious killers in my time, but I haven't ever doubted it was only that someone had killed them first. Someone like me.

I don't want to tell lies, not any more than I have to anyway. The first thing I ever thought of Emily was I'd like to fuck that girl. So I was shit. But it was a matter of fate, or something to that effect, what would bring us together, regardless if I ever deserved her. And if my life got fucked it wasn't her fault. I should say that now.

CHAPTER TWO

I took the Greyhound to go see Madison at Rutgers. She was staying in the dorms and her bed was small for two people, so it was uncomfortable. But at least her roommate had gone home for the weekend. Madison didn't like her roommate. She said she was snotty. I asked why her roommate had gone home. She said the girl's grandmother had died. I said that was too bad. She said, "Screw her."

I was to stay two nights. Madison took me to parties. But it was more like I followed her to parties. We went out with all her new girlfriends from the dorm. All the girls were best friends already. They clattered out into the night. They shouted at cars. Madison shouted at all the cars.

The parties were shit. The kids didn't do drugs; they just drank beer. Random dudes knew Madison. She had been at Rutgers only a month and they knew her. It was on account of Madison could dance like a real bad-assed slut. That was one thing about her, and that was fine and whatever, just it got a little awkward when you were the one who was there at the party with the girl who was on top of the bar, fucking a spirit. It got so you were at a loss for things to do in the meantime.

We had come to a frat house, to a basement done out in plywood, some kind of beer-pong sex dungeon, everything dismal as murder. They were playing a song that was popular then. It was a song about making all the females crawl on the floor and jizzing on the females and stuff. Madison couldn't help herself. I lost her somewhere. I went and stood off to the side of the room to wait for this to be over.

All I had was a pitcher of Natural Ice, but it was cold and I was low enough on money so that it tasted really good. Then Jessie came by. Jessie was one of Madison's girlfriends from the dorm. I will remember Jessie: Jessie had amazing tits and she was nice to me. She looked at me all sad for a second; and then she said, "Bad news, kid. Madison's playing you."

THE MORNING I was supposed to go back to Cleveland we didn't have any condoms, and Madison was big on using them even though she was on the pill. I don't know what her problem was. I said to her, "We don't really need stupid fucking condoms, do we?"

She said we did. She said there was a machine in the bathroom. That was good since all I had was change. But it was a girls' dorm, so it was a girls' bathroom.

I said, "Can't you get it?"

She said, "Go get it."

I was half-dressed and I found the machine, but it was all sold out except for some shit called Black Velvets. I just wanted to get out of the girls' bathroom so I bought one of those and I went back to Madison's little bed, where we started up again.

It was time to put on the condom.

The condom was black as licorice jelly beans. My thighs were pale. The condom was made out of the same stuff they use to make galoshes. It looked like I had a fake dick on.

I didn't care if I fucked her or not. I was tired of fucking her. It was always a big production: she needed condoms, mix CDs, an overnight bag. One time I had gone over to her house; she'd said she was going to blow me, and she did, but she made me eat a bag of popcorn and watch an entire baseball game first.

This can't be love, I thought.

I ate her out for the last time.

I rode the bus back to Cleveland, starving.

CHAPTER THREE

The shoe store was at the end of Promenade 3, next to the Dillard's. My boss was giving me a hard time because I'd worn flip-flops.

"This is a shoe store," he said.

I knew he knew I was on acid.

Then Johnny Carson walked in. He said, "Kid, I need your help."

He needed a pair of white tennis shoes.

"All white. And none of the jazzy designs on them either. Nine and a half wide. I have a wide foot."

I said I'd do what I could. "But most all the shoes have the jazzy designs on them nowadays."

He said he understood.

"Just do the best you can," he said.

It took two hours but I came through for him. I'd had trouble reading the boxes. That, and I wasn't any good at colors. I kept grabbing my crotch real fast because I thought I'd pissed myself.

I sensed an uneasiness in this customer.

I wanted to tell him everything.

I wanted to be clean.

By the time it was over it had been an ordeal. There were shoe boxes everywhere. Tissue paper was everywhere. The remnants of despair and hesitation. He had almost walked away, not once, not twice, but I had begged him not to go: "I understand perfectly," I'd said. "I am like *you*."

Now he was glad he'd stayed. He had the shoes he'd wanted,

or something close to them. He was more complete. He said to me, "Let me tell you something, kid. . . . You're going places. . . . You stuck to the sale. . . . You're going places."

When work was over I took the 32X, and got off at South Belvoir and walked. It had been a warm day. Now the sun was setting. I saw the shadows of the birds in the hedges. I guessed sparrows. Lights were coming on in the houses, and I was slithering in the post-peak euphoria. I had a Rubella song in my head, one of the *William Whales*, "The Great Pink Hope." I said to myself I'd sing a little.

I did. I sang:

Said I could disappoint you with a smile
Found out that's true
After swimming forty miles
Yer ghost is my biggest fear
I've heard that it's nice in Greenland this time of year

I ran in—to an elec-tric eeeel
Tried to teach me—about a scarlet whee-el

I was going along like that, while to the right of me the sky burned down. And I felt something. My heart was pressurized. I wanted desperately to be nice to someone.

I called Madison.

I said, "I miss you. What are you doing?"

She said, "Oh, gross. You sound fucked up."

"I actually am not."

"Then why do you sound like that?"

"It's just cuz I miss you so much."

"What do you want?"

"I want to talk to you."

"I can't talk right now."

"Why not?"

"I have to go."

"Don't."

"Good*bye*."

"Wait?"

"What?"

". . . I'm scared."

She hung up.

I'd made it to Fairmount. I went into Russo's to buy some more cigarettes, and I ran into some Shaker kids I knew. They gave me Xanax. I had some ecstasies on me so I passed a couple out and took one. Outside it was dark. The Shaker kids said they were going to a party at this girl Maggie's house. I went with them. It wasn't far. The house was on Inverness. A brick house. We walked up the driveway around the back and through a garden gate, and I saw Emily. She was standing under a trellis strung with lights, wearing a white summer dress. And she was laughing.

She said, "Is that you?"

I said it was.

"You know these people?"

"Kind of."

She said, "Small world, huh?"

"Yeah. So do you know Maggie, or?"

"Holy shit! Your pupils are huge."

"I'm on ecstasy."

"How is it?"

"It's pretty good. I'm sorry I don't have any more, I'd give you some."

She said that was okay. "I already turned some down. This weird guy offered me some. He said I should pop the ecstasy in my butt. Those were his exact words. Pop it in my butt."

"Who was it? I'm gonna knock him down."

"Don't. He was just lonely. It could have happened to anyone."

"It's kind of fucking disrespectful."

"That's just how some boys talk."

"Who is this motherfucker?"

"I don't know. He's not here anymore. Please don't worry about it. I thought it was funny. I didn't mean to upset you."

"I'm sorry. It's just that that shit ain't fuckin right, you know? This motherfucker talking to you like that."

She took both my hands. "Forget it."

I said, "I'm really glad you're here."

"Why's that?" she said.

"Cuz I like you a lot."

"Shut up."

"No, I really do."

"Hmmm."

"What?"

"I was just thinking."

". . . Yeah?"

"I was just thinking . . . that you're shady."

WE WALKED back together, Emily and I, all the way along the tree lawns and with the headlights going by us. Neither one of us was wearing shoes. She hadn't worn shoes to the party and I was carrying my flip-flops because I wanted her to think I was nice.

"You don't have to do that," she said.

I said, "I feel like I do."

"Look at you," she said. "You *are* shady, aren't you?"

"You've got me all wrong."

We went like that. And we came to the room where we kissed for the first time. Where she looked away and said, "Do whatever you want, man."

WE WERE awake in the morning. I had to be at work in two hours. Then the shoe store called and said I was fired. I said I understood and I hung up and went back to bed. I said to Emily, "There's been a change of plans. I just got fired."

She said, "Oh, fuck. I'm so sorry."

"No, it's alright," I said. "It's a good thing. Now I don't have to go to work."

"Was that the revisionist fat man you told me about?"

"It was his mother."

"Your boss had his mother fire you?"

"Yeah."

"What a fucking pussy!"

"Right? I told you he was no good, didn't I?"

"What are you going to do?"

"I dunno. But I'll think of something. . . . Hey."

"Yeah?"

"Thanks for taking my side on this whole me-getting-fired thing. You're a really nice lady."

She smiled.

I said, "I think I adore you."

"Stop it. Did you see my bra?"

She bent over and felt around under the bed; and I was thinking, No one's ever had a better one of those.

I reached for her hips. "You're fucking beautiful."

"Hmm . . . fuck! Where did it go?"

"You don't need it."

"Yes I do. It's my best one."

"You're an angel."

"Help me find it."

"No. I won't. I'm sorry."

"Fuck you."

". . . You're killing me."

"Goddamnit."

"Come back. . . . Please. I'm fucking serious."

"Oh yeah?"

She was gushing.

CHAPTER FOUR

You'll have friends. Usually it's nothing. James Lightfoot was alright though. He'd remember your birthday, didn't ever start shit. Strictly a pacifist. He had a lazy eye and half a heart. Born that way. Wore his hair long. Brown hair. Lived at his mom's house. It had been a while since his mom had lived at his mom's house; still it was done up like a family place. There were pictures on the wall, showed James growing up, year in and year out. School pictures. And the one eye, all the way back, fucking him up.

Tuesday he drove me to the bank. He'd just bought a $300 GTI. Faded blue. I could have walked to the bank, but I thought well of James Lightfoot and I thought well of his GTI so I went for a ride with him. The sun was shining on us that day: we had burned a peach White Owl with Train Wreck in it, and so we were high as fuck. Roy was with us. Roy painted houses but he wasn't working that day. He was riding in the front seat. Roy was tall. Black hair. I was riding in the back. James Lightfoot had a noise rock album going on the stereo; it was like TV static set to blast beats; I thought it wasn't possible that he could actually like the album. I thought maybe he was being full of shit about it, but it was his car.

James Lightfoot was yelling at Roy. Roy's cousin Joe had been saying he would join the Marines. And James Lightfoot didn't want Joe to join the Marines. But Roy was more or less okay with it and James was yelling at Roy about this now. Earlier he had said that Roy needed to talk Joe out of joining the Marines.

"IT IS THE OBLIGATION OF YOUR LOVE," he had said.

"YOUR LOVE FOR YOUR COUSIN, WHOM WE ALL LOVE SO MUCH."

And now he was yelling at him again about this shit with Joe and the Marines and I couldn't hear what he was saying, but I saw James waving his arm around and I couldn't help noticing that he looked helpless and that probably no one would ever listen to him as long as he lived.

I had received a letter earlier that afternoon. The bank said I owed them money. It was a mistake. I was going to sort it out. James Lightfoot parked the car and Roy got out and put the seat forward so I could get out and I went into the bank and waited in line. I hadn't thought about how much I smelled like Train Wreck. One of my shoes was coming apart, and I looked like my life was more fucked than it really was. But I was in earnest. I had a receipt and that was as good as the truth. I had their letter with me and I had the receipt and I was going to have the mistake sorted out. This wasn't gonna be a problem.

I said to the lady behind the counter, "You guys sent me this overdraft notice but it isn't right. I paid this off already."

I showed her the receipt. The receipt was from the other day. I hadn't taken any money out since then. She typed me into her computer.

"This is a new overdraft," she said.

"But that's impossible. I haven't made a withdrawal since the last deposit. I put a hundred and sixty dollars in."

"That deposit brought your account up to ten dollars' credit, but there was an additional overdraft charge against your account that put you back into the negative."

"How could you charge me another overdraft fee after I'd paid it off?"

"The deposit didn't clear in time."

"I paid it in cash. Right here."

"It didn't *clear*, sir."

"It was fucking cash."

"It. Didn't. Clear."

I went outside and the car was on fire. Smoke was pouring out from under the hood. James and Roy were watching it go. I walked over to where they were, and I stood beside them.

I said to James, "I'm sorry about your car."

He asked me if I'd got my money back.

I said I hadn't.

We took what we could from the car: the tags, the CDs, what stereo equipment we could carry. We started walking to James's mom's house. Roy had some Train Wreck and he packed it in a bowl and passed it to James.

We said nothing.

We hit the Train Wreck and we felt like we were winning again.

EMILY KEPT leaving her hair ties in my bed and I would give them back to her. One thing about Emily was her parents had divorced when she was 13. She was always saying how she thought love didn't really exist, how it was just pheromones playing tricks on people and I was probably a dog and a liar. She told me about how she'd been the first one in her family to find out about her dad's affair; she'd been eavesdropping on the phone. I asked her why she'd been eavesdropping in the first place.

She said, "You're being a fucking jerk."

"I'm sorry," I said. "I mean, that must have been awful."

"I confronted him about it, and he tried to buy me off. He said he would send me to volleyball camp if I promised not to tell my mom."

"Goddamn."

"I wanted to go to volleyball camp," she said.

"What did you do?"

"I told my mom."

"Did you ever get to go to volleyball camp?"

"No."

She had a habit of disappearing. Sometimes I'd go looking for her. It wasn't always easy; she might be hard to find. I'd found her under a grate in the sidewalk before. I asked her how she'd got down there. She said she didn't know.

"Let's go for a walk," I said.

She said she'd have to think about it.

"Whatcha doin down there anyway?" I asked.

"Studyin."

"You been down there very long?"

"Uh-huh."

"Are you hungry?"

She held something up to the light.

"I brought a little bag of Cheerios," she said.

"What'll you do if it rains?"

"Drown, I guess."

And then there was Rollerblades. She was hanging out with him more than I'd have liked. So I said to her, "Why's that fucking asshole always got those stupid Rollerblades on?"

And she said that I was the fucking asshole, that they were just friends and they'd never done anything.

"He's so respectful," she said.

I said, "You don't actually believe that shit, do you? God knows what he's got planned."

"What about your girlfriend?"

She could be vicious like that.

MADISON FOUND one of Emily's hair ties over Thanksgiving. But she didn't make a big deal out of it because there was everything and we both knew that. So we were fine.

You couldn't hurt Madison.

She wasn't the type.

She was cold-blooded.

Really she was a murderer.

But then for all her being a murderer she could be lovely. Like

I remembered a day the past April when I'd been on a headful of acid and she'd been fucking around on a trampoline. How it had been to see her like that, her light blue shirt spinning tracers in the air. Her laughter panning in the treetops. How it had made me cry. But she wasn't the hill I was meant to die on.

CHAPTER FIVE

Emily worked nights in the Science Building. She cleaned out the cages and killed the lab mice with the little guillotine that the scientists made her use. She cut the mice's heads off and squeezed the blood out of their bodies. She didn't like it, but she figured the mice were doomed anyway and she needed the money. Her dad was some kind of special dentist, and he made enough money to see to it that she wasn't ever going to get much help from the financial aid people. But he didn't give her any of his money. And her mom wasn't any help. So Emily'd do shit like walk an extra half mile in the fucking rain on account of Marc's sold popcorn and diet soda a few cents cheaper than Russo's did. She was doing shit like that while I was off doing whatever I wanted because I was a soft kid and my parents gave me everything I needed. And I could make up for whatever I didn't need by selling drugs to the kids at school. Which was an easy thing to do. Emily half-thought I was a dirtbag, but then she was kind of into that so it was okay. All the same she liked to make a point of telling me she didn't trust me in the least. And when I'd try and say something nice to her she had a tendency to laugh in my face. She couldn't help that though. She was a tough girl.

It went like that and our first semester was over. Emily was going home to Elba for the winter break. And she had come over. She was lying on my bed. We weren't doing anything but waiting to say goodbye. And I was just looking at her and how her body was so light and delicate, her expression all composed and enigmatic, and I knew that the girl could take my life if she ever felt like it, yet all I could think was that I never wanted her to come to any harm.

And like a fucking idiot I said, "I love you."

The words had come out on their own volition, so I must have meant them. Now she was looking dead at me, not saying anything.

Then after a little while (I don't know how long because time had stopped) she said, "Thank you."

And that was it. She left. I wouldn't see her again till mid-January, when school started up again.

And the whole time she was gone I was thinking, She loves you.

CHAPTER SIX

Can you look back to when you met the one you loved the most and remember exactly how it was? Not as in where you were or what she was wearing or what you ate for lunch that day, but rather as in what it was you saw in her that made you say, Yes, this is what I came here for.

I could say some dumb shit, but I really don't know.

I liked the way she cussed. She cussed with great beauty.

And her body.

She was the best fuck. She really fucked you, or she really let you fuck her. She didn't hold back. She always gave you everything and she wasn't ever fake about it.

The way she smiled when she was nervous.

I don't know what she saw in me. When we first were together we used to hook up in this empty chapel at school. And there was this altar. On the wall behind the altar were these ornaments. The ornaments were stick figures depicting the Stations of the Cross, metallic stick Jesuses hossing the crosses around. Sometimes Jesus would have the cross about upright. In other places He'd be about collapsed under its weight. I said to Emily that it looked like a man suffering an accident while setting up a basketball hoop. And she laughed like she'd die laughing. Maybe that was it.

The day I met her we went for a walk after class and we ended up in her dorm room. We talked for a while there and then for whatever reason I got to crying, like really bawling-my-fucking-eyes-out crying. I said I didn't want to live because

I'd already seen everything that was going to happen and it was a nightmare. Something like that. And she was really sweet to me. I don't think there was ever anyone who felt more compassion for weak motherfuckers.

CHAPTER SEVEN

And it was January and Emily was back. She was having me watch a movie with her. Her mother had given her a $20 Best Buy gift card for Christmas, and she'd bought this movie on DVD with it. It was her favorite movie, she said. The movie was about different people who had all these intricate experiences of profound sadness, and some of the people freebased orchids. And there were car accidents.

We were in this room at school that had a TV and a sofa in it. And there was a microwave too. But the room wasn't bigger than a very large closet. It didn't seem like anyone ever came here. It was a room you wouldn't know about. Emily had a gift for finding rooms you wouldn't know about.

I checked my phone and I saw I had a voice mail. No one had tried calling; there was just a voice mail somehow. I listened to it. It was Madison Kowalski getting fucked in the voicemail. And there was a guy saying, "Madison's so hot. Madison's so hot. Madison's so hot."

It sounded like he was wearing wraparound sunglasses.

Then Madison took the phone:

"And *yer* just mad," she said, "cuz *you* can't have it."

I said to Emily, "You gotta hear this shit."

I cued up the voice mail for her. She listened to it.

"Holy shit!" she said. "Such a bitch. . . . Baby, I'm so sorry. . . . I'm so sorry you had to be with her."

"I told you it didn't matter. The chick is a fucking cunt. She always was. I just didn't know any better."

Emily got quiet.

"What's wrong?"

She looked away.

I said, "What's the matter? What did I do?"

". . . I hope you never say that I'm a cunt."

"Of course I'm never gonna say you're a cunt. I love you. That's what I've been trying to tell you."

"I love you too."

And we were on each other.

I started working on her belt.

She said, "Wait. . . . I'm on my period."

I said I didn't care.

She said, "Fuck it. . . . No, wait."

"What?"

"We can't. The sofa. I don't want to get blood on it."

"Fuck, you're right."

"Here. Stand up," she said.

She was being real serious about it. She went as far as she could, and she caught her breath.

"Do whatever you have to do to come," she said.

I brushed her hair back and tried to be nice about it, and I came and she swallowed it.

I kissed her chin. Her chin was wet.

I said thanks.

She said, "Don't mention it."

AND THAT'S when we were in love. And I felt lucky for a while. Till it all got fucked up about a month later, when she said she'd be leaving for good at the end of the semester. She wanted to go to school in Canada. That was what she said. And I thought it was just like a girl to go and say some shit like that.

CHAPTER EIGHT

I was fucking off school pretty bad and I tried to balance that out by getting a job helping make the pizzas at Gerasene's. It was okay so long as Old Man Gerasene wasn't there. But when he was, watch out.

I had just started when he caught me trying to learn how to throw the dough in the air and all that. He was hardly five feet tall with a slight frame, and he had his little grey suit on so he looked like a puppet. I saw him and I thought, Oh, here comes a nice old man.

He said, "Come on. Let me see you do it."

So I tried, but the dough didn't get much spin on it, and it came down in roughly the same shape as it had begun. There'd been an all-encompassing sadness in its trajectory. I didn't have the magic. The old guy went nuts on me.

"WHAT THE FUCK WAS THAT, YOU COCKSUCKER? YOU'RE ALL WRONG, COCKSUCKER. DO IT AGAIN. THIS TIME, DO IT BETTER."

I did it again. Worse.

"NO. FUCK. SHIT. NO NO NO. SHIT FUCK. DO IT AGAIN, COCKSUCKER."

I did it again, about as bad, and the old fuck pantomimed a series of simpering motions so as to insinuate that I threw dough like a queen. Then he wheeled around and said, "THROW IT HIGH. HIGH. SO THEY CAN HEAR IT IN THE DINING ROOM."

I didn't understand what was happening.

He said, "WHAT THE FUCK IS THE MATTER WITH YOU? ARE YOU A MAN OR WHAT?"

Obviously the pay wasn't good, but on the bright side nobody apart from Old Man Gerasene seemed to mind if you took a fuckload of cigarette breaks. So that was good and I spent a lot of time hanging out behind the restaurant, bullshitting.

There was a young waiter who went to the same school I did. He was a skinny white kid like I was, except he smoked Newports and I smoked Winstons. He told me he was fucking one of Gerasene's granddaughters.

Old Man Gerasene had half a dozen daughters and granddaughters. They all drove Escalades or Denalis or whatever and they liked soap operas and *The Sopranos* and shit like that. They all worked at the restaurant, not doing very much. I don't know if Old Man Gerasene had any sons or grandsons, but if he did they didn't go to the restaurant.

Anyway. The waiter told me how he was fucking Gabriella. Gabriella was 21. She had a pretty face and she was stacked. She always wore fuck-me shoes, rain or shine. She seemed nice enough, but the waiter didn't give a shit one way or another.

"She's dumb as a rock," he said.

I couldn't see how it mattered.

"She likes getting that ass stretched out, though," he said. "And she buys me clothes."

There was nothing worth saying, so I just looked up at the sky. Clearly this guy had the magic.

I went back inside and there were a few tickets up, so I started in on throwing the dough again, and every time I threw the dough and it spread out in the air I couldn't help thinking about Gabriella and her dilating asshole.

I'D MEANT to drop out of school, but I took a 5mg Klonopin and drank half a 40 of Olde English and blacked out at the art museum. So I fucked off the deadline for dropping classes and I ended up having to fail out.

I got a letter saying I had to go see Father Whomever so he could tell me I was finished at the university. Which he did. And he asked me if I'd ever traveled outside of the United States. I told him I'd been to Spain once. He said I was lucky. He'd been all of 60 the first time he ever got to go overseas. And here I was, so young and already been to Spain! Then he asked me what I was going to do, and I told him I was probably gonna mind my own goddamn business.

BY MAY I had moved out of my parents' house and gone to live in a duplex on Murray Hill with my friend Roy and his cousin Joe and whoever else happened to be there (primarily James Lightfoot). Roy was a big Irish kid, and he wore the same fucked-up sport coat every day and drank 40s and rolled cigarettes with pipe tobacco. Joe was a pretty little wop. He couldn't not get laid all the time. It was really something. He was adopted; that's how he was Roy's cousin. He was the toughest one of the three of us. He was tough as shit. We used to beat the shit out of each other to prove how tough we were, so that's how we knew.

Joe painted houses with Roy. And they actually made okay money. But then Joe signed up with the Marines, so he'd be done painting houses for a while. He was leaving for Parris Island in a few weeks.

Roy didn't ever join the Marines, but he did call up Gerasene's for me and lied and told them I'd broken my arm skateboarding at Cain Park. They said that was fine. And he got me hired at a restaurant on Mayfield, a nice place with two big dining rooms, high coffered ceilings, and one toilet. The owner was a dick but not too bad and all the waitresses were gorgeous and you could make money there. They had these Turkish guys working in the kitchen who'd pull a knife on you over nothing, so you felt like you were really alive. The manager started me off busing tables, but I didn't have enough personality for it and my shoes were all wrong, so he stuck me making salads.

EMILY WAS leaving in three days. She was going home to Elba. She'd be in Montreal by the end of the summer. I had put together a picnic lunch: some fruit, some cold ravioli, some caprese salad, and some bottles of cheap red wine. The plan was that Emily and I would have a picnic down by the pond in back of the art museum. Instead we had it in Roy's attic. We drank one of the bottles of wine, and we fucked there, in the attic. She was above me, concentrating. I could tell she was concentrating because her jaw would go a little sideways when she concentrated like that. Which was absolutely the most beautiful thing in the world.

It was a clear day and the sun was going pretty well so the attic became unbearably hot and we did eventually make it down to the pond, where a good number of people of all shapes and persuasions were out enjoying the weather. Emily and I sat by the water and talked about all the things we thought we were going to do. I said I wouldn't go if she didn't go.

She said, "Fuck you."

And I guess I was wrong to try her like that. It was only that it had been such a good day, and I thought most of the days would have been as good.

I WENT into work at six. It was supposed to be a big night. The owner was throwing a party after we closed at twelve and the salad station was being converted into an extra bar and I'd get to serve drinks. I'd told Emily and Roy and Joe to be sure they came through so they could drink for free. They'd said they would come. And they did.

I saw Roy and Joe first. They were talking to the owner. Joe was saying how in three weeks' time he'd be at basic training.

The owner listened intently. He liked Joe because Joe looked like a TV dago; he said, "Parris Island . . . that's Marines, isn't it?"

Joe said, "Yeah."

"But that's a good way to go to heaven."

I got Roy's attention. I asked him where Emily was.

He said, "She's around here somewhere."

"Okay. That doesn't really help me but thanks."

"Gosh, look who's on his period."

"Man, what the fuck!"

"What?"

"Who the fuck is he?"

"How the fuck should I know?"

He was standing real close to her. And she brought him with her when she came over to the bar/salad station.

She said hi.

I looked at her.

"This is Benji," she said. "Benji's from Ghana. He goes to Case."

I said what's up to Benji. He flashed a smile at me and just as quickly turned back to Emily.

"I know this great restaurant," he said. "It is called Mi Aldea. The food is so good there. I must take you sometime."

She said, "Mmm. That sounds good."

I came around from behind the bar/salad station and I put my arm around Emily and kissed her on the top of her head. But I was drunk and I accidentally dropped a lit cigarette into the hood of her sweatshirt.

Benji said, "Watch out. He has dropped his cigarette in your hoodie."

"Get it out, man!" she said to me.

I didn't understand at first. I got the cigarette out, but not before it had burned a hole through the material.

"Is it okay?" she asked.

"It's fine," I said. "Can we please talk somewhere?"

"What?"

"Let's go over here."

"You're being an asshole."

"Shh. Listen to me. Nobody thinks the food at Mi Aldea is good. The only reason he wants to take you there is cuz they don't card and he wants to get you drunk and fuck you in the ass."

"What the fuck is your problem, man?"

I couldn't say anything right.

Roy came up.

I said, "What's up, Roy?"

He said, "You want me to punch that guy in the dick?"

"Not yet."

Emily said, "I'm fucking done with this."

She walked out in a hurry. Roy and Joe left after her. They said it'd probably be alright. I didn't know but I had to stay where I was. I had to look after the bar/salad station. And that's what I did. And I felt like shit. Around one-thirty the manager told me to shut it down. Then one of the real bartenders, a guy named Chris, said I should look after one of the patrons for him, a guy named Tommy.

"Tommy just got out of prison," he said. "Tommy's a real stand-up guy."

Tommy was drunk as fuck. I was supposed to help him to not throw up on anybody or goose a slut or whatever it was they thought he might do. Tommy had been in prison 20 years, which meant he'd gone away in the early '80s, which meant he'd been locked up longer than I'd been alive. He had big plastic eyeglasses and a grey bowl cut and a shiny red bowling jacket. He said everybody was full of shit and they were all a bunch of fakes. He meant some of the guys you would see in the area who acted like they were real Cosa Nostra motherfuckers. Tommy said all these guys liked to talk the big game. "But they don't have the balls . . . to put a gun to the guy's head and BLOW HIS BRAINS OUT."

That's what he kept saying, the stuff about the brains. He'd start talking about this punk and that peckerhead and the other turkey, and he'd finish up by saying that they didn't have the balls to put a gun to the guy's head and BLOW HIS BRAINS OUT.

Then he got to asking me about what I did. I said I didn't do much but I was going to join the Army soon.

"Don't be a fool," he said. "Those people don't give a shit about you."

I said I already knew that.

"So what the fuck are you thinking?"

"I don't know. But I don't have any other ideas."

"But do you have the balls . . . to put a gun to the guy's head and BLOW HIS BRAINS OUT?"

"I don't know."

"AGGH! You'll be alright."

The night was about over and I said, "Listen, Tommy, I've got to help close. If you need anything, let me know, alright?"

And I went around the place, pushing tables and chairs around, spraying things and wiping them off and sweeping and mopping. I was really moving because I needed to get out of there and I needed to see Emily.

I got done and I went outside, and there was Tommy standing out on the sidewalk in front of the restaurant, looking like a lost child.

"Tommy," I said, "you alright?"

"Yeah. What are you doing?"

"I'm all done. I'm about to walk home."

"You need a ride? I'll give yaz a ride."

"I can walk. I'm not even five minutes that way."

"No, come on. I'll give yaz a ride."

"Alright. But hold on a second cuz I'm gonna go run over to the bakery and buy a cake."

"Whatcha buyin a cake for?"

"My girl. She's leaving town and I want to buy her a cake."

"Don't waste your money."

"It'll just take a second."

There was a 24-hour bakery across the street and up toward the hill a little ways. They didn't have any cakes to sell me and I had to settle for a dozen cheesecake muffins. But they were impressive muffins and I thought it was just as well.

Tommy said, "Let's go. You ready or what?"

He was driving the blue Chevy Astrovan that was parallel-parked next to the restaurant. We hopped in and Tommy fired up the engine. He ran into the car in front of us and backed into another car before he could get us into the lane. I glanced over and he looked like he was feeling real ill. All of a sudden he stopped the van and opened his door to retch. He retched for a minute. Violently. When he was done retching he leaned against the driver seat. He was going, "Oh, Jesus. Oh, Jesus Jesus Jesus."

In the dome light I saw that he had caught himself with a fair amount of the vomit.

I said, "Bad news, Tommy. You threw up on your sleeve."

Tommy looked down and saw what he had done to the right sleeve of his shiny red bowling jacket.

He went, "AGHH RATS!"

I said, "Don't worry, Tommy. We can fix it."

There was a paper grocery bag on the floor of the van. I tore it into napkinesque shapes that Tommy could use to scrape the lion's share of the vomit off his sleeve. They didn't work like magic or anything, but they did alright.

Tommy said, "Close enough for rock and roll."

And we resumed our drive up the street. We only had another ten houses to go and we were there. Tommy ran over the curb for good measure. I thanked him for the ride and asked that he be careful getting home. He said he would be okay. I gave him one of the muffins and I never saw him again.

EMILY WAS still awake when I got upstairs. She'd been drinking and I joined her at that. I gave her the box of muffins and said I was sorry about earlier when I was being an asshole. I said I understood that she hadn't meant anything by bringing Benji around and that she was just a sweetheart who believed in diversity and developing countries and stuff like that and that she wanted friends. I said there was supposed to be a dozen muffins but I had given one to Tommy and Tommy was a good man and he had needed to eat something. She said that it was all very nice of me and that I was forgiven. Then I saw that she was crying. I hadn't ever seen her cry before and I asked her what was wrong and that just made her cry more. She said she didn't know what was wrong. It was a while before she stopped crying. I asked her if she was alright. She said she was alright.

I said, "This is fucking crazy, isn't it?"

She said, "Yeah. It is."

And we laughed about it.

And we fucked around.

And we went to sleep.

PART TWO

ADVENTURE

CHAPTER NINE

Staff Sergeant Kelly had the face like Death and the every other word out of his mouth was *joker*; he had the black sweater and the green slacks, the patent leather shoes. A fuckload of piss cups was in his desk drawer. He said the latrine was at the end of the hallway. "Go left out the door and follow it around," he said. "You can't miss it."

My piss was clean, so Kelly told me how his wife was a Korean. He told me how he drove a government car and got BAH and TRICARE. He made it sound real good. I had to show him I could do 20 push-ups and 20 sit-ups; then he took me next door to the Bally Total Fitness so I could show him a mile on one of the treadmills. I was wearing Vans (Geoff Rowleys, vegan shoes) and my pants kept trying to fall down, but I did okay. We went back to the Armed Forces Career Center, and I took a practice ASVAB so Kelly could be sure I wasn't a subnormal. He checked it over when I was done, and he said I'd scored in the 85th percentile. He said I could have any MOS I wanted if I did as well on the real thing. I could tell he was excited. This was the first week of 2005, and for a while the news mostly had been about kids going off and getting themselves killed and maimed, so Kelly and his like were having a hard time getting enough kids to sign up. But there I was, and I was too easy; I'd made his day.

We went to talk to his boss, Sergeant First Class Space, and Kelly said, "Pardon me, Sarr, but I have a joker here says he wants to be a ninety-one whiskey, says he's tryin to go ASAP."

All Space's teeth were gold and he was one long and thin

motherfucker. I hadn't known that people could be named Space. He said, "Have a seat, Mister Ninety-One Whiskey."

I told him the same shit I'd told Kelly, and Space agreed that I was going about things the right way. He said I'd made a smart choice because 91Ws had it made in the Army; then he got on the phone, and when the other end picked up he said, "Hamburger hamburger hamburger," and laughed like this was real funny.

And for whatever reason I wanted to say hamburger hamburger hamburger too, even though I knew he was laughing at me.

JOE CAME and got me from Severance and we went and got drunk with Roy. We made a big deal out of the drinking, the way you will when you're young and you drink and a day's momentous. Joe was just back from Camp Lejeune, and he'd be in town for a few weeks before his reserve battalion left for Fort Irwin and then Iraq. And now I was enlisting in the Army because I'd been saying I would. So we thought we were hot shit. It was Tuesday night.

We ended up at a bar on Mayfield. The place was dead, but we got to meet a Knight of Columbus. He had a black leather jacket on and his hair coiffed like he was Frankie Avalon or Robert Blake or one of those guys. He looked to be in his 50s. He asked us what we were carrying on about, and Roy explained it for him, and he approved. He said, "You know I used to teach hand-to-hand combat to the Special Forces guys down there at Camp Lee-Joon."

Joe said he'd just come from SOI there.

"What's SOI?"

"School of Infantry."

"Yeah I forgot."

The Knight of Columbus liked Joe because Joe looked like a TV dago, and so we had his company.

As for the barmaid, she was in her late 20s. She had white-blond hair and a tan that cost money, and she was skinny except for she had a little pooch in the front that gave a false impression of her being some months pregnant. We had been there before and we had seen her then; the pooch didn't change, and she'd always act stuck-up like she was the one who served drinks to Ben Affleck or somefuckingbody. At first I'd just assumed she was a cunt, but then I'd come to wonder if there wasn't a sadness in it.

The Knight of Columbus had been showing us fighting moves, and now he wanted to buy us a round. That's how I saw that the barmaid wasn't shitty to him. She even called him Mr. Something-or-Other. And I thought, There's something to be learned here. But before I could figure out what it was, the Knight of Columbus made a toast.

"I bet you make it home alive, Joe," he said. "Your friend here I'm not so sure about. . . . Sah-*loo*!"

We drank the drinks. Roy said he was going to enlist in the Marines as a machine gunner. Everyone agreed it would be a fine thing for him to do. I said I had to go take a piss. So I did. I punched the bathroom mirror on accident when I was washing my hands. The mirror fell off the wall and took the sink with it.

I didn't stay.

It had been a tremendous fucking crash and I needed to warn my friends. The barmaid was making for the wreckage. "We gotta go," I said. "I mean like *we gotta go right fuckin now.*"

The barmaid was cussing in the bathroom and we said goodbye to the Knight of Columbus. He said not to worry about the barmaid. "That whore has had two abortions," he said.

We didn't have far to run to get home, and we had a fistfight in the driveway till one of the neighbors said he'd come down and shoot us if we didn't be quiet and go to bed. So we went inside.

I called Emily. I wanted her to tell me I was good, maybe thank me or something. But she had her mind made up to give me grief, and I shook my head because I didn't understand. I said, "Dearest, I told you before that I was gonna do this and you didn't say anything then."

She said, "That's because I thought you were full of shit, baby."

I WENT and saw my parents the following evening. They were doing alright. They thought the shit with the Army was dumb, but they were doing alright. They'd just bought a house, a nice house with plenty of room. I wanted nothing to do with it.

I said I was going Thursday to MEPS for a physical and some other tests, and if those went well I'd be at basic in a couple weeks. Sergeant First Class Space had said I'd fill out a wish list of the duty stations I'd like to be assigned to in order of preference, and since practically everybody got one of their top three, I was more or less guaranteed to stay close to Ohio. So I'd be able to visit often. And the life insurance policy was good for $300K if I opted to pay for the kicker.

My dad said, "Are you sure there isn't *any*thing else that you would rather do?"

I said I didn't know what else there was to do.

My mom said, "I don't see why you don't wish to continue with your studies."

I said, "What studies? I failed out of school eight months ago."

"You can always go back," she said.

"And I might. And if I do, the Army will pay for it. Sergeant First Class Space said—"

"Who the fuck is this sonofabitch? I'd like to speak to him."

I said that couldn't happen.

She said, "Why not?"

I said it was something I was doing on my own.

. . .

THURSDAY I found out I was color-blind. It wouldn't be a problem though because 91W was one of the few MOSs you could hold in the Army while color-blind. "Because you already know what color blood is," they said.

There was a lot of standing in line, and our legs ached because we weren't used to it. They had us strip down to our underwear and duckwalk the circuit of a big room. The big room smelled like balls (unwashed) and feet (ditto) and open ass (regardless), and there was a lot of inadequacy to be seen in the big room. Fat kids. Acne. Acne on the face. Acne on the body. Skinny kids. I was a skinny kid. I wasn't strong. We looked like shit. We'd grown up on high-fructose corn syrup, with plenty of television; our bodies were full of pus; our brains skittered. They called us one by one into another room, a smaller room wherein there was a man whose job it was to check everybody's asshole. He had you bend at the waist and spread your ass apart with your hands so he could get a good look at it, and when he had seen enough he said, "Okay."

They took me. By three in the afternoon I had signed a contract and I was sworn in. Roy came and got me from MEPS, and he drove me up to Elba so that I could stay with Emily my last two weeks as a civilian. Joe had come along for the ride. Snow was falling when we passed Erie. By the time we had passed the exit for Jamestown, it was all-out night and the traffic on 90 was bound up in a proper storm. We were boxed in by semis. They were all around us, rattling against the wind. Were one of them to jackknife, were one of them to not see us and then change lanes, we'd have had a fair chance of death by machines out on the roadway. But we didn't worry about it. We had Roy's car and we had cigarettes; we had heat and music; and all the way through the tolls outside Elba, we didn't ever doubt that we were some of the ones who wouldn't be killed.

It was ten o'clock when we got to Emily's. They dropped me off and turned the car around and went home.

THIS WAS my first time seeing Emily in her hometown. All the last summer she'd been saving up to go to school in Montreal. She'd worked a third shift six nights a week at a Walgreens. And she'd been living with her aunt, and her aunt was religious. So there'd been no time or place for me then.

I had gone to see her in Montreal just as soon as she'd moved there. That was late August. Twenty hours' worth of Greyhound each way, and it was worth it: to be alone with her in a strange city (the Paris of Canada), to only know each other, to smoke Player's with pictures of cancer or black heart on the packages. To stick our heads out onto the fire escape, to make dinner in her kitchenette, to drink liquor and have wild fucking arguments about different things—God, Oasis, my insufferable arrogance—whatever she felt like. We would get to screaming at one another, then fuck and sleep like young wolves in a shoe box. It was like a dream. And like in dreams I didn't get to stay. And neither did she. Something to do with money. She dropped out and moved back to Elba. She rented an apartment and got a job at a Giant Eagle. She was waiting for the spring semester to start up at the local school.

It was strange with us not fighting at all. Now and then she'd say she thought the Army was a bad idea. But I didn't know as it was a good idea either; it was only something that was happening. So there was nothing to fight about.

When she went to work I'd do jumping jacks and read Kurt Vonnegut books and chain-smoke. When she came home we'd fuck and take naps, listen to the Lead Belly CD we'd bought at the Borders down the street, drink gin. The girl loved gin; she'd drink gin and then she'd want to kiss you.

It wasn't like I didn't know I was better off there, but what was done was done and I wasn't supposed to stay. The days ran out and she drove me back to Cleveland.

They put the recruits up in a hotel downtown. I was in a room with a kid my age from Steubenville who had enlisted as a military policeman in the Ohio National Guard. He said when he came home from basic he was going to wear his Class A uniform with his patches and his ribbons and take his fiancée out to dinner.

I wished him luck.

He wished me luck.

CHAPTER TEN

Fort Leonard Wood, Missouri. The head shavers were civilians—a fat fuck and his women. The women had silver-blue permanents; there were two of them and they were awful. So was the fat fuck. It wasn't enough for them that we had to pay them money for these haircuts that we were ordered to get; they talked shit to us too. They cut a kid's head so it was bleeding pretty good and he let on that he minded and they said he was a sissy. They wanted to know if he was from San Fran-sissy-co. Then they cut another kid and the blood was running down and they thought it was funny. They didn't get bored of it. They had special vacuum clippers that sucked the hair up as they cut. The suction pulled the scalp up into the blades; that was how come they drew blood so much. The fat fuck and his women had to talk real loud so they could hear themselves over the sucking sounds. I wished death upon them.

Then we got a hundred fucking shots. We got all our Army stuff: uniforms, boots, helmets, shit like that. We took our papers with us everywhere. They signed our papers. This was in-processing. When we weren't in-processing we sat in an auditorium and they taught us things: left face, right face, the Army song, whatever. When it was time to eat we acted like the food was really bad even though it wasn't that bad.

One kid said, "I'm a spook. That's counterintelligence."

Another kid said, "I'm an eleven bravo."

That was infantry.

But he couldn't be an 11B because all the 11Bs went through at Fort Benning. Now we knew he was a liar.

The group I came in with was B1, as in bravo one. That night another group came in, B2.

We thought the B2s were decadent children.

We said, "These bravo twos are ate-the-fuck-up."

We said, "They sure are."

The B2s thought we were weird losers.

The mutual enmity between B1s and B2s lasted three days; then we were redistributed at random into three platoons called Alpha Company, and no one could remember who anyone was. The universal baldness made it difficult to recognize people. They packed us into cattle cars and we rode up the hill to boot camp.

IT WAS a lot of yelling. They called us names like High Speed and Dick With Ears. Our hands were dick skinners. Our mouths were cock holsters. Our enemy was Haji. Our friends were battle buddies. It was real trashy.

There were girls in our company. They couldn't do the exercises. We carried their equipment for them. It was a hassle. There were dudes who were fucked up too, but nothing like the girls.

The drill sergeants pretended they were real angry. They said not to come close to them because they could wig out and snap our necks. PTSD, they said. And a drill sergeant did choke a recruit. The kid was unconscious. He had choked the kid out. It wasn't because of PTSD, though; the drill sergeant had no combat patch, he hadn't ever been anywhere. He was full of shit.

We had drill sergeants who had been to Iraq, and they were full of shit too. They said they'd killed children over there. They said in Iraq there were children who tried to sneak up on American soldiers so as to blow them up with hand grenades. When it came to those types of situations, they said, it's either you or the kid, so you had better kill the kid. One of the drill sergeants was an 88M, a truck driver. He said he had run over the hand grenade children with his truck. He said that was why he was crazy.

I stayed out of the way most of the time, and so I didn't get fucked with much. Still there was no avoiding it entirely. Like when I told Drill Sergeant Cordero I needed to trade my Country Captain Chicken MRE for a vegetarian one because I was a vegetarian. Cordero got angry as fuck. He said, "WHY DON'T YOU EAT MEAT, PRIVATE? ARE YOU RICH?"

He talked like a Chicano Macho Man Randy Savage.

I said I wasn't rich.

He said, "I SAW A SHOW ON TV. IT SAID THAT PEOPLE WHO DON'T EAT MEAT HAVE WEAK MINDS. THEY ARE EASY TO BRAINWASH. THAT MEANS THAT YOU ARE EASY TO BRAINWASH."

"YES, DRILL SERGEANT."

One day I was shooting my rifle at some silhouettes on a practice range, and I was sucking because I couldn't see the silhouettes too well. The silhouettes on this range were light green, whereas normally they were something darker: black, I think. And Cordero was standing over me, losing his fucking mind. He said, "SHOOT THE TARGET, PRIVATE. WHAT THE FUCK IS THE MATTER WITH YOU?"

I said, "I'M HAVING A HARD TIME SEEING THE SIL-HOUETTES, DRILL SERGEANT."

"WHY CAN YOU NOT SEE THE SILHOUETTES?"

"I'M COLOR-BLIND, DRILL SERGEANT. RED-GREEN."

"WELL THEN MAYBE, SINCE YOU ARE *COLOR*-BLIND, YOU SHOULD NOT HAVE JOINED THE UNITED! STATES! ARMY!"

He bent the brass cleaning rod he was holding on account of his hitting me on the head with it. But I wasn't hurt because I was wearing a helmet. I left the range. I had to be patted down: NO BRASS, NO AMMO. Drill Sergeant Cole punched me in the penis for no reason. You'd have that though. You just had to remember it was all make-believe. The drill sergeants were just pretending to be drill sergeants. We were pretending to be soldiers. The Army was pretending to be the Army.

The only thing I worried about was Emily. Dave from the Giant Eagle was gonna try to fuck her. I'd met him two nights before I left Elba. Emily had invited him over after they got off of work. He'd been rude as shit to me. I knew what he was about. I'd said to Emily, "That guy's gonna try to fuck you."

She said he wasn't like that.

I said, "That's exactly what he's like."

I CRAWLED out of the barracks window to use the pay phone. It was night. I had a calling card. The phone rang. She picked up. "Hello?"

"Can you hear me?"

"Hello?"

I was talking low. "It's me."

"Oh, hi!"

"How are you?"

"What?"

"How are you doing?"

"I'm fine. What about you? I'm surprised you're calling."

"I snuck out of the barracks."

"Are you alright?"

"I'm good now. Whatcha up to?"

"Oh, nothing. Just hanging out with some friends from work. . . . Hello?"

"Yeah."

"Are you okay?"

"Yeah. I'm fine. I miss you."

"I miss you too."

"I can't stop thinking about you. I snuck out the window to call you."

"Can you hold on a second?"

"Yeah, sure."

"..."

"..."

"..."

"..."

"...Are you still there?"

"Yeah, I'm still here."

"So how have you been? What's it like? What have you been doing?"

"Oh, I'm fine. It's not really terrible. Just this, that, and the other thing, you know? I snuck out the window. Third-story window. No big deal though. There's ledges. I'm not supposed to be out here."

"I can barely hear you."

"I've got to talk quietly. If I get caught out here I'm fucked."

"You said you snuck out the window? I can barely hear you."

"Fuck."

"What did you say?"

"Nothing. I miss you."

"I miss you too."

"I wish I was there right now."

"I wish you were here too."

"Listen. I have to go. If I get caught out here I'm absolutely fucked. I have to get back inside."

"Okay."

"I'll try and call again soon."

"Okay."

"I love you."

"I love you too."

"Sweet dreams."

"You too."

CHAPTER ELEVEN

Sundays were easy because we had the morning off just to clean the barracks and do whatever and we could go to a religious service if we wanted to. I identified with the Hare Krishnas, but they didn't have a Hare Krishna service so I went to the Buddhist one. You couldn't go alone. You had to go with a battle buddy. Specialist Kovak was a Buddhist too. We went to talk to the cadre.

I said, "We're going to a religious service, Drill Sergeant."

He said, "What religious service are you going to?"

"Buddhist, Drill Sergeant."

"Go."

And we went and it was alright and there were a lot of people at the service because the Buddhists gave out mini Reese's cups. But there was more to the services than just that. We would start off with some deep breathing. Then we would chant for a while, something like twenty minutes' worth of breathing and chanting. After that the Buddhists would tell us things about Buddhism and they'd ask questions and if you knew the answer *then* they'd throw candy at you.

On this day Staff Sergeant Rockaway joined us. He said to call him Sergeant Rock. He was real into Buddhism. He said since he started being a Buddhist he had bought a car (paid off) and a motorcycle (paid off). Buddhism had changed his life for the better. He said he'd started being a Buddhist when he was in boot camp, going to the services on Sundays.

"Just like y'all are now," he said.

. . .

THE NEXT day we learned unarmed combatives. Drill Sergeant Cole was teaching us. He taught us the Sleeveless Choke. He taught us the Tokyo Choke. There were all different kinds of chokes we could do. And we all sat in a circle and we were supposed to take turns choking each other. They sent two of us at a time into the middle of the circle, and the object was one of us was to choke the other one out. I was paired with Specialist Kovak because we were about the same size. I choked the shit out of him. When it was over I got the idea that I had surprised him and I felt bad about it. The next time I let him choke the shit out of me. Still I felt bad about it. Kovak was my battle buddy, and I'd choked him.

THE ONLY way not to graduate basic was to try and kill yourself. One kid tried hanging himself from the drop ceiling in the latrine. It didn't work. He brought the ceiling down. So he didn't die. But he didn't graduate either.

My parents came down for the graduation. A lot of people's families came. A lot of people's families didn't come. We marched around on the stage in an auditorium and did cadences. The Toby Keith song was played and we were all dismissed with a day pass good till 21:00. My parents took me to Chili's. I ordered a veggie burger.

My mom said, "I bet that's the first veggie burger you've had in a while."

"Actually, no," I said. "MRE number twelve is a veggie burger in barbecue sauce. It's not bad, but this is much better."

We had time to kill, so we hung out at the hotel room they had in the town by the base. My mom took a lot of pictures of me in my Class A uniform. And I smoked cigarettes (Winston Reds), and those were really good. And after a little while we went back to Fort Leonard Wood, and we said goodbye to one another there.

CHAPTER TWELVE

Those of us who were healthcare-specialists–to-be got on a bus. We were going to Fort Sam Houston in San Antonio, Texas. The bus driver was a Vietnam vet with a right hand that had been melted into a red fleshy claw back in his white phosphorus days. He was an agreeable man, and he encouraged us to drink and smoke on the bus. When we got to Fort Sam there were all-new drill sergeants who yelled at us, but the whole drill sergeant thing was played out by then and we didn't give a fuck if they yelled or not. All the same we pretended like we were scared shitless so they'd overlook our being beer-drunk and smelling like cigarettes.

We were in the intake a few days, waiting for groups to show up from the other basics. Then everybody was there and we found out we were called Charlie Company and we got on a bus to go to our next barracks. There was a girl from North Dakota named Private Harlow, and she told everyone on the bus how she liked dipping Copenhagen and getting gangbanged. So she was popular. And we all thought about what it would be like to gangbang Private Harlow.

WE ARRIVED at the company. The prior service were there already. The prior service either could be military personnel changing their MOSs and branches of service or could be ex-military people who had enlisted again after they'd been failures in the civilian world. They'd get trained with us. Most of them looked like shit. And they were bad for morale; they ruined our expectations as far as what we thought we were about to become.

The training battalion had a mantra: Warrior Medic. Naturally everyone thought it was stupid. Yet the cadre were supposed to call us Warrior Medics. So it was like that. And it was to last 14 weeks. But we were supposed to get weekend passes after a while.

It was all classroom instruction in the beginning, which was a welcome change from basic, from digging graves and freezing our asses off in the woods and getting gassed. We had EMT textbooks, and we listened to lectures. It was a lot of PowerPoint, and some Faces of Death now and then. The Faces of Death was meant to get us used to mortality. We watched a guy break his neck when his car rolled. We saw an eviscerated motorcycle rider. We saw a chick who had got stabbed about a million times.

There were two instructors per platoon, an E-6 (staff sergeant) and a civilian paramedic. Our civilian paramedic was Ms. Grey. She was hot and probably a lesbian. But never mind. She was an expert. She worked on the Life Flight out of a hospital in San Antonio and she knew more than most Army medics put together.

The E-6 looked like Harold Ramis, and he chain-smoked mentholated Camels. He'd been in the Army 15 years and he told us shit he thought we needed to know about it: namely the ways people died in the Army. He also told us you could use tampons to treat gunshot wounds. He said you ought to use unscented tampons. I asked him if he had ever been stationed at Fort Drum. He said, "Why do you ask, Warrior Medic?"

I said I wanted to go to Fort Drum because my girl lived in Elba, New York, and it was just a couple hours away.

He said, "Don't ever ask to go to Fort Drum. You'll spend more time in the field there than you will anywhere else, it gets cold as hell, and she's just going to cheat on you."

CHAPTER THIRTEEN

Drill Sergeant Masters was a perfect honky if ever there were such a thing. He addressed the company formation: "WAR-RIOR MEDICS, YOU WERE TOLD TO COME UP WITH A COMPANY CHEER. YOU WERE GIVEN A WEEK TO DO THIS. THIS IS WHAT IS CALLED A DEADLINE. AS OF NOW YOU HAVE MISSED THE DEADLINE. . . . OPEN RANKS."

We said, "OPEN RANKS."

"HALF-LEFT . . . FACE."

We did a half-left face. Which was bad news. It meant the fucker was going to smoke us.

"FRONT."

This was even worse news. It meant Front-Back-Go's. When he said "FRONT," we were supposed to drop down and start doing push-ups till he said otherwise.

So we did.

". . . BACK."

Now we were supposed to roll over and start doing sit-ups. I didn't like sit-ups, especially on concrete. They made my ass hurt.

". . . GO!"

Now we were supposed to jump up and run in place like *Sweatin' to the Oldies.* And we'd do that till he said "FRONT" or "BACK" again. Front, Back, and Go could come in any order at any interval for any duration.

"FRONT . . . BACK . . . GO!—FRONT!—BACK! . . . GO!—BACK . . . GO!—FRONT—BACK—GO!—FRONT—GO!"

Etc. Etc.

This went on till the company lay prone on the concrete, in a pool of its own sweat, unable to front, back, or go anymore.

Then Masters had us form up again.

"NOW, SINCE YOU HAVE FAILED TO COME UP WITH A COMPANY CHEER, I HAVE TAKEN WHAT IS CALLED THE INITIATIVE AND COME UP WITH ONE *FOR* YOU. ONE WHICH YOU WILL HAVE TO LEARN *NOW*."

This is what he had come up with:

Warrior Medics in the fight!
On the double day and night!
We will beat out all the rest!
Charlie Company is the best!
Don't stop! Get it, get it!
Soldier on, Warrior Medic!
Don't stop! Get it, get it!
Woooooooooooooooooooooooooooooo-
OoooooooooooooooooooooOOOOOOOO-
OOOOOOOOOOOOOOOOOOOOOOOOOOOAAH!
MAKE! Way! Here come the Warrior Medics!
Oo! Ta-ah! Here come the Warrior Medics!
MAKE! Way! Here come the Warrior Medics!
Oo! Ta-ah! Here come the Warrior Medics!
MAKE! Way! Here come the Warrior Medics!
Oo! Ta-ah! Here come the Warrior Medics!

The refrain was to go on indefinitely, till we were signaled to stop. That's how it went. And from that day on, whenever the company was called to attention (something that happened no less than a million times on any given day), the company cheer was to be recited in its entirety. No exceptions. To make matters worse, after a while it got to be expected that the guidon bearer would do the robot throughout the refrain.

So don't ever join the fucking Army.

CHAPTER FOURTEEN

Private Harlow was in my platoon. She'd get in trouble for wearing makeup.

They'd say, "Harlow, don't think I don't see that makeup!"

"Harlow, you better wash that makeup off your face!"

"Don't let me catch you out here with makeup on again, Private!"

When we learned to take vital signs I got paired up with her. She was the casualty first. She lay on her back. She'd taken her BDU top off so it'd be easier to take her blood pressure; she just had her brown T-shirt on and she was cold because they kept the air-conditioning going full blast in the classrooms.

I was on my knees beside her with the stethoscope in my ears. I was getting the blood pressure cuff on her arm.

She said, "I'm freezing. Don't look at my tits."

I hadn't looked at her tits.

Now I did.

She had nice tits.

Her tits didn't get all flat and sideways when she lay on her back.

"I feel like I'm gonna get tea-bagged," she said.

She smiled when I didn't look at her.

I blew up the BP cuff.

"Do you shave your balls?"

"Goddamn."

"*That's* a yeah!"

"I can't hear the thing when you're talking."

"Sorry. I'll be quiet. . . . Drill Sergeant Masters shaves his balls."

"A hundred and ten over sixty."

"You and Drill Sergeant Masters have something in common."

"Please don't say stuff like that."

"I'm sorry. I'll never say it again."

I thought probably she was telling the truth about the guy's balls. It was by no means unknown that the cadre fucked the female recruits sometimes. We knew they did that at Leonard Wood. It was the trade-off, I guess: the girls didn't have to carry their equipment but the drill sergeants would fuck them, or some of them anyway. I was depressed.

When we formed up to go back to the barracks, Harlow was slow getting in formation. Masters pulled her up. She had some dip in her mouth. She was busted. Masters told her to swallow it. She fished the dip out to throw it away and he said no, she had to swallow it. She put the dip back in her mouth and swallowed it. She smiled at him. When he went away she threw up in the grass.

CHAPTER FIFTEEN

It was Wednesday. We were five weeks in and coming up on our first weekend pass. Emily was flying down to see me. She'd arrive on Friday. It was going to be amazing. She was the hottest girl in the universe, and I was dying to get laid.

But it was still Wednesday, and it was 16:00, so we had to form up for Close of Business. And the first sergeant came out and told us he was fucking us. He said he wasn't giving us full weekend passes just yet. He said he was only letting us out Saturday night so he could see how we'd do. If things went alright then he'd give us a full weekend pass next time. He said it like it was cool, like he wasn't fucking us, like it wasn't just an arbitrary fucking, in broad daylight, at four o'clock in the goddamn afternoon.

"I know what you're thinking," he said. "You're thinking it isn't fair. You're thinking, The other companies don't do it this way. . . . Well here's the news, Warrior Medics. This ain't other companies. This is Charlie Company, and we do things differently. That's why we're number one."

I called Emily and told her the bad news. She was mad as fuck, but she said she was flying down anyway. She'd already arranged to take off from work. She said she'd come to town that Friday.

When Friday came around I couldn't not see her. She was at the Super 8 off the highway by the base. She was close. I said fuck it. I took a chance. The company gave us an hour free every day in the afternoon for taking care of PX-type bullshit. An hour would be enough. Fifteen minutes to get there. Fifteen minutes to get back. Half an hour with Emily. I had no choice. I had to try.

I caught a cab at the big PX. I said take me to the Super 8 motel. It wasn't five minutes from the gate. The cab let me out in front of the office. I went looking for her room; it was on the second floor. I found it. She opened the door, and the way she looked, there was nothing else for it.

SATURDAY she said, "I hate this."

I said, "What can I do? I'm in it now."

"Fuck!"

"What?"

"You act like you had no choice. But you did."

"You act like *I'm* the one who left *you*."

"You can't even compare the two things," she said.

"Why not?"

"I changed what school I was going to. You still could have come to see me whenever you wanted, and it wouldn't have been like this. I wouldn't have said, 'Oh, well gee, sweetheart, I wish I could stay, but Sergeant Fuckass says I have to be in bed at FOUR O'CLOCK IN THE AFTERNOON."

She'd spent Friday night alone at the Super 8. She'd be spending Sunday night alone too. She was flying back to Elba on Monday morning. All we had was Saturday.

She said I was an asshole.

I said I understood that but I had done the best I could and it wasn't like it had been the easiest thing in the world getting off-post Friday afternoon. I about hadn't made it back on time and I'd have been so fucked.

About Friday she said she'd thought we could have at least talked a little first.

I said I hadn't known she felt that way.

I said I'd thought it was the romantic thing to do.

. . .

SUNDAY MORNING Emily came along with me when I went back to the company. I had to go upstairs to the barracks and change into my PT clothes so I'd be ready when they called formation. I came back down in my PT shorts and my PT shirt, some ASICS running shoes on. The shorts said: ARMY. The shirt said: ARMY. I was wearing the reflector belt we always had to wear. It went diagonally across the chest. I looked like a fucking douche bag. Emily cried. She cried till it was time for her to get in a cab and leave. And the whole time I was trying to act like I was tough because I thought I was tough and I was supposed to be tough. But I wasn't. And I can tell you now that there are many things better than to try and be tough, not the least of which is to be young and fuck your girl and leave it at that.

CHAPTER SIXTEEN

There was a fake river in San Antonio. It was like the Pirates of the Caribbean ride except instead of pirates and pirate ships you got fat drunks and chain restaurants.

I was down by the Fake River. Kovak was with me. We were walking around. It was night, the weekend after Emily. We had our first full weekend pass. It was Friday.

Kovak was an Air Force brat from Nevada who'd had some bad luck on account of he liked speedballs too much. Then he'd joined the Army. He was 23, so he'd made the liquor run early that afternoon. I'd put away a fifth of Seagram's gin already. I missed Emily. Longing devoured my liver; I felt like Prometheus with his fucking birds. Now it was getting late and I thought I ought to eat something.

We passed what was advertised as a pub and grille. You could see inside. There were bagpipes on the walls, different types of flags, whatever. There were waitresses in plaid skirts. I didn't care. They had a veggie burger on the menu so I wanted in, but the guy out front, who was wearing a kilt, wouldn't let me in because I was only 20. I said I wasn't trying to drink, I just wanted the veggie burger. Still he said no. I said I'd order one to go. He wouldn't let me do that either. I got inarticulate. I told Kovak to go ahead without me. I almost walked backwards into the Fake River, but I was lucky and didn't. I took the stairs up to street level, and the Alamo was there. A bum asked me for a cigarette. I gave him one and I told him about how I'd got fucked around on the Fake River. He said they were dirty motherfuckers for fucking me around like that. He was wearing an old Expos cap pulled down low and I couldn't see his eyes, but he sounded sincere. He said there was a Denny's nearby. I said Denny's was good. I asked him if he wanted to go get some Denny's. He said he didn't have money. I said I'd pay.

We got a booth in the smoking section, and the waitress took our orders right away. I was talking-drunk, so I asked the bum about his situation and how he'd got to be a bum. He said his life had got fucked about the time he went to prison.

"What were you in prison for?"

"Murder."

The pancakes arrived.

"A fool raped my sister. So I shot him dead."

"That's understandable."

The bum was on parole, and his parole officer gave him a hard time because he didn't have a job. But he couldn't get a job because he was mentally ill.

"Leave your parole officer to me," I said. "I'm in the Army. We've got a lot of juice these days. What's his contact info?"

He gave me his parole officer's name and telephone number. We parted ways outside the Denny's. I assured him I'd have things straightened out for him soon.

MONDAY AFTERNOON Ms. Grey told us about the bad weekend she'd had. Life Flight had been called out to a barbecue party in the countryside. A young woman, the mother of young children, crashed a four-wheeler into a barbecue pavilion at a campground and hemorrhaged in her head and died on the scene in front of the whole barbecue party. Her head turned purple. A lot of bad swelling. Kids there and everything. Ms. Grey said things like this happened all the time.

We filled out our wish lists. I'd given it a lot of thought and had decided I'd like to be stationed at either Walter Reed Army Hospital or Aberdeen Proving Ground or Brooke Army Medical Center or, should those fall through, Fort Drum. Harold Ramis had said Fort Drum was a bad time. But it was near Elba, so it was near Emily, and if it was as bad as it was supposed to be I was a shoo-in.

I called the bum's parole officer that evening. I wanted to leave a message, put the ball in his court as it were. I said who I was, and I said I was in the Army and I'd taken an interest in the welfare of one Mr. Charley Pride. I said Mr. Pride had some bad mental illnesses he was dealing with and he couldn't rightfully be held accountable for his not having a job and I was prepared to go through the proper channels if the situation wasn't resolved soon.

THERE WAS a lot of fucking around with mannequins. There were mannequins that were just trunks with heads. There were entire mannequins with arms and legs. There were mannequins with rubber lungs. There were mannequins with rubber bone sticking out of their legs. There were mannequins that could squirt fake blood. There were even little baby mannequins with cherubim faces. Any mannequin you could think of had been provided for the training of Warrior Medics, and we crawled around on the floor, going from mannequin to mannequin while the cadre read scenarios to us:

"Blood pressure dropped to seventy over twenty."

(You pretended to start a line on the mannequin and push imaginary fluids.)

"Your patient is vomiting."

(You rolled the mannequin over on its side and cleared out its make-believe airway before it make-believe aspirated on make-believe vomit and make-believe died.)

"Sucking chest wound."

(An occlusive dressing was the thing for one of those.)

"Patient shows tracheal deviation."

(A make-believe tension pneumothorax called for a make-believe needle chest decompression on the midclavicular line of the make-believe third intercostal space.)

"Severe facial burns around the mouth and nose."

(A mannequin like that would need a make-believe crico-thyroidotomy.)

Eventually we did stick one another's real-life veins with 14ga needle-catheters, and we drew one another's real-life blood with butterflies. I drew some of Harlow's blood. She didn't like needles; they made her tremble.

She said, "Please be gentle."

CHAPTER SEVENTEEN

I tried to be good. But I was fucked up. Emily'd got a job as a shot girl, and I got wasted. I was kicking around a hallway on one of the floors of the Fake River Hyatt, and Kovak was helping me to not get arrested. I kept saying how it sounded slutty as fuck: shot girl. And Emily wasn't picking up her phone. I said, Kovak, doesn't it sound slutty as fuck? He said he didn't know what to tell me. I said he was a useless motherfucker. I said, If yer just gonna say useless shit I'd rather you shut the fuck up.

Then I saw Harlow coming down the hall. She was with five prior service, all dudes. She asked me what I was doing. I said the Fake River was shit because they carded everywhere. She said, Really? She said she didn't get carded. She asked if that was Kovak. I said yeah, that was Kovak. She said, Hi, Kovak. Kovak said hi. The prior service got impatient and they were dicks about it. I told the one that he was a rapist. He asked me if I was supposed to be Captain Save-a-Ho. I punched him in the mouth. He got ahold of me. I tried to get around him so I could choke him out, but I only got him in a headlock. I was at a loss for what to do then. I tried running his head into the door but it didn't work; I couldn't get enough momentum. He said, Let go of me. And his voice was all froggy and it made it so I couldn't concentrate. This fucking rapist was once a child, I thought. His friends were on me. I got punched in the jaw, and it clicked for days after. Kovak tried to help me and he punched me in the neck. A woman was shouting behind the door, "I CALLED SECURITY." We all scattered. Harlow and Kovak and I ran down the stairs and out of the hotel. We went back to the Fake River. The Fake

River was shit. It was Top 40 music. It was stale Bud Light and it was cargo shorts. It was quesadillas and Axe body spray. It was everything I was guilty of.

Harlow had a glow about her. She cleaned up nice. She asked me for a cigarette and I held out the pack and she touched my wrist. I held out a lighter for her, and she held my arm at the elbow when she leaned toward me. We walked for an hour before we felt like it was safe to go back to the hotel. She stood real close in the elevator. The room was on the seventh floor. Kovak ordered a movie on pay per view. I made a gin and tonic. Harlow wanted one as well. She sat next to me on the edge of the bed. She kept brushing her tits against my arm and breathing on me on accident. I told her that I had a girlfriend and that it was serious. But we're scared, she said, and it's okay to do things when we're scared. I said I was sorry. She fucked Kovak in the bathroom. You could hear she was really going. She liked dick a lot.

CHAPTER EIGHTEEN

We all got our orders on the same day. My orders said I was going to Fort Hood in Killeen, Texas.

Fort Hood hadn't been on my wish list.

There were two divisions at Fort Hood, the 1st Cavalry Division and the 4th Infantry Division. I knew I wasn't going to 1st Cav because people going to 1st Cav had orders that were different from mine. Theirs said 1st Cav and mine didn't. Mine only said III Corps. But that meant 4th ID.

It wasn't five minutes before I'd found out that 4th ID was deploying to Iraq that fall. And I was thinking, Emily will be mad at me.

Kovak's orders said he was going to work in a hospital on a base in Alaska. He wasn't happy about it, but I envied him.

I walked to the stairs. A girl was there. She was crying into her cell phone. "They're sending me to Walter Reed, Mom.... No.... But, Mom...but, Mom...MOM...Mom, I'm a WARRIOR Medic!"

Life is strange.

I HAD read in the news that Joe's battalion was in some bad shit that summer. There had been one week when his battalion lost 19 killed, all kids from Ohio.

I'd tried getting in touch with Joe by email and I hadn't heard back from him. I did talk to Roy, though. He said his cousin was still alive and in one piece. He said he would let me know if anything changed as far as that went.

. . .

WEEKEND PASSES had come to an end because clinicals were to start that week, so we were stuck on post. It was 21:00. We were formed up and waiting on Drill Sergeant Masters to come down and do accountability. Masters was a fuck, and he had got it in his head to go upstairs and inspect the barracks. I didn't remember having locked up my aid bag, and sure enough when Masters came down the stairs, he was holding it up like he'd really done something.

"WHO IS NUMBER EIGHTY-NINE?" he said. "WHOSE AID BAG IS THIS?"

I raised my hand, and he had me get out of ranks and stand at attention.

"FRONT LEANING REST POSITION . . . MOVE."

I got in the front leaning rest, and he left me that way while he went about telling us what the black market was.

"HAS ANYBODY HERE EVER HEARD OF THE BLACK MARKET?"

We assumed this was a rhetorical question.

"WARRIOR MEDICS, SOME OF YOU WILL BE GO-ING TO IRAQ AND AFGHANISTAN SOON. IN IRAQ, IN AFGHANISTAN, THEY HAVE THE BLACK MARKET. THE PEOPLE THERE ARE POORER THAN DIRT. THEY WILL STEAL ANYTHING THAT IS LEFT UNSECURED AND SELL IT ON THE BLACK MARKET."

He picked up my aid bag and opened it and dumped its contents onto the ground. The contents—a few field dressings, some Ace wraps, two Israeli bandages, a dusty-looking combitube set, an oral pharyngeal, a nasal pharyngeal, an unpackaged syringe, some IV tubing, two 500-cc bags of lactated Ringer's, maybe half a dozen 14ga needle catheters—had little to no monetary value.

He tossed the bag aside: "MEDICAL EQUIPMENT IS A BIG SELLER ON THE BLACK MARKET."

He bent down to address me face-to-face. "WARRIOR MEDIC, YOUR BATTLE BUDDY HAS JUST DIED BECAUSE YOU DID NOT SECURE YOUR AID BAG AND IT WAS STOLEN AND SOLD ON THE BLACK MARKET. WHEN HE GOT HIT YOU COULD DO NOTHING TO HELP HIM. YOUR BATTLE BUDDY IS DEAD AND IT IS YOUR FAULT. YOU HAVE JUST KILLED YOUR BATTLE BUDDY, WARRIOR MEDIC. WHAT ARE YOU GOING TO TELL HIS FAMILY?"

He had me do push-ups till I reached muscle failure. It didn't take three minutes to get there. Still I did a lot of push-ups. I was good at them. Most of us could do push-ups. And were the outcomes of all the wars decided by push-ups and idle talk, America might never lose.

CHAPTER NINETEEN

Brooke Army Medical Center, BAMC, was the hospital on Fort Sam. It treated civilians as well as military. The floors were very clean. It was a nice hospital. We did clinicals there, two weeks. We were supposed to go to BAMC and act like we knew what we were doing. There were five us on the floor I was on, five trainees. They split us up. We each made our rounds.

There was a guy who had been in a motorcycle wreck. His leg was broken. His wife was there in the room. I put the BP cuff on inside out, and it blew up like a life raft when I turned the machine on. He was cool about it, but his wife thought I was a total asshole. I kept on with my rounds. A man had been stabbed up in some kind of hobo war. The smell of his body was overpowering. I was to give him a sponge bath. I lifted up his balls and everything. I was storing treasure in heaven, where no thief can get to it.

One of the patients was a soft man in his 30s who had been run over by a car while crossing a street. The car had snatched off his penis and left him no-bullshit retarded. His mother was at his bedside, and her grief was so intense that to look at her was like to stare into the sun. I was glad to have the blood pressure cuff figured out by then because they were nice people, and I'd have hated myself were I to give them any more cause for sorrow.

At the end of one of the corridors was a sealed room with a kid who'd been burned up in Iraq. A soldier, a kid: no difference. The room was off-limits because his burns made him ultravulnerable to infection. But there was a window that looked in on him, so you could see him in there, where his whole life had led him to.

I GOT through clinicals without accidentally murdering anyone. And I guess I was proud of myself. The feeling lasted well into Friday evening, up till the moment my balls died suddenly and unexpectedly.

I had got punched in the balls.

As a joke.

An Army joke.

I knew something was wrong, but I waited till my balls had swollen up real bad before I told the cadre. I went back to BAMC, this time as a patient. They took X-rays in the ER. The doctor said some shit about an inguinal hernia. I didn't know what that was. He said I wouldn't need surgery, at least not as far as he could tell. Still there was the swelling and my balls hurt like a motherfucker.

I was laid out on a gurney in the ER, and the hospital staff wheeled in a guy who'd been picked up off the street. The guy was beat up pretty bad and sobbing. They put him next to me. Through the curtain I heard the nurses talking. They said the guy was concussed and he'd swallowed some teeth and he had broken ribs and somebody had poured bleach in his eyes.

They called his mother.

His mother got there.

She wouldn't stop talking.

"Who did this to you, honey? . . . Honey, did they take your billfold? . . . Did they take your billfold? They did? Honey, did they take your billfold?"

Jesus.

I got out of the hospital early in the morning with a week's supply of 800mg ibuprofens and a light-duty profile. I was glad to still have my balls, but I didn't know if I'd get to do the big field training exercise that was coming up that week. It was the last thing before graduation, and I didn't think I could graduate if I didn't go. I'd get kicked down to Delta Company and they were a month behind, so I'd be stuck at Fort Sam an extra month. I couldn't let that happen. I was supposed to go home for three weeks after graduation. I'd do it. Balls be damned.

I didn't make it through the first day of the field training exercise. It was one of those deals where they gave you a rubber M16 and you were supposed to go around saying BANG BANG BANG. I was with a squad riding up a ridge in a deuce and a half, and when we got to the top of the ridge we were all supposed to jump out of the back and get ready to say BANG BANG BANG. But when I jumped out something went wrong in my crotch and I crumpled to the ground. They took me from the field on a litter and brought me to the aid station. The medics had a look at my balls. My balls weren't doing so good. I had bled into them and they had turned royal blue. The supervising medic of the aid station had all his medics come through to look at my balls. They discussed my balls in front of me. The company first sergeant came in, and he looked at my balls. He thought it was funny. I went to the hospital and a man stuck his finger up my ass. He didn't tell me he was going to do it; he just let me have it. Then there was another man who came to talk with me, and he told me that the bleeding into my balls had inflamed my epididymis. At last I got some morphine. Then I felt better: the morphine was super nice. The bed was very comfortable. The hospital menu had a veggie burger and I ordered one and it was good and I was about ready to turn in for a night's rest when a doctor showed up with a group of interns so they could all have a look at my balls and talk about them.

I WENT back to the field the next morning with a bottle of penicillin, a three-day supply of Percocet, and a bed rest profile. There was a company formation. The first sergeant and the captain were out in front, being dicks, and the first sergeant said, "Hey, where's old Smurf Balls at? He back yet?"

I was obliged to raise my hand.

The first sergeant said to the captain, "That's the one I was telling you about. His balls turned blue."

The formation was dismissed and I was told to go see the first sergeant and the captain.

"Well, Smurf Balls," said the first sergeant, "how did you like BAMC?"

"It was alright, First Sarr."

"Good. Take good care of you, did they?"

"Yes, First Sarr."

The captain said, "Did they put you on any kind of a profile?"

"Bed rest, First Sarr."

I'd just fucked up. You didn't call a captain a first sergeant, you called him a sir. But I was dehydrated and had a couple Percocets in me, so I'd accidentally demoted him.

He was displeased. "I'm the captain, son. You call me sir. You got that?"

"I'm the first sergeant, son. What the fuck's wrong with you?"

"Do they have you on any pain medication?"

"Percocet, sir."

"You'd better let me have that."

So I was tired and dismayed. But then I got some good news too. The good news was that I was going to graduate on time even though I wasn't taking part in the FTX. And then I'd go home. And I'd see Emily.

THE DAY the company did the mass-casualty exercise part of the scenery was a lot of old ripped-up fake-bloody Air Force uniforms for the fake casualties to make them look fake-bloodier. I was on a one-man laundry detail cleaning these uniforms. There wasn't going to be any bed rest for me, never mind that

I was practically fucking crippled. I was carrying an armload of these fake-bloody Air Force uniforms up to the shack with the washing machine in it when I ran into a make-believe perimeter patrol from the make-believe forward operating base.

Somebody said, "HALT! . . . HALT! . . . *HAAALT!* . . . YEAH, YOU."

I knew him of course. I had punched him in the mouth before, at the Fake River Hyatt. We didn't like each other, and he out-ranked me. He was an E-5, a sergeant; and I was an E-2, nothing. I was at a disadvantage. I said to him, "I'm not part of this shit. I'm on the laundry detail."

"What laundry detail?"

"*This* laundry detail. What do you think I'm carrying these uniforms for?"

"Who authorized the detail?"

"You're insane, and you have no idea."

"What did you say?"

"Eat a fucking dick."

He turned to the trainee beside him and handed her his rubber M16. "Hold my weapon, Warrior Medic."

I said, "Shit."

He picked me up off the ground and body-slammed me. Fake-bloody Air Force uniforms went all over the place. He pinned my arms behind my back, while he was digging his knee into my right kidney, putting as much of his body weight into it as he could manage. I'd landed with my face on a little anthill, and ants crawled out and all over my face and bit me. I suppose I deserved it.

"Are you done mouthing off?"

"Fuck. You. Bitch."

He wouldn't let me go. I could see some of his make-believe patrol out of the corner of my eye. Kovak was with them.

I said, "Kovak, what the fuck is the matter with you?"

He said, "Hey, stop. That's the guy who hurt his balls."

. . .

WE GRADUATED. They played the Toby Keith song. We were free to leave. My balls were getting back to normal, but the penicillin I'd been taking for my epididymitis had made me ultrasensitive to sunlight and I was badly sunburned. Plus, there were the ant bites. I ran into Private Harlow just as I was leaving for the airport, and she saw me and she laughed in my face.

CHAPTER TWENTY

E mily was driving.

She said, "What if I chopped off your feet?"

I said, "No."

"What? You'd like it. You're fucking lazy. You could just sit around and smoke dope all day. Think about it. Save you the trip."

"I think you'd get in trouble if you cut off my feet, baby."

"Not if you don't press charges."

"Destruction of government property."

"Seriously?"

"I'm afraid so. It'd be out of my hands."

"Hmm."

"They think of everything."

"I wish I could chop your feet off."

"I know, baby."

"It isn't fair."

"No, it isn't."

Emily'd be with me the whole time I was home, and she drove me around when I had to go places. Things were good. She was between jobs. She wasn't a shot girl anymore. She had saved money up. She was caught up on her loans. She was caught up at school. She'd got all As. I was so proud of her. I was glad she wasn't a shot girl anymore.

I had three weeks. The only catch was I had to spend two weeks doing some shit called Hometown Recruiting. I got to see Kelly and Space again. They didn't remember me. That was fine. There was recruiting to be done at a fair in Mayfield. Sergeant

Bellamy and I had brought the Army of One rock-climbing wall along with us. But the only people at the fair who wanted anything to do with it were the babies. I'd put the babies into harnesses and clip them to ropes attached to automatic belaying devices atop the Army of One rock-climbing wall. The belaying devices were good because the babies didn't break their necks. But the problem was that the babies didn't weigh enough and the devices pulled them up directly to the top of the wall. I'd clip a baby to a rope and up the wall the baby would go. I asked Bellamy what I ought to do. Bellamy was a recruiter who had come aboard at the Severance Armed Forces Career Center in the time since I'd gone through there that past January. He was a short paunchy man with dirty eyes, and he had a mouth full of gold like Space.

I said, "What am I supposed to do, Sarr? These kids can't get on the thing right. They're too light. They fly straight up and get stuck at the top."

He said, "Just make it work, Pri."

So I did what the man said and I kept hooking babies to the ropes and the babies kept flying away and I'd have to climb up the wall and fetch them down again. This went on for a long time. I don't know where they got all the babies from but they did. They kept bringing me baby after baby till a thunderstorm came along to drive everybody away from the fair. And we took the Army of One rock-climbing wall down so it wouldn't get struck by lightning.

Bellamy rode off in his late-model Dodge Durango. I hung around in the deluge and waited for Emily to come get me. I liked rain and I was already soaked so it didn't make a difference if I stood in the rain or not. When Emily pulled up she looked perfect. She was very good to me.

We went to meet my parents at a Mexican restaurant. My dad asked me how things had gone at the fair and I recounted the babies for him and everyone agreed it was funny. We all had a nice time. And I couldn't help but think that it was too bad that I was supposed to go to Iraq in a few weeks. But it couldn't be helped. You make your bed, you lie in it.

I ASSUMED I'd be piss-tested about as soon as I got to Fort Hood, so I was trying to get a lot of weed smoking in early on. Most everyone I knew lived near enough to Severance, and this was easily done.

I had an hour before I had to be back at the Armed Forces Career Center. Emily picked me up and drove me over to James Lightfoot's mom's house. James Lightfoot and I got blazed as shit. Emily didn't smoke weed. She only fucked with pills. I'd brought a razor with me, and I was shaving at the kitchen sink. I was cutting the shit out of myself, and James Lightfoot was telling me about Kashi the Indian. Kashi had been living in Cleveland the past four years, studying at Case. Now his student visa was up and he'd have to leave the country soon if he didn't do something, and he was thinking about enlisting in the Army as a means of becoming an American citizen.

"Why does he want to be an American citizen?"

"It beats me. I guess he likes it here better than India."

"Huh. . . . Do you have any Clear Eyes?"

I was five minutes late getting back. I had needed the extra time to get myself together. I was still blazed as shit. Bellamy was the only guy in the office when I came in. The rest of the recruiters had already left for the big freestyle basketball tournament downtown. Bellamy was pissed at me. He told me to start doing push-ups, and I went about doing that; then I said, "I apologize for being late, Sarr, but I have a good reason. I think I may have found somebody who wants to sign up."

"Recover," he said. "Tell me about it in the Durango."

Once we were on our way I gave Bellamy the details about Kashi, and he made me promise not to tell any of the other recruiters. I said I wouldn't.

Our stand was set up in a parking lot across the street from the arena. A great deal of basketball-related shit was taking place there. I milled around the crowd and tried to hand out flyers. Someone asked me what suburb I was from. His face was youthful at first glance, but then I saw the crow's-feet and the laugh lines. He was missing a front tooth. He had his dirty-blond hair done up in cornrows, and he was wearing Cavs shorts and a Tall T. He said his name was Jug. I tried to recruit Jug for the Army but he said he wouldn't do it because Vice President Cheney had conspired with the Illuminati to knock down the Twin Towers and take control of the world's oil supply. I admitted that I hadn't heard this.

"And yet here you are," he said, "yer ignorant ass tryin to hoodwink all these young niggaz into spilling their blood for Dick the Devil and the Illuminati."

I told him I had to be going because Sergeant Bellamy was probably looking for me.

He asked if I'd ever been to Iraq.

"I'm supposed to go this fall."

"Better tell them people yer gay. Go to Canada or some shit."

I said I didn't think there was any way out of it.

He said, "Yer gonna die."

CHAPTER TWENTY-ONE

Fort Hood was bleak, a new kind of desert, engineered to induce fatalism in the young. It worked like a charm.

4th ID put me in an armor battalion. It wasn't all armor though. The battalions were getting mixed up then. There were two armor companies (Alpha and Bravo) and two infantry companies (Delta and Echo) and an engineer company (Charlie), along with a support company (Foxtrot) and a headquarters company (HHC). The latter two had a lot of different shit in them: cooks, mechanics, scouts, mortars, intelligence, finance. The medic platoon was part of HHC. I went there first. I'd either stay there as part of the aid station or get attached to one of the line companies (Alpha through Echo).

I didn't like it in the medic platoon; most everybody in it was older than I was, and they put a premium on a kind of talking I wasn't any good at. So I told the guy running the platoon that I wanted to be in one of the line companies and he attached me to Echo. That's how I got into the infantry.

It was September. We were deploying in November. The company was a tight group. So it went about as you'd expect. There was a lot of Who the fuck are you?

Sergeant Shoo was my boss. Big kind of bro-ish motherfucker. The other two medics attached to Echo were joes, lower enlisted, like I was. PFC Yuri and PFC Burnes. They were good people. Yuri was arrogant as fuck but it was alright, and the 11Bs liked him on account of he was batshit crazy in the heavy metal sense of the words. As for Burnes, he was maybe too smart to be in the Army. You could see it was killing him, how dumb it was.

He kept to himself mostly and spent his off time studying differential calculus and drinking Icehouse beer. He was planning a career in politics. He was in his early 30s and seemed old as fuck to all of us who were just kids really.

I WAS lucky in that my roommates in the barracks were laid-back and not excessively patriotic. They were infantry from Delta Company: PFC Grace and Private Carranza. Grace was from Oregon. He was 20 like I was. He looked like Jean-Michel Basquiat and he talked like a surfer. He was my assigned roommate. Carranza was staying there unofficially on Grace's invitation. Carranza was married so he got BAH, the basic housing allowance, which meant he couldn't get a place in the barracks. He had an apartment off-post in Killeen but, for whatever reason, Mrs. Carranza was pissed at him and he was kind of homeless.

It so happened that Grace and Carranza were fucking the same 17-year-old girl from Harker Heights. Carranza explained it all to me. "That's my little snow bunny," he said. "I'm keeping her on ice."

Then Grace married her and that sorted it out. But the three of them still hung out together, and they watched *Casino* five or six times a week. Grace was going to die in Iraq and Carranza's face would get destroyed there, but this was before any of those things happened, so hearts were light.

Apparently Grace was some kind of dynamo in the fucking department because the girl would go nuts whenever he fucked her. You could hear her through the wall. They'd go for hours. You got the idea that it was true love, sacred and unguarded. But it was none of my business. I was in the business of being lonely all the time. Weekends I'd go to the movies in Killeen. It was one of those big shopping center movie theaters, and I'd spent so much time there I'd run out of movies I hadn't seen.

I talked to Emily as much as I could. I'd call her up after nine, when the minutes were free and it was ten her time so she'd usually be done with work. She was waiting tables at a chain restaurant. They served Caribbean food there. She said it was good. She worked full-time. She went to school full-time. She did all the homework. It was hard to imagine having the energy for all that. She was working her ass off. And it was good that we could at least talk, but there was a distance. I'd been in the Army going on nine months by then.

"People think you don't exist," she said. "They think I'm making you up."

I said I was sorry about that.

"I never see you," she said. "It isn't normal. Why don't I get to have a boyfriend I can see?"

I said, "I think I'll have the chance to make it up there around Columbus Day. Maybe Veterans Day at the latest."

". . . Okay."

"Just hold on for me, you know?"

"I miss you."

"I miss you too."

And it was always that. That was most of all what we said to one another.

SINCE I was the Fucking New Guy, I got sent with the company when it went out to the field to train. It was considered a hassle to go and sit out there for days and do nothing, and it would have been a hassle for a Shoo or a Yuri or a Burnes, who'd done it a million and a half times already, but I didn't mind. I would have just been lonely as shit anyway and I could smoke cigarettes as I pleased.

The weather had been dry for months, and when the company trained with live ammunition the tracer rounds set the grass on fire. I'd go out and run around with a square rubber mat on the end of a long stick and slap at the fires to put them out. Sometimes the grass fires crept into a tree and the tree would go up like a match. Which I liked.

. . .

IT WAS good to go AWOL. There wasn't any training on the calendar for Columbus Day weekend, so there was a window. As long as I could make it back in time for the 06:00 formation that Tuesday, no one would know I'd been gone.

As I was going AWOL I couldn't use the Killeen airport; there was a chance the Army would have some goons there checking paperwork. Fortunately Yuri had a pathological aversion to authority types, and he said he'd drive me to the regional airport in Temple. From there I could fly to Bush Intercontinental in Houston and make a connecting flight north.

When work was over we got out of town, Lamb of God blaring in his Honda Accord. I didn't know how he could listen to that shit and not kill himself. But I was grateful to him.

IT RAINED all weekend in Elba. Emily and I lay around and slept through the days. We would go out and drive around at night. It was fall and you could really feel that it was fall. There was that ache. You were crushed by the beauty of it all: all the bare trees and the black sky and the streetlights. It was two years since we had met. We were older now; we both had money saved and we had our jobs and we were very much on our own. She'd be 21 in a month. We were so sure that we had grown up. We would get married before I went to Iraq. She brought it up this time. She said it made practical sense. If we were married I'd get paid more and she could be on my health insurance. And I'd get to marry Emily.

"But we're going to get divorced," she said.

I said that was fine.

I said, "We'll get divorced if that's what you want."

CHAPTER TWENTY-TWO

Emily and I were married in Elba by a justice of the peace the Tuesday after Veterans Day. Joe and Roy had made the drive over from Cleveland to visit Emily and me that Friday night, and Joe head-butted me in the face. It was all in good fun though. He hadn't meant anything by it. He didn't know that Emily and I were getting married. No one did. She didn't want anyone to know.

My nose was busted and there was still blood on my windbreaker and we had no rings. Emily was wearing a blue mechanic's jacket with a name tag on it that read MARIO. She looked like an angel. And we knew that at that moment we were the two most beautiful things in the world. How long it lasted, I don't know, but it was true for at least a few minutes. Six billion people in the world and no one had it on us.

After we got married she drove me to the airport and we sat in her car in the parking lot and cried like babies till it was time for me to go.

PART THREE

CHERRY

CHAPTER TWENTY-THREE

Unless you happen to have been there, you've never heard of where we were, so it doesn't matter. There was a FOB, a forward operating base. The FOB had been built up around a power plant beside the river. The power plant was a monster of a thing and made all kind of noise. It burned oil so oil was everywhere. Oil was in the air. Oil covered the ground. We lived in the shadow of the power plant, by the North Gate, in the Russian Village, which was a few buildings, concrete buildings, close together. That was our company area, where we slept and lived and all that. Delta Company was down at the other end of the motor pool. The aid station was down that way too, next to the LZ. The rest of the battalion was in the Tent City on the east end of the FOB, on the other side of the power plant, past the haji shops, towards the Main Gate. The battalion TOC was up that way, next to the Tent City. At first I thought people were saying "talk" because the radios were in the TOC and people talk on radios. But it wasn't talk; it was TOC. And TOC stood for something and somebody had to tell me that or I'd have always had it wrong probably. So TOC. The battalion had its TOC. Each company had its own TOC. There were many TOCs. TOCs abounded. The battalion TOC was the big one though, two stories. It faced the road that ran along the north wall of the FOB. The road ran west to where we were, by the North Gate, where you could look out and see the river on the left-hand side and Route Martha going up through the fields and the palm groves. Route Martha wasn't two lanes' worth of tar.

We showed up in December. We were taking over for some

Nasty Girls, the Mississippi Rifles. They weren't big on cere-mony. They said we were ate-the-fuck-up. They had pictures of their kills and they'd collated them into a PowerPoint slide show called "Towelhead Takedown." We phased in as they phased out. We did right-seat/left-seat rides. The last of the Mississippi Rifles was on his way home by Christmas. Christmas was our first day on our own.

Third Platoon was on QRF1. I was Third Platoon's medic. We were staging by the power plant when Haji shot the battalion TOC with a rocket. Three were wounded. But we didn't see any-thing. We were 200 meters from where the rocket hit, and there were buildings in the way. It was a great disappointment. In the beginning you wanted to be where the action was.

QRF1 meant we were supposed to go out if anything hap-pened in the battalion's area of operations. Should a patrol get hit or make contact, we were its backup. Should EOD get called, we were its escort. So it didn't make sense when we were sent out to pull security while one of the miscellaneous sergeants from our headquarters platoon flew a small, remote-controlled airplane around outside the base. The little airplane was called a Raptor. I didn't like it.

You were wide awake when you got out on the ground out-side the wire for the first time. You expected to get shot any moment. We had stopped at a random spot where you couldn't see anyone around but you were nevertheless sure that there was a haji out there who had been waiting all day just to shoot *you*. And you were as ready for it as you could get, but it didn't happen. The sergeant fucked around with his airplane. The sun went down. The sergeant got his airplane back and we mounted up and left. It had got dark fast. On our way back we heard the battalion net saying a Charlie Company patrol was hit out on Route Polk. And we were supposed to get there. The problem was we had been out fucking around with the little airplane and we were on the wrong side of the FOB. We had to go through the Main Gate on the southeast end, then cut through the FOB to get out at the North Gate. We went half a klick on Martha and turned right onto Route Grove, which got us to Polk. If we had been on the FOB to start with we'd have made it in five minutes. As it was it took us close to thirty minutes. Half the battalion had beaten us to the spot. A long column of vehicles was between us and the Charlie Company Patrol.

It had gone out over the net that there were five casualties from an IED: two KIAs, three WIAs. I was in Lieutenant Heyward's truck, and I asked him if I ought to go and help out, seeing as I was supposed to be a medic. He sent Specialist Sullivan with me.

An up-armored Humvee was overturned and on fire in a bomb crater. There were three wounded lying on the road near the truck and two dead in the truck, in the fire. The wounded were stable—broken bones, minor burns, concussions, shit like that, nothing life-threatening. The Charlie Company medic had done well getting the wounded ready for medevac. Some medics from HHC had come out, and they'd helped him.

The medevac helicopter touched down in a field to the left of the road. We took up the litters with the wounded and carried them out into the dark and over the broken ground. We were all crouching down low well before we were under the rotor blades, and with what little light there was I could see the man on the litter I was helping carry. His eyes were wild and grieving. He was in his lizard brain. We made eye contact; and I said, "I got you."

I said it real loud so he could hear me over the helicopters. And then I was embarrassed because it was a stupid and melodramatic thing to have said and I had said it.

Back at the road the upside-down Humvee wasn't on fire anymore. There was a wrecker trying to take it out of the hole in the road, and a lot of people were in the way trying to get a look at the bodies that were still inside the truck. A master sergeant was ground-guiding the wrecker, and he got to yelling, "EVERYONE OUT OF THE WAY. THIS AIN'T A FUCKIN SHOW."

Sullivan and I were in the way. So we walked back to Heyward's truck, and Sullivan said, "Did you see those bodies? You could see all the bones."

When we got back to the FOB, guys were waiting for us in the motor pool. They asked us what all had happened and who had got killed and what we had seen. I wasn't much good for telling them anything. I went and talked to Shoo. Shoo thought it was funny that I was being such a bitch about it. He was laughing at me some. He said I'd just got my cherry popped. I went back to the room I stayed in. Some of the others who stayed in the room were there. Burnes, Yuri, Lessing, Fuentes, Cheetah: they were there. All of them but Arnold were there. They wanted to know what had happened. I didn't really know what had happened but I told them anyway. Fuentes left to go to the company TOC. He had to go on radio guard. He left the room solemnly, like he was off to embalm his own grandmother.

Arnold came in. Fuentes had relieved him. He said he'd heard on the radio that the three guys we had put on the helicopter were dead. It fucked me up; I was kind of devastated. They hadn't looked like they were going to die. What had we missed?

Arnold's boss, Staff Sergeant Drummond, came in, and I said, "Sarr, is it true the guys we put on the medevac are dead?"

"No. Who told you that?"

"Arnold said he heard on the net that they were dead."

"Arnold's a retard."

"I thought that was what I heard, Sarr."

"Shut up, Arnold. And you, calm down and don't get so excited. You're acting like a woman."

Drummond left.

Yuri said, "That guy's an asshole."

We all smoked cigarettes.

Lessing was pissed off; he said, "We got our asses kicked today."

Lessing was from Chicago.

Burnes was doing some math. "We took eight casualties today," he said, "out of a population of what? Maybe eight hundred?"

"And we're here for a fucking year," I said, "a year's worth of fucking days."

Yuri said we were fucked.

Lessing said, "What did you guys think you were coming here to do?"

CHAPTER TWENTY-FOUR

A few days after Christmas, Second Platoon had an IED go off on one of their patrols. A Humvee was torn up and on fire. All the soldiers got out of the truck okay, but a reporter was still inside. The reporter's head was fucked up pretty well from the blast, and he was unconscious in the backseat of the burning truck, next to the ammo boxes. Sergeant Thorpe went back into the truck to get the reporter. This was brave of him to do since the truck was on fire, plus he thought he was getting shot at. The shots he heard were rounds cooking off.

Thorpe pulled the reporter out of the truck and got himself shot by a cooked-off round in the process. He was hit on the inside of the thigh. But he wasn't hurt bad—just a flesh wound, as they say.

The reporter was the worse for wear. He was burned on his face and upper body and had what would prove to be some brain damage. But Burnes, who was Second Platoon's medic, helped him out and kept him from dying till they could put him on a helicopter. The guy ended up living. So Burnes had done well and Thorpe was a hero—a no-bullshit, shot hero.

THORPE'S WIFE was pregnant. She was in the Army too. She was with 4th ID but she hadn't deployed. She was with the rear detachment back at Fort Hood, and she'd got knocked up there.

Seeing as Mr. and Mrs. Sergeant Thorpe had said goodbye to one another in November, and seeing as it was still December, you'd think she'd have tried telling him the baby was his. But the thing was she couldn't. The reason being Mr. and Mrs. Sergeant Thorpe were white people and Mrs. Sergeant Thorpe had got knocked up by a black guy.

When she first told her husband about this, she said it was a consensual thing between her and the black guy. Then she said the black guy had raped her. The police must have believed her because the black guy was in jail.

Sergeant Thorpe more or less lost his mind over all this. And he'd talk to anyone who'd listen about what had happened to him. He'd get all philosophical about it and quote Top 40 radio songs. He had this look in his eyes, like he'd about died; she'd almost killed him.

Staff Sergeant Drummond said, "I could've told you ol girl was a whore." Thorpe was on radio guard and we were talking about him behind his back because we all felt bad for him, even Drummond, who wasn't big on sympathy. He said, "Me and my wife had those two over to our house for supper one time, and this was in September, and she told me and my wife, right in front of her husband, how she'd screwed her first-line supervisor in a Porta-John when she was deployed back in oh-three. She said it right there at the table while we were eatin supper. My wife couldn't believe it. She thinks that woman's trash. I felt bad for Thorpe. I knew it was going to turn out bad for him. But what could I say to him? Your wife's a no-good straight piece-of-trash whore? No! Now old Thorpe, he's not the sharpest tack in the box. He's a good man, so don't get me wrong. He's better'n most of the idiots we've got in this company. Still he should've known better than to get hisself hitched to a whore like that one. Cripes! Foolin around on him with a gosh-dang porch ape, son."

THERE WERE two rows of chemical toilets: one in front of the company area, atop the berm that came up to the motor pool; the other in the back, atop the berm that went up to the road that took you through the power plant. All told we had a dozen chemical toilets. Most of the shitting, pissing, and masturbating to be done inside the wire would be done in these.

Once a week this permanently sunburned Russian came around in a special truck and sucked all the shit and piss and jizz and etcetera out of the chemical toilets with a big hose and he sprayed the chemical toilets down with a pressure washer, looking like an old fisherman in a gale. He was a friendly guy too. He always smiled and gave you the thumbs-up if you waved to him. I've often wondered if he was a spy.

If you wanted to buy something you went to the haji shops, little plywood shacks that sold more or less all the shit you needed and some more shit you didn't need. I went and bought a carton of Miamis for $5. It was a good deal at 50¢ a pack, so good it made up for the Miamis tasting like bug spray. I bought three cans of Wild Tiger too, and a box of Metro bars. Metro bars were alright. Wild Tiger was fucking great. It was like Red Bull but with nicotine in it. It was real expensive by haji shop standards, but it was so good it didn't matter. It was New Year's Day. Happy New Year.

I went to the phone tent because the phones were back on and I could call Emily. The phones had been off since Christmas on account of the casualties. There was a line and I had to wait awhile till a phone opened up and I sat down. I'd had the calling card in my hand already for a half an hour and I put the card number in and put Emily's number in and I got through.

"How are you?" she asked.

"Better now. So much better. Goddamn. The sound of your voice, you know. I miss you."

"I miss you too. I've been waiting for you to call. Are you alright?"

"Yeah. How are things?"

"Things are good."

"Anything new?"

"Nothing really. I made a new friend."

"That's good," I said. "Who's your new friend?"

"He's *interesting*, man. He's from Puerto Rico and he robs ATM machines."

"You don't say."

"Yeah, he robs ATM machines. But don't worry. He's really nice. He's a cool guy."

"Are you fucking with me?"

"What?"

"Nothing. How old is this guy?"

"Twenty-five."

"Uh-huh. That's nice. How did you meet him?"

"At a party with some people from work."

"Great. May I ask you something?"

"Of course."

"Do you seriously think the twenty-five-year-old Puerto Rican guy who robs ATM machines wants to be your friend? Don't you think it's more realistic that he just wants to fuck you? . . . You there?"

"He's just a nice guy. He's cool."

"Sweetheart, I love you, but that's the stupidest fucking thing I've ever heard you say."

". . . What's your fucking problem, man? Don't you trust me?"

"I trust you. It's just that there's no such thing as a nice guy. Believe me. I'm as nice as they get and I'm a total piece of shit."

"You don't have to worry about me."

"I'm not worried about you. I'm worried about this motherfucker."

"You don't trust me."

"I trust you."

"But you *don't*."

"I *do*. I fucking *do*. So shut up and I love you a lot, okay?"

"I love you too."

"Really though. I mean you're it, you know? Like you're it for me."

"I feel the same way."

"Just watch out, okay. Cuz, this guy, I have a feelin he's bad news."

"It'll be okay. You can trust me."

"I trust you. That's not it. It's just I think he might be bad news."

CHAPTER TWENTY-FIVE

The infantry were fired up and eager to kill. They were impatient to begin killing. They wanted to kill so bad. There was a profligate confidence in our firepower. There was a bullshit comradery. But sometimes having all the guns and ammo lying around was a problem, like when PFC Borges told Corporal Lockhart that Lockhart was a faggot and that Lockhart's wife knew he was a faggot but she'd married him just to take all his money. Borges was kind of fat and could be a real nasty motherfucker. That and the meth had got his face. He'd done some pimping before he joined the Army. He had liked pimping but his country needed him. He said his bitches still wrote. Borges had the devil's own luck. Not Lockhart though. Lockhart was one of those ones to say people took his kindness for weakness. Really it was just the weakness they took for weakness though, as it always is. And that night Lockhart pulled a 12ga on Borges and Borges said, "Do it, faggot."

And Lockhart said he was going to do it.

But he didn't.

I was riding with Sergeant North and his fire team in the lead Humvee. We were going to an Iraqi Army base. They'd sent us to win the hearts and minds of the IAs there. We didn't know what that meant, but we would see what happened. We arrived at the base without incident and had falafel and Zamzam colas with the IAs. The patrol leader went and talked to whomever. He got done and we mounted up to head back to the FOB. It was after curfew.

We took a wrong turn somewhere and got lost and ended up on the opposite side of the river from the FOB. We could see the FOB from where we were, but nobody knew how to get there. We were traveling on a narrow strip of road and we were driving fast without headlights. (You didn't ever use headlights.) A white sedan came around a bend in the road, and North radioed back. The last Humvee turned so as to block the road off, and the white sedan didn't try to go around. If it had it would have been lit up. So it didn't.

North and I left the truck and walked to where the white sedan was. North looked like Morrissey. As far as I know that was all he had in common with Morrissey. North was a killer. And he was from Idaho. But he looked like Morrissey. I think he was about 23 then.

Two hajis were standing on the road with their legs apart and their arms out, getting frisked. They were both wearing man dresses and sandals. The older of the two of them had thick strangler wrists and a no-fucking-around mustache. The younger was wiry and clean-shaven, and he had the young-Elvis hair like a lot of the hajis did.

Some joes searched the car. Two joes covered the hajis. One joe was saying that the two hajis were probably boyfriends, and the other thought that was funny and said the two faggots had no clue how close they'd just come to getting smoked.

The patrol leader asked the mustache haji questions about what he was doing out so late and where he was coming from and where he was going. An interpreter translated.

The car was clean.

The radio said to let the hajis go on their way.

The patrol leader said to the interpreter, "Tell them that from now on they must respect the curfew. It's for their own safety. They could've been hurt out here tonight and we don't want that to happen."

And the interpreter said something. As far as what he said, we'd have to trust him. So that was that.

The white sedan went on its way, going south by southeast. We mounted up and continued on, heading north by northwest. And we hadn't been driving a full minute when North said, "Stop stop *stop*."

There was an EFP on the side of the road. EFPs could cut through anything. The Iranians liked them. But this isn't a big deal. North spotted the EFP, and the driver stopped short of the pressure plate. It was close, but *close* is just another word for nothing. So nothing happened. And we made it back that night.

A POG got the first confirmed kill.

(Personnel Other Than Grunt.)

The POG was a cook.

She did it with a fifty-cal.

Foxtrot was bringing a KBR convoy out of Baghdad to set up a DFAC on our FOB. (Kellogg Brown & Root; dining facility.) PFC Livingston was up in the turret of one of the Humvees. Presumably somebody had put her up there as a joke, because I don't think she weighed more than 100 pounds and a fifty-cal. weighed about a million pounds and it wasn't like the turrets moved so easy either.

So.

The convoy was ambushed—IED, then small-arms fire. But Livingston kept her cool. And maybe she saw the haji in the palm grove before she lit him up . . .

The infantry were sick when they found out about her kill. It was dishonor: a fucking POG, a fucking girl.

And she'd have got promoted, but she kept getting caught getting fucked because she'd get fucked for money. And there was an E-6 who'd lose his stripes fucking her in a guard tower.

(The sergeant of the guard.) They said he was hitting her in the ass.

She was definitely fuckable.

She had a nice face.

And she was hard-core.

One of God's diamonds.

CHAPTER TWENTY-SIX

The Big Shia City was well south of the FOB. Getting there meant driving an hour down a four-lane highway called Route Carentan. Traffic was usually heavy on Carentan, but it served to clear the route so that you didn't have to worry too much about pressure plates.

There was a point where Carentan crossed the river and you'd have to cross on a pontoon bridge since the actual bridge had been bombed during the invasion. Bravo Company kept a bridge guard there, and lots of haji kids hung around in the day-time to beg MREs off the soldiers on the banks of the river. The kids were skinny shoeless boys mostly. There was also a little girl you'd see sometimes who might have been seven or eight, or she might have been older only more malnourished. She had dusty brown hair that was like a bird's nest, and her dress was like something out of the Flintstones.

We called her Pebbles.

We kept two rifle squads at the Iraqi Police station in the city center. But it was whatever. We didn't control the city. Neither did the IPs. It was the Mahdi militia who controlled the city. We had a cease-fire with the Mahdi on account of the higher-ups having decided they were too much of a pain in the ass to fight. The Mahdi were Shia. And they were backed by Iran. So we weren't allowed to fuck with the Mahdi and we weren't allowed to patrol the city. We could drive to the police station and leave the same way we had come in. That was all.

The police station was three stories high with a walled court-yard in front and another in back. There was a jail and it was packed with prisoners. One time the prisoners all sang together and you could hear them outside the jail and it was very beautiful and it made you feel like an asshole.

Some of the IPs were alright. Some of them were fucks. But that was whatever too. And there was a special haji SWAT team sort of deal there and the hajis on the haji SWAT team thought they were the hottest shit going; they were absolutely fucking delusional but this was what they thought. They rode around in a shitty compact pickup with a machine gun in the back and them all piled on top of one another looking like a lot of goddamn fools. We hated the shit out of them because they'd got some kicks out of showing us grainy IED videos on a portable DVD player; they'd pointed at the screen and said, "You see? Good. You see? You see? Good, yes?"

Yes, we were for killing them and it would have been easy. But orders were orders, and we'd been told to endure them for the sake of their hearts and minds. So we did.

I WAS on the roof of the police station, on a guard shift, trying to figure out the sniper scope on an M14. This wasn't my job but I had got stuck up on the roof with this M14 and I was doing my best. We didn't ever have near as many guys as we were supposed to have.

An IP walked up behind me and said, "Mister."

He offered me a cigarette, a Miami. He called me brother. It was a windy day. You had to be careful smoking Miamis on a windy day; one false move and the Miami would turn to ash in a great flash of light. I cupped the cigarette. The haji cop admired my form. He smiled knowingly, and said he wanted to ask me something. I said alright.

He gave me a long windup about this crippled wife of his: "The leg is very sick, you see."

He asked if I had any morphine I could spare.

"You want me to give you morphine?"

"Aha! You did not know. But you see, I too know things about medicine."

"I'm sorry but I have no morphine I can give you."

"You have the morphine, yes?"

"If I give you morphine I'll get in trouble."

"You can give the morphine to me?"

"No."

He stopped smiling and he said something in Arabic. Sounded like "motherfucker."

Going home, the Humvees stopped to wait to cross the pontoon bridge. Sergeant North saw the shoeless haji kids and Pebbles standing out there and he got an idea. He opened his door and called to Pebbles. He held out an MRE and waved to her. She hurried towards him, reaching out for the MRE, and North, who incidentally survived the tour without a scratch, pulled the MRE out of her reach just when she got there and he shut the up-armored door and thought it was funny.

ON DAYS when it wasn't our turn to go to the police station we'd get sent out to the middle of fucking nowhere to collect unexploded ordnance. A couple of us would have mine detectors. Sometimes we'd walk in old minefields. It was boring as hell.

We were out this way around an old barracks complex. It had been bombed in one of the wars, and all the buildings were in ruins. I wandered around. I got to thinking of Emily and I tried to picture what she was doing. I pictured her eating her lunch, probably something with lentils. Then I remembered it wasn't lunchtime where she was.

There was an old Air Force bomb lying out on the desert floor. It hadn't exploded whenever it was dropped. It was cracked open and there was green foam that had come out of it. Our people took turns posing with the bomb, having their pictures taken.

The lieutenant called it in.

The radio came back and said to get away from the bomb.

So they all got away from the bomb.

That same day three vans full of explosives went off and killed more than 140 outside the mosque near the police station. First Platoon was there when it happened. Some of them stood on the roof of the police station and filmed what they could get of it with their digital cameras. I saw the videos they took and you couldn't really see anything.

OUR FIRST raid was on an apartment complex north of the Big Shia City. We came up in a wedge formation over a long stretch of open ground looking up at a lot of windows. It had been raining. I thought, This isn't a bad way of drawing fire.

All I had was a 9mm pistol and everyone else had a proper gun and I felt like a fool. I asked the sergeant nearest me, "Am I supposed to have my weapon drawn? Cuz I don't know. It seems kind of stupid."

Staff Sergeant Greene had been an NYPD cop. He had enlisted after September 11. They said he'd killed 15 hajis in 2003. He was no faker.

He said, "Shut up."

So I drew my pistol and I did my best, but I had my mind made up to look into getting a better gun when I got back to the FOB.

A lot of bomb-making material was found in the apartment of an IP captain, and he was detained. We also found a few dozen mortar rounds and 155mm shells all around the grounds behind the buildings. One-five-fives were the big ones. You hit an IED with a couple one-five-fives in it and you were having a bad day, probably your last bad day. So we gathered up all of those and brought them back with us and rode back to the FOB with them rolling around on the floors of the tracks, wondering if we'd suddenly disappear.

. . .

WE WENT back to the Big Shia City for the Ashura. One hundred thousand pilgrims would be there. At least 100,000. We expected attacks. We were staying at the police station through the week, a whole platoon's worth of us.

I was doing a turn on radio guard. It was the middle of the night. Valentine's Day was coming up and there was a laptop with Internet in the radio room, so I got an idea about ordering Emily some flowers. I had my debit card on me. I asked Staff Sergeant Castro and he said I could use the computer. Castro was laid-back. I went online and found an affordable orchid for $110. It had to be an orchid; nothing else would do.

I couldn't come up with anything good to put on the card. I was tired, I guess. I ended up typing the bouquet of parentheses from *Seymour: An Introduction*. I thought she'd know what it was. I signed "love" and my initials.

Staff Sergeant Castro asked me if I was a rich kid.

I said not especially but we never starved or nothin.

In the morning I was in the back courtyard, guarding things as I often was, and it was getting on in the morning because the shit flies were out. The shit flies landed on your lips and walked around. Then they went to go get more shit on their feet. There was shit everywhere so it was easy enough and they'd come back and they'd walk around on your lips some more. It got so you only noticed when they weren't around.

I heard some shit like yelling, and two IPs crashed through a door into the courtyard. They were wrestling over a 9mm Glock. Both of the IPs were wearing plain clothes. They looked like 1970s TV detectives with their slacks and their mustaches and their leather jackets. I knew the gun was loaded; people don't usually wrestle over unloaded guns. And it was a Glock so there was no safety switch on it. I didn't know if I was supposed to shoot them.

So I just stood there. Some more haji cops ran out and they pulled the two apart and one of them got run off and somebody threw a shoe.

THE PILGRIMS came out under a white sky. The imam had been martyred where the big mosque was and that had been 1000 years ago and the mosque was named for him. That's what the intelligence officer had said.

The minaret broadcast verses and a great slow drum sounded and the men struck themselves with knives in unison. I was standing on top of the barricade and I saw all this. A sea of black. Dust clouds rising into the air and disappearing. Nothing changed in 1000 years.

And now when I try to remember the way the verses went, the way the drum went, I can't get all the way back there. I am forever outside of it. I know how it was, how it looked, but I can't see it. I didn't have a camera. I didn't believe in taking a camera out with me. I suppose I thought if the Haj ever took me alive I wouldn't want him filming me with my own camera when I got my head sawed off.

Some IPs came back and showed me their cuts from where they had been cutting their own heads. The cuts were unimpressive. It was like they almost really had and then hadn't.

On the last night of the Ashura a haji tried to sneak over the wall behind the police station, and Sergeant Bautista shot him in the ass with a star-cluster flare. I was there too. The haji got away. We could have shot him a lot more and with real bullets and nobody would have given us a hard time about it. But we were fakers, so we didn't.

At the bridge on the way back, I gave Pebbles an MRE. She held it tight against her chest and ran off with it. But one of the shoeless boys caught her and punched her in the head and took the MRE away from her. She was sitting in the dust when we drove away.

CHAPTER TWENTY-SEVEN

We didn't get much in the way of prior notice; then the sergeants were at us, going:

"Git yer shit."

"Chop chop, dalli dalli."

So on and so forth.

PFC Borges was huffing computer duster with his battle buddy, Specialist Roche, when Staff Sergeant Castro came banging on the door. Borges went to get it but he was too fucked up and he fell and busted his lip. He had to go to the aid station to get stitches real fast.

It was an inauspicious start to Operation Honor Bright. Yet we rode out, north by northwest.

Our work was tiring and we wouldn't have much luck because Haji knew we were coming, because when you were mech you didn't ever surprise anyone.

It was a lot of women and children, some old men. You didn't see men of fighting age when you were out there. Either they were with the IAs or they were with the IPs or they were dead or they were detained or they were hiding or they were somewhere else.

A rifle squad walked the road that ran along the riverbank. Shooting broke out in a clutch of houses on the other side of the river. Grenades going off, machine-gun fire—it sounded like something real. The squad took cover on the back side of the road. Except Borges and I. We slid down the shooting side and scanned the far bank of the river. This was my first day carrying a rifle. I'd traded my pistol to Yuri for it. Now I was looking to see if there was anybody I could shoot bullets into.

Not a minute, not 30 seconds. The shooting stopped. And maybe it was real, but it was nothing to do with us. Staff Sergeant North and Staff Sergeant Castro were laughing on the far side of the road. They'd done this kind of thing before. North, who had just got his E-6, had been with the battalion in '03, and he had shot a haji off a rooftop. Castro, a former Marine, had been at Fallujah in '04. He said, "C'mon, doc. Don't be fucked up. You're supposed to go away from the shooting."

I said something. I was still a retard.

"Okay," he said. "Whatever you say. Next time, the other direction."

Even Borges was laughing at me and he'd done the exact same shit I'd done. Really I'd just been following his lead. And he had about wiped out sliding down the berm. But nobody would bust his balls over it; Borges was on his second tour, so if he wanted to fuck up and get himself shot, that was on him.

We went back the way we came, and we stopped at an empty house facing the river. Halfway across the river was an island that was overgrown with date palms. North cocked a high-explosive round in his two-oh-three and sent it into the island, where it worked about as you'd expect. That was just North acting out. He was disappointed because we were on the wrong side of the river and he knew he wasn't going to get to kill anybody.

LIEUTENANT HEYWARD had been fired. It was because he kept having us all put in bullshit paperwork. He'd made up a bunch of sworn statements for all of us who had been on QRF1 that Christmas. The sworn statements said we had all been within 50 meters of the battalion TOC when the rocket hit it. This wasn't true. We had been much farther away than that. But had we been within 50 meters we would get credit for having been in combat and Heyward would get a Combat Infantryman Badge, which was good for promotion points if for nothing else. So 50 meters it was. And he had us all sign these statements he had written up on our behalf and he turned them in. When they got kicked back he printed out a new batch and had us sign again. Then he turned the new batch in and got himself fired that way.

EVEN WHEN the people were shooting, my mind was somewhere else. I was out of sorts. I'd asked Emily if she'd got the orchid I'd sent her and she'd said yeah, she'd got it. Well what did she think? She thought it was dumb. Why had she thought it was dumb? What did the card mean? It was the bouquet of parentheses from *Seymour: An Introduction*. Well, what the fuck was that? She didn't know. I'd given her that book around the time we met. I'd thought she'd like the story with the quiet old man who smoked and drank liquor. She'd said she liked the book. Had she even read the book?

I'd told some of this to Yuri. I said, "She's fucking hiding something, isn't she?"

He said I was a fucking idiot.

Did that mean he thought she was hiding something?

I said, "Yuri, just tell me yes or no. Is she hiding something?"

CHAPTER TWENTY-EIGHT

It was 22:00 and Delta Company had just hit their umpteenth IED in eight hours. The battalion had been taking casualties. We were sent on a raid. The ramp dropped and we weren't far from some houses. Our company first sergeant, First Sergeant Hightower, had come along. He was a stout man, built like a coconut; he seemed excited. The door on the first house was made of sheet metal like all the doors were. But this one had bullet holes all over it, and the light inside the house glared through the holes. We lifted our NVGs and we were hesitating; then Staff Sergeant Hueso-Santiago came running up like the movies and kicked the door in and we went in after him. Inside were the ubiquitous women and children, the ubiquitous old man. They were all along the wall. The television was on. We searched the room. The wooden chest on the table in the corner was packed full of clothes, and there was an AK-47 wrapped up in a shirt with two loaded magazines. This wasn't a big deal because they were allowed to have these things. But the first sergeant either didn't know or had momentarily forgotten because he took the AK-47 away and he was talking to it when he went outside, saying, "Yes, I've got you. I've got you, yes."

This was the first sergeant's first rodeo.

There was ground to cover before the next house, but we didn't make a big deal out of it and we got there. We stacked up and rushed through the front door and came into a room that had another four doors off it. Everything was in night vision. Nobody was talking. We were making it up as we went. We each took a door. I was in front of a door and I'd never kicked a door in before and I was worried I'd kick it ineffectually. The sheet metal gave way easy enough, and the bolt came out of the slot. It was a small room. There were no hajis, only some goats: a mama goat and her baby goats.

Some shit was happening behind me and I turned around and saw a naked haji was caught up wrestling with Private Miller. Miller had been in Echo Company all of three days. He was just out of basic. Now this shit. He brought a heel down on the inside of the haji's knee and he dragged it down the length of the tibia. Even before Hueso-Santiago could jump in, it was over. The naked haji was down on the floor. He was young, fighting age. There was a young woman too. She was backed up against the far wall of the bedroom. She had wrapped herself in a sheet. An AK-47 leaned against the wall in the corner across from the door.

Miller said, "He was going for the AK, Sarr."

He said it like he thought he was in trouble.

Hueso-Santiago said, "You did right."

Somebody brought an old man and his old wife out from one of the rooms. The old man and his wife saw what had happened, and the old man got to yelling and the old lady started to shake. The first sergeant wanted to question the old man. But the old man wasn't having it. He said something to the interpreter; sounded like *What the fuck is this?* And the first sergeant pointed at me and told the old man I was a doctor.

Somebody asked if the leg was broken.

I moved the leg. I felt it. I listened for crepitation. I got the impression that I didn't know what I was doing. I said, "It might be fractured."

Moving the leg caused him pain.

He was still naked.

I said, "Can somebody please get a fucking man dress or something for this guy?"

I told the interpreter to say the haji needed to go to a hospital.

The interpreter was wearing a ski mask.

I gave the haji some 800mg ibuprofens. Miller had wrapped a man dress around his waist. I put a few more ibuprofens in a little Ziploc bag for him and I laid the little Ziploc bag beside him on the floor because his hands were Zip-Cuffed behind his back.

The hajis were sitting on the floor, covered by rifles and looking sullen. The joes smoked cigarettes and the first sergeant did his questions.

The radio said don't detain anybody.

It was time to go.

"No harm, no foul," said the first sergeant.

WE LEFT and moved on to the next house.

The sun had come up. Some of us got to meet the new platoon leader for Third Platoon. Second Lieutenant Evans. He was sort of a tall goofy-looking motherfucker, like a young Tom Hanks. But he seemed reasonable enough.

We were at the assembly area in the desert outside of town. I was in the troop compartment of the Bradley that was now Evans's, and I was listening to the battalion net. Miller was there too, in the back of the track. The radio said one of our guys had got fucked up somewhere. The battle roster number went out: hotel hotel charlie echo yankee tree tree six six.

I said, "That's Yuri!"

Miller didn't know who Yuri was.

We cleared house all day.

Borges shot a dog in the face.

Seven. Six. Two.

Nothing else happened.

CHAPTER TWENTY-NINE

The last day of Operation Honor Bright some of us were sent to a schoolhouse to set up a clinic for the hajis. A lot of hajis were lined up outside. One old haji had deep lacerations on his wrists. He said the lacerations were from when he'd been Zip-Cuffed a few days back. I washed the lacerations out with saline and dressed them with bacitracin and gauze. One of his hands was swollen and shaking real bad. To me it looked like it was serious. But I didn't know and I didn't know what to tell him either. So I went to ask the two senior medics, two sergeants from HHC who had come along to help with the clinic. They were asleep in a five-ton outside. I woke them up and told them about the old haji and asked them what they thought was wrong with him. The senior medic said it was cellulitis.

I said, "I don't have antibiotics or anything. Do you?"

He said, "No."

"What can I do for this guy?"

"Nothing."

"What should I tell him?"

"Tell him to eat shit and die."

I went back and I told the interpreter to tell the old haji to go to a hospital and try and get some antibiotics from a doctor because I didn't have any medicine.

I didn't have anything.

I didn't know anything.

A mother had brought her kid in. The kid was about seven. He had a deep laceration on his right hand. There was nothing I could do but bandage it. A photographer from the *Army Times* took our picture when I was putting the bandage on. This was the kind of shit that happened.

The infantry were pulling security outside. About a dozen kids were hanging around, and Borges was teaching them the shocker. He arranged his fingers just so.

He said, "Two in the pink. One in the stink."

They went, "YAYAYAYAYAYAYAYA!"

WE WERE on the road heading back to the FOB. I was in the troop compartment of Evans's track and I realized I was by myself for the first time since I'd left Fort Hood. So I jerked off into some MRE toilet paper. Then I pissed into a liter water bottle. I filled it up pretty far and I put the jizz in the bottle with the piss and threw everything out the hatch on the ramp. I went to sleep. I didn't dream. When I woke up we were stopped. I banged on the turret door. It opened and I asked the gunner why we were stopped. The gunner said we'd run over an IED but it hadn't gone off. The track had crushed the battery so the bomb couldn't detonate. EOD was taking it apart with a robot. "Three one-five-fives," he said.

Jesus.

CHAPTER THIRTY

PFC Cecco and Specialist Greenwald were in the aid station overnight. Black Hawks would take them to Baghdad in the morning. From Baghdad they'd go to Kuwait, Kuwait to Germany, Germany to the States. They'd get their coffins somewhere on the way.

There was a battalion formation on the LZ. It was only our second time taking dead, and the lifers were still making a big deal out of it like somehow you were the asshole. And you went along with it.

Cecco and Greenwald. They were just names to me. I hadn't ever talked to them. If I'd ever seen them before I didn't know. It was IPs who'd done it. It had happened on Route Carentan. The EFP went through the up-armor no problem. It smashed Cecco's head. It cut Greenwald at the waist—he spilled on the gunner's platform.

The Black Hawks didn't spend two minutes on the LZ. Some medics carried the body bags out. When the medics were clear the Black Hawks went on their way. The battalion sergeant major told us to fall out. Then two other helicopters were coming in. They showed up a ways off against the grey sky, and we stayed around to see what they were about.

The second pair of Black Hawks landed, and all these beautiful women came out of them. And the women waved and bounced and they had white teeth. And they didn't know or whatever but still it was goddamn awful.

The Denver Mustangs Cheerleaders were on display at the DFAC for an hour, talking to the soldiers, taking pictures with the soldiers. Beautiful women with skin like expensive cream. And they were there, albeit not for long.

I didn't go see them. It wasn't like they were going to fuck you. And that was what this was all about: you were supposed to want to fuck them and they were supposed to not fuck you.

If you were a ballplayer they'd fuck you.

If you were a ballplayer they'd let you do everything to them. They'd let you disgrace them.

But you weren't a ballplayer.

WE NEVER did anything to the IPs. But some of us from Echo were put out on a cordon on the edge of the Big Shia City one night about a week after Cecco and Greenwald. We were supposed to block anyone from going in or out while Special Forces raided a Mahdi compound.

A voice came over the net, sounded like death metal, said they were ready.

And they killed a lot of hajis, 40 of the poor motherfuckers. It only took a few minutes. We didn't do anything but stay in place. We didn't even hear it. I wouldn't ever have known about the 40 dead hajis if I hadn't read about them on Yahoo! News the next morning. I wondered how it was they'd done it.

Anyway. That's when I figured out we weren't there to do shit. We'd do for getting fucked-up-or-killed-by-bombs purposes, and everyday-waste-of-your-fucking-time purposes, but no one thought we could do the actual fighting, whatever that was.

SINCE YURI was done, as in all fucked up and not going to be back, First Platoon was without a medic of their own for a while, and I ended up on most of their patrols, on top of the ones I was doing with Third Platoon. So I was on a fuckload of patrols. I was getting pretty dull already from exhaustion, but then again

I was on edge all the time because I was waiting for the war to happen to me.

When I went out with First Platoon I usually rode in Sergeant Caves's truck. Private Rodgers did the driving. Specialist Clover did the gunning. They were all tough guys and they weren't trying to lie about shit. They said they wanted to kill somebody, really anybody if it came to it. It was that simple. But there wasn't anybody for them to kill, so we just rode around, and when we weren't on the move we'd talk about what drugs we had done and what shit we had done and what we had paid for ecstasy when we were in the world, things of that nature. Clover had got his ecstasy the cheapest. But Rodgers had seen a guy get Uzied to death one time. So he was the winner.

I took my helmet off. Clover looked down from where he was, up in the turret, and he saw the card I had taped on the front of the inside of my helmet.

"What's that?"

"It's Herman Thompson," I said, "the running back."

"Why do you have Herman Thompson taped inside your k pot?"

"My wife used to have a crush on him back when she was in grade school, back in the early nineties when he ran the ball for Buffalo and they were in the championship every year. I made fun of her about it once, so she sent me this card with a letter the other day telling me to be careful cuz if I got killed she was gonna fuck Herman Thompson. So I have the card taped in the front of my helmet as a sort of reminder for me not to get killed."

"That's fucked up."

"I paid a hundred and ten dollars for an orchid on Valentine's Day and she gave it to her grandmother."

"Fuck."

Rodgers asked me if I was scared of getting hit. I said I'd prefer not to get hit if I had any say in it. Rodgers said he wanted to get hit because he'd get free hunting and fishing licenses for life if he had a Purple Heart.

"You don't want a Purple Heart, doc?" Clover asked.

"Not especially."

"Hey, doc," Caves said, "check this out."

He was holding a hand grenade by the pin.

I said, "Nice hand grenade."

He said, "I brought it back with me from Afghanistan."

I knew why they were fucking with me. They thought I was an asshole. I'd been fucking up and they'd heard about it. I had gone out with QRF a few nights before when one of the battalion's snipers had fallen down and said he was hurt. He'd said he was hurt so bad that he needed morphine before he could be evacuated to the aid station. I wasn't the type to deny anyone morphine and I was going to stick him in the leg with a 15mm auto injector of it, but I was holding the fucking thing backwards and the needle shot through my thumb and came out my thumbnail, spraying morphine on the ground. A number of people had seen this happen. And there'd been another fuckup whereby I came to appreciate how difficult it could be to start an IV on a real-life heat casualty. You got a real heat casualty and his skin was like rubber, and the needle as dull as a spoon. Evans had seen me stick the same heat casualty five times in a row without starting a line. I was sure I'd get sent back to the aid station. But I stayed where I was.

ALL OF us cherries got our combat patches on Easter. The combat patch wasn't like a CIB or a Combat Medic Badge or something that you at least had to get shot at or whatever to get. The combat patch had nothing to do with actual combat, not even pseudocombat. It was just a unit patch, usually a division patch, that you wore on your right sleeve so everybody would know you'd been deployed to a theater of operations and stayed a little while once. In short it was a big fucking nothing. But all of us in the company who weren't outside the wire, who were just hanging around waiting, maybe getting some sleep or cleaning weapons or breaking track or watching porno or playing cards or huffing duster, got rounded up by the squad leaders and told to stop whatever it was we were doing and go up to the motor pool and form up as a company.

They'd brought a boom box out. It was on the pavement, hooked up to an extension cord that ran from the mechanics' shed. So we knew something was up, and then we found out we were getting our combat patches. No one gave a shit. Really this was an inconvenience. So we bitched. Rodgers said real loud that they could keep the patch if he could get to see some combat.

First Sergeant Hightower came out and called the company to attention; then the captain came out to say a few words. He thanked us for our hard work, said some other things. And when he'd said all he was going to say, he had the first sergeant hit the play button on the boom box and the Toby Keith song started playing. Then right when it got to the big crescendoing part where Toby gets to talking about putting boots in people's asses and that's what Americans do, the captain gave the order: "Present . . . patches!"

It was too fucking funny and we couldn't help laughing in his face. We didn't want to do it; just it couldn't be helped. The patches went around. It was awkward but they went around and we got them. You could see the first sergeant was upset about us not being as solemn as he'd have liked, and after all the patches were passed out he had us close ranks and he right-faced us and marched us to the back of the motor pool, where he went about smoking the dogshit out of us for a while on the blacktop in the noon heat. He really gave us the works: Front-Back-Go's and Starmans—Starmans being a simply infamous form of exercise. He had us do that shit, and what was crazier was everybody staff sergeant and below got caught up in it. That was about the craziest shit in the world to us joes since none of us had ever seen an NCO get misused like that before.

I DON'T know if it was two weeks after that. I went out on a census patrol with Third Platoon. Cheetah was driving. Cheetah was a shitbag. He was big into Faces of Death and what was almost certainly child pornography. He would buy all the stupid gaudy knives the haji shops sold and mount them on the plywood wall above his bunk. He was driving that morning, and I thought it was stupid since he wasn't even a grunt. He was the lowest ranking of three supply POGs in the company, and he wasn't even good at that because he kept getting himself Article-Fifteened for being a moody knife-pulling shitbag. Yet he was leaving the wire with us and he was even driving. It was something to do with him having assured the first sergeant that he wouldn't be such a shitbag all the time if he could only leave the wire a little and feel like part of the team.

Lieutenant Evans was riding shotgun. Perez was in the turret. I was in the back. Neither Cheetah nor Perez was an American citizen. Cheetah was from Somalia. Perez was from Mexico somewhere. I wondered about the implications of this. I think they both liked America more than I did. What was my problem? We were the lead Humvee of three that had left on the patrol. It was midmorning. The three Humvees drove north on Route Polk and took a right turn off the highway and onto a trail that hooked around a main irrigation canal. The trail ended some 150 meters short of some houses where the day's censusing was to be done. I told Evans he shouldn't try to drive over the ground between the trail and the houses. I said we ought to dismount and walk the rest of the way.

"Why can't we drive?"

"The trucks can't drive through that shit, sir. They're too heavy. They'll get stuck."

"It looks fine to me."

"It only looks fine because it's dry on top from the fucking sun. But it's all shit under the surface. Trust me. I've seen shit identical to this before. Lieutenant Heyward got four vehicles stuck trying to drive through identical shit as this. You don't remember Lieutenant Heyward because he got fired before you came to the company, sir."

"I don't know," he said. "I think we'll try anyway."

The truck didn't go 20 meters and it was stuck. Evans told Cheetah to back out, but the truck couldn't go back either, and it didn't help that Cheetah didn't know what he was doing. So then Evans wanted North's truck to come up and pull us out, and I said, "You don't want to do that, sir. That's what Lieutenant Heyward did and it didn't work. You'll only make things harder for QRF when they get here. You need a Bradley with a tow cable."

"Hush."

So after the three trucks were stuck Evans radioed the FOB for QRF to come and fetch us out. It was either that or he could defect to the hajis.

QRF arrived. They were from First Platoon, a Bradley in front of three Humvees. The Bradley came tearing up the fucking trail and went directly into the shit and buried its track up to the skirt. So ended the rescue. It looked like we were going to be stuck awhile, like all day, and I took a turn up in the turret. A haji was watching us from where the houses were. I watched him watching us. I thought it must have been that he was amused by our situation, so I let it go. He got bored after a while and he went away.

Sergeant Caves was there. He had come up with QRF and he was bullshitting with North. They were talking about what a clusterfuck the day had turned into. They talked about where they would go hunting when they got back to the States. The battalion radioed and told QRF to return to the FOB and come back to us with a wrecker. The Bradley would have to stay put.

The order went around. QRF headed back and Caves departed with them.

We heard the dull thump. We saw the smoke streaming into the sky. I asked Evans if QRF had a medic with them. He got on the radio, "Echo one six, this is echo tree six actual."

A voice came back on the net. It was Lieutenant Nathan. "Um . . . this—uh—isn't a good time."

QRF wasn't far away. Evans sent North with some dismounts and some fire extinguishers to try and get there and help out. The quickest way back to the hardball was across the irrigation canal. It was deep enough and wide enough that we had to get in it and swim across. We were loaded down with fire extinguishers, guns, body armor, assault packs, all that shit, and we were having a hard time not drowning in the motherfucker. Perez almost drowned and Cheetah had to pull him out. I was the first one to get across. I crawled up the bank and got to my feet just as a white bongo truck was coming down the road, going the way we were going. I pulled my rifle up and aimed where I guessed the driver's face was. I took my left hand off the grip and signaled him to stop. If he didn't stop I was going to try and murder him. But he stopped. I moved up to the driver door. It was two hajis in the cab. I saw North and the interpreter coming up on my right. North told the interpreter to tell the hajis to take us down the road. We piled in the truck bed. We stopped about 100 meters short of the QRF element and ran the last part of the way.

On the other side of the rear Humvee there was a hole in the road and farther on a Humvee was burning. A charred seat was lying on its side on the road. Specialist Farley was standing there looking. I said, "Where are the casualties?" He said, "They're all dead, you fucking asshole." I looked again at the body of the gunner. He was burned away, scraps of IBAS clung to his torso, legs folded up, femurs and tibias and fibulas with black tissue, arms melted, body eviscerated and lying on its guts, face gone, head a skull. The smell is something you already know. It's coded in your blood. The smoke gets into every pore and into every gland, your mouth full of it to where you may as well be eating it. Soldiers are getting water out of the paddies on either side of the road with a Gatorade cooler, ammo cans, whatever else and making a chain from the water to the fire. The fire extinguishers are used up quick. First Platoon's new medic, a lifer named Jackson, is yelling about how somebody needs to pull security. He's the only one on the road who gives a fuck about security, and he's right but nobody gives a fuck. I've got my helmet off and I'm going back and forth with it from the water to the fire, carrying water in it, and it's not register- ing with me that this is idiotic, but we are all obsessed with getting the fire out even though everybody's fucking dead and there's really no reason to hurry. The fire's out and the three dead make four counting the one on the road: Caves, Rodgers, Clover, and I don't know who the fourth is. Half the battalion is lined up on the road. I go down the road and wave at the gun- ner of the first track I see. I hold four fingers up to the gunner, and I mouth the words *body bags*. I go to turn back, but I look twice because Clover's walking up the road. I say, I thought you were dead. I say I thought he had been in the truck. He says he was supposed to go on midtour leave this morning. Says the flight out got canceled though. I say, Fuck, I thought he was a ghost just now, and fuck, sorry about those guys because I know they were tight and who was the gunner? He says Easton. I say, Fuck. What about the fourth guy? He says Dewitt. The four body bags come. The captain is there by the truck now. Dewitt is curled on the platform under the turret. The face is gone so you couldn't know who it was unless you knew because Clover just told you. A burned-up hot-white skull, empty sockets, teeth clenched like they'll shatter. The captain gives a look to say, Pick up the body. I take it by the top half and he takes it by the legs. Muscle tissue is slick black, hot enough that the latex gloves break on contact. Hands burning too much, I've got to set him down. Set the body down. Set him down. Pick it up again. Somebody helps, supports the body under the ass burnt off. The penis and testicles, his dick and his balls, are burned off, and it's a tab of flesh there, not a centimeter of it. We shuffle back some steps to the body bag laid open on the ground. Lay him in the bag. Close the bag. Go to the water. Throw away what's left of the latex gloves. Back on the road some guys are picking up Easton. They stop and one's saying, *Holdupholdupholdup*. His guts are coming out. They have Easton on his back now. The part of his face that was lying against the pavement hasn't burned away. It's a circle of flesh. The right eye hasn't burned away. You can tell just from the eye that it's Easton—blue eye—and this kid looking down crying says, *"That's Easton. That's my friend."* Caves and Rodgers are in the front seats, Caves leaning forward against the dash. It's easy getting him out because his IBAS is mostly intact and it keeps his guts where they are. The hand grenade is still attached to his IBAS. I don't remember that it's there. I send him back to the aid station with the hand grenade strapped to him. They have to call EOD to deal with it. Rodgers is in the driver seat and I know because he was Caves's driver. Otherwise I wouldn't know. Caves and Rodgers have no faces. All faces burned off. No faces anymore. Rodgers is in the body bag. A shook-up sergeant named Edwards tells me he thinks there's some more of him still in the truck. He points to a string of fat running along what's left of the driver seat, the frame of it. I don't know what to do. I skim it off with my fingers, roll a ball of it, and throw it in the water. Then I walk down the road, gory as fuck, not making sense.

CHAPTER THIRTY-ONE

I went home on midtour leave in May. Two weeks. And I got disappointed: Emily was only around a little while. She said she couldn't hang around too long in Cleveland because she had got a job in Washington State somewhere and it couldn't wait. Something to do with Nature. Whatever it was she couldn't miss it. There were other girls who'd have fucked me. And they were beautiful. I should have fucked them all. But I didn't because I was supposed to be married, even though I wasn't supposed to tell anyone. I went back.

CHAPTER THIRTY-TWO

Some nights we walked what seemed like forever; some nights we didn't walk far; some nights somebody shot a dog out of boredom. This night there were five of us, a fire team. North was leading it. We took the road as far as OP1, the first observation post, then veered off to the right and down into the fields between Route Martha and Route Polk.

We settled into an empty field from which we could see neither of the two roads. North wasn't interested in the roads. He thought he could catch a haji out in the fields. The curfew was sundown, and our ROE was to shoot anybody we caught out after dark. Even with the sand flies it was easy to fall asleep. Night vision was tedious and all this was nothing. We sat still for some hours. Nobody talked. Nobody moved. The bugs ate us.

North got up to leave and we followed him. We filed to the edge of the field and brushed through the tall grass and into a dooryard. There was a haji on a bed outside in front of the house. I heard him breathe and stumble when he took off running. North radioed the company TOC and the TOC said go ahead and shoot him.

The haji had gone left and we spread out in a line to turn him up. I was scanning a ditch, hoping I wouldn't see him as I didn't feel especially ready to shoot him right that minute. It was Sullivan who spotted him, and he called out as much. The haji was up and running, 30 meters in front. Private Dallas—a brand-new cherry we had with us—went chasing after him. Dallas crossed into my line of fire and I didn't shoot. But the rest of the fire team opened up. Never mind the cherry.

We came up with our rifles shouldered, and the haji was laid out on his back. He had blood on his white tank top. He wasn't wearing shoes. He was good-looking, young. Twenty-five at most. He was quiet—eyes staring—thinking probably he was going to die.

I was supposed to work on him. The entry wound might have been over his stomach. I didn't know. There was a splash of blood from the wound, but there was no blood coming out of it now. Just fat pushed out of it. I balled up some gauze and pressed it into the wound. I covered the gauze with a Ziploc bag, taped the plastic down on three sides, and asked Sullivan to keep pressure on the dressing for me. I was looking for an exit wound. There wasn't any exit wound I could see on the upper body, and since five-five-six rounds tumble, I could only guess where the bullet might have gone once it was in. I cut the haji's sweatpants off with trauma shears. The haji had a big dick and he was shaved. That got a laugh out of Sergeant Bautista. But there was no exit wound.

I should have packed the haji full of gauze. I should have kept packing the wound till I couldn't pack it anymore, till it was packed tight. But I didn't. I should have had him lie on the side he was wounded on. But I forgot. I said I was going to prop the haji's feet up on my helmet because the haji could go into shock if his feet weren't propped up like that. And even though this was true I was only saying it just to say things because there was no exit wound and I didn't know what to do. The haji's eyes rolled up in his head and then came back, focused again, rolled up again. I was trying to start a line but his veins were flat. I said I was going to give him morphine to keep him from going into shock.

North said, "Do what you have to do, doc. You don't have to tell us."

I gave the haji morphine, so I could look like I was doing something right. I stuck him on his right thigh and went back to working on a line. His arm was thin. I couldn't get a flash. Then I got a flash, but he moved and I lost it.

I said, "Keep still, you fuck! I'm trying to help you!"

North said, "Be quiet, doc."

North had called for a medevac. That was one of the first things you were supposed to do. I'd told him to call it in as an urgent surgical. But the medevac wasn't coming.

The haji started choking on vomit. The vomit was white and viscous, and I was clearing it out of his throat with my fingertips when he lost consciousness.

He had no breath. No pulse. I put the bag ventilator together with the CPR mask. I had Bautista do the chest compressions and I did the ventilations. A little of that and the haji came back and he was breathing on his own again.

Then he croaked.

We tried CPR another few minutes. His ribs were broken from the chest compressions and you could hear them popping. It was over with.

North radioed back to the company TOC and said the haji was dead and we didn't need the medevac anymore. The haji was a corpse, and we had no practical way of taking him back to the FOB with us. We needed QRF to come out and get us, and they'd need to bring a body bag with them because we didn't have one of those either. The TOC said QRF wouldn't come out till after the sun was up. Better they be able to see the road, better safe than sorry. We stayed put.

The sun came up. That's when I saw the other house. An old lady in black came out of the house and she saw the naked haji laid out on the ground.

North called to her, "Do you know him?"

He indicated the naked corpse.

She turned away and went back inside the house.

North said, "She knows him."

The dismounts from QRF showed up. Castro was the first to reach us. He saw how I was looking and he said to me:

"This your first dead body, doc?"

I said no. Like he was asking.

Somebody gave me a body bag. I spread it out on the ground next to the dead naked haji and rolled him up inside it. That was when things got worse.

The old lady came out of the house again and was screaming her fucking head off. She tried to get to the body bag but a couple soldiers pulled her back and she fell on her knees and screamed some more and kept screaming. She started taking handfuls of dirt and pouring them over her head. She hit her face against the ground. Then she rose back up on her knees and went through the whole thing again. I closed the body bag. A young woman, real pregnant, had come out of the house, and she started doing the same shit the old lady was doing. And there were two boys. Very young. And they were screaming. Four soldiers took the body bag, and the old lady got up and ran after them. She tried to pry the body bag away from them. I was about to cry and maybe shoot myself when the AK-47 let loose. Full-automatic. Three long bursts. Stopped all that. Everybody scattered.

We took cover in a ditch. The infantry were returning fire. I was on the far left of our line, scanning the left flank because I thought a haji might try and pick some of us off that way.

Castro was in charge because his date of rank went back further than North's did. He was on the radio and the radio told him to secure the dead haji. He called cease-fire: "THEY SAY WE HAVE TO GET THE BODY. GIVE ME FOUR VOLUNTEERS."

Only three hands went up. I waited. Still no more hands. So I added a fourth since, all things considered, I had to.

I didn't know where the shooter was, so I emptied a magazine into a cow standing in front of the house, figuring this was the safest course of action. Private Dallas was to my left, on his knees, firing an M14. He said, "DOC, I'VE GOT A WOODY!"

I left my aid bag in the ditch and threw red smoke as far ahead as I could get it. When the smoke popped we went. It was 20 meters to the body bag. The old lady was there. She was black cloth on the ground.

Running there wasn't bad. Coming back the other way was more interesting. I was waiting on an AK round to come along and punch my brain out through my face. Yet I was calm, hadn't ever been so calm. I closed my eyes and I saw Emily, clear as day.

No such round and I was back in the ditch. More firing. We did the bounding overwatch routine to the next ditch back. Dallas left off shooting and ran back to where I'd got to. He had my aid bag with him. I'd fucked up real bad and left it in the first ditch. My NVGs were in the bag, and if I'd left that shit out there I'd have never lived it down. The cherry just saved my ass.

I said, "Thanks."

We fell back some more, shooting everything and nothing in particular. I shot the cow some more with a new magazine. Apaches were in the air now and the shooter was long gone and we were making fools of ourselves. No one was shooting back at us.

On the way back to the road there was a shit canal. So we made a bridge out of some branches and tried to drag the body bag across. But the body bag rolled off the branches and fell into the shit canal. I went in after it. It wasn't easy getting it out of the water. The body was heavy and there were holes in the bag and the water ran out of the holes and into my face, like the dead haji was pissing on me.

We were nearly back to the road and I was dragging the body bag behind me with the haji in it and I could feel his head bounce in and out of the furrows in the field and we were out in the open and my hands were full, my rifle slung, and we'd just been shot at and my karma was fucked and I was jumpy. Dallas said something to me. But I didn't know what he was saying. I said, "Don't fucking talk to me! Pull fucking security!"

You weren't supposed to let your nerves show like that.

When we got back to the road somebody told me to drape the dead haji on the front of one of the QRF tracks so no one would have to ride back to the FOB with the dead haji in the troop compartment with him.

I MISSED breakfast because I was up at the Main Gate waiting for the IPs to come and get the dead haji. Sergeant Castro was there too. He'd stayed to see that it went alright. I was so tired that my face hurt. I had just done my ninth patrol in four days. The IPs arrived.

Nobody said anything. I opened the body bag. We looked at the dead haji. The IPs took him and loaded him up and left. Castro saw how I was looking and he said, "You did what you could for him, right?"

I said I had.

"Then don't beat yourself up about it."

Evans was the first guy I saw when I got back to the company. He said he'd been in the company TOC when we'd been out there killing the haji.

"I know it's a lousy thing to say," he said, "but I was hoping that the guy wouldn't make it. Who knows what kind of stuff he would have said."

"Yeah," I said. "That's understandable."

"The people up there are making a fuss," he said. "They say we left another body up there."

"Who?"

"We don't know. But we're going back up there tonight. I'm taking two squads up there myself. We're expecting retaliation. Will you be ready to go?"

I said, "Yeah, no problem."
And we were back out that night.
And nothing happened.

IT WAS Sullivan who told me how he'd seen the old lady get hit with our fire that morning. And I knew it was true because Sullivan didn't lie and he wouldn't have said it if he wasn't sure.

CHAPTER THIRTY-THREE

The battle roster number was EAJ-0888, and we were trying to think of who that was. We knew it was a guy from First Platoon because Staff Sergeant White had called it in. We knew it wasn't Specialist Jackson, First Platoon's medic, since line medics were attached to Echo from HHC and if the dead guy were Jackson the battle roster number would have started with *HHC* and not *E*. The first initial being *A* wasn't much help as we weren't in the habit of calling one another by our first names. It took us the better part of ten minutes to come up with a guy from First Platoon whose last name started with the letter *J*.

Private Jimenez.

We cleared houses like we normally did when these things happened. It had been just a klick away, south of us, past the bend in the road, down a little past OP1, so we didn't need to go anywhere. And with nothing to the west but a short field and the river, we turned east off the road and went about it.

A blind retard was chained to a palm tree in front of the first house we came to. An old woman, presumably the retard's mother, stood near the gate of the courtyard, and some of us filed in. There were four rooms around the courtyard so we split off to see about each one and I kicked a door in and went into an unlit room. The room was empty except for a haji lying on the floor with his eyes closed. I said, "Get the fuck up, motherfucker."

But he didn't move.

I moved closer to him, rifle trained down on him. "GET THE FUCK UP, MOTHERFUCKER."

He opened one eye and looked at me, stayed unmoved, closed

the eye. So I had my mind made up to kick him in the face. I didn't go around kicking hajis in the face for no reason and I didn't know anyone who did, but Jimenez was dead and I was going to kick the haji in the face. I brought the kick as hard as I could, aiming center mass. But I stopped halfway to connecting. It was all I could do to stay on the one foot and not fall on my ass. The haji got up and stretched and he shuffled out of the room. I can't remember when it had occurred to me that maybe he was also retarded. I unfucked myself and went outside to see where the haji had gone. He was heading off into the fields, looking up into the sun. Nobody touched him.

Jimenez was a cherry. He was one of the replacements who had come to the company after First Platoon lost the four guys killed out on Route Polk. He hadn't been around two months and he was dead. It was unlucky.

Sometimes the dead guy was really an asshole, or you could make the case that he was. Not so with Jimenez. For all intents and purposes Jimenez was a saint. That's why he stuck out like a sore thumb in an infantry company.

The thing is your average infantryman is no worse than your garden-variety sonofabitch. But he talks in dick jokes and aspires to murder and it doesn't come off as a very saintly mode of being. Yet Jimenez was a saint. It wasn't like he was soft or anything like that; he was a tough kid. He'd only just turned 19 but he was strong with a deep chest and the kind of unbreakable wrists one gets from working with his hands. And he'd work. The sergeants liked him for that. But he was so goddamn nice that he drove people crazy sometimes. Like he'd play poker with the poker players and he'd play bad hands. Dealt a queen-four off-suited, he was liable to call two preflop raises and hit a boat on the river. And when people got mad at him for playing garbage he'd apologize and try to give them back their chips. But it didn't work like that.

The last time I saw Jimenez was about eight hours before

Haji killed him. He'd been boxing Staff Sergeant Castro in the weight room, sparring, and Castro had popped him on the nose pretty good so his nose was bleeding—not broken or anything, just bleeding. And Castro told him to go see a medic and Jimenez did what he was told and when he came around looking for a medic I gave him a hard time. I said, "What the fuck are you coming to me about a bloody fucking nose for, cherry?"

And he didn't say anything. He just smiled, all awkward, like he was embarrassed for me.

I said, "C'mon, cherry. I'm tired. Please don't come to me with dumb shit, okay? I'm really fucking tired, you know?"

He went out with a fire team in the morning. They set up a TCP on Route Martha. They'd gone out when it was still dark and they hadn't had a good look at the spot where they were set up and they didn't know Haji had laid a one-five-five round underneath the road there. The road was just a paved berm and it was easy to mine. And the Haj was watching them. He saw Jimenez stand on the spot he had mined.

I heard Koljo talk about it. It was later that same day. He was telling some joes what it had been like. He said, "It looked like something out of a horror movie."

The one-five-five round took off both Jimenez's legs and severed one of his arms almost completely. But he was still awake and he knew what was happening. He was screaming. The fire team traded shots with two fucking murderers, but the murderers got away, north through a palm grove. The fire team couldn't go after them because they couldn't leave Jimenez there by himself.

CHAPTER THIRTY-FOUR

A lot of Internet pornography went around the FOB. The biggest file had been passed down to us from the Mississippi Rifles, who had inherited it from the Marines, who had inherited it from the 10th Mountain Division, who had inherited it from whomever. We watched the Fuck Van a lot. The Fuck Van was the last thing we needed to see. The way the Fuck Van worked was the Fuck Van would cruise around looking for young women to video getting fucked in the Fuck Van. Several bros would ride in the Fuck Van and they'd be on the lookout. Then one bro would go *"look!"* and he'd point out a young woman walking down the side of the road and maybe she'd have a bag of groceries or something like that. It would always begin innocently enough. The bros would call out to the young woman and offer her a ride. At first she'd be reluctant to accept the ride because the Fuck Van was a panel van and she associated this type of van with rapists and laborers and these were strange bros. But the bros would overcome her misgivings with their bro charms and she'd inevitably accept the ride. Once they got her in the Fuck Van the bros would make fun of the young woman and call her stupid so as to make her feel insecure about herself and they'd ask her questions that got rather personal and after a few minutes they'd ask her to take off her shirt. She would decline at first. So the bros would offer her cash. Once the cash came out things changed. Before long the woman would be completely naked, sucking off several bros at once, and they'd have her do things like say the ABCs with a dick in her mouth and she'd do it. When the bros were done with her they'd take turns coming on her face. Then she'd get dressed and the Fuck Van would pull over at a random spot where the bros would kick the young woman out of the Fuck Van and throw her groceries at her and call her a whore and drive away.

One day the Fuck Van happened to be playing on a laptop on the card table and Sergeant Thorpe happened to see it. A young blond woman with a British accent was getting double-penetrated by some bros in the Fuck Van. Thorpe noticed something and he stopped the video.

"She's a slut," he said. "Look! The slut's wearing a wedding ring!"

He dragged the timer back to a point in the video when there was a close-up of the young woman fingering her clitoris, and you could definitely see she was wearing a wedding ring.

A married woman in the Fuck Van!

Thorpe couldn't watch the Fuck Van after that.

It was too bad for Thorpe. He was still all fucked up from what his old lady had done to him. It was sad as fuck. And he wasn't the only one. A lot of us were getting fucked around.

The Fuck Van was bad for morale. Guys argued about whether the Fuck Van was actually real. But it had to be real because it was there and we could see it. And we knew then that life was just a murderous fuckgame and that we had been dumb enough to fall for some bullshit.

THIRD PLATOON was on QRF1 the night that Haji took some paratroopers alive at an OP north of Checkpoint 9. It was a straight shot up Route Martha to get there, and we could have made it fast, but we were held up on account of a lot of last-minute additions to the patrol roster. Then the blue force tracker went down. That was our GPS, and we weren't allowed to leave the FOB without it working. So we were stuck waiting with the trucks staged at the North Gate.

Specialist Jeffries said, "We're sitting ducks out here."

Jeffries was a little fucker and he didn't know how ate-the-fuck-up he was. He thought he was alright because he'd been in the 82nd Airborne once. But nobody gave a rat's ass that he'd been in the 82nd Airborne. The only reason Jeffries was on the roster that night was the captain's usual driver was on midtour leave and they'd had to have somebody fill in. And Jeffries was worried about light discipline.

"I've got to say something!" he said. "I've *got* to!"

He went to tell whomever that we were sitting ducks. When he came back he was looking chastised.

"I can't be*lieve* this!" he said. "Freaking *am*ateurs!"

It was more than an hour before we were on our way. We went up north, past Checkpoint 9. The trucks stopped to let us out. Hueso-Santiago led a squad into some fields west of the road. North led a fire team heading northeast. And Lieutenant Evans, First Sergeant Hightower, Castro, and I went off due east of the road. There was no shortage of aircraft above us. Through one came word of a target house. We were going to clear it.

Evans said, "This is the target house."

The first sergeant asked if he was sure.

"They say we're right on top of it."

The target house was twenty-five meters away. No lights on. Without any words it was determined that the lieutenant and the first sergeant would cover Castro and me from the tall grass on the edge of the yard while we kicked the door in and cleared the house. So Castro and I crossed the yard and stopped next to the door. I'd kick the door in. I was pretty sure I was about to die but it would have been lame if I'd pussied out, so I flicked the safety switch to burst and I didn't think about it. We went in. I went left and Castro went right. There was nobody in the entire room. I scanned a smaller room from a doorway and again there was nobody. There was a stairway in the back corner of the room and we saw it and we didn't hesitate before we were going up because we didn't give a fuck about dying and really we had figured out by then that this target house was bullshit.

Back at the road, Greene was giving Jeffries a hard time. He said he'd personally shoot Jeffries if Jeffries ever touched a radio again. He said he was serious.

I asked Sullivan what it was about.

He said, "Numbnuts over there green-lighted an airstrike on Hueso's squad. Almost got them all killed."

"No shit?"

"Yeah. Hueso's people don't have IR beacons on their shit because they're all from fucking Bradley crews. The aircraft thought they were the Haj. But that's what happens when you send Bradley crews out as dismounts. Ate. The fuck. Up. The fucking aircraft radioed the captain to see if all our people were accounted for, but the captain wasn't in his truck and numbnuts, fucking Jeffries, radioed back on his own and said all our people were accounted for. Meanwhile Hueso's out there and this big IR beam comes down on him like some shit out of a fucking UFO and he radios on the company net and says, Um, I think I'm about to get lit up by one of our aircraft. So Greene figures out what's going on, and he runs over to the captain's truck, yelling like he's fucking gone crazy, and he pulls numbnuts off the radio, calls the fucking shit off, thank God."

"Fuck."

We regrouped at the road. The target house had been cleared. So there was nothing left to do but search everywhere else till somebody found the missing paratroopers.

Everywhere else was connected by paths through tall grass and palm groves and shit canals. The paths were very narrow and turned a lot and you couldn't tell what was around the bends. We cleared some houses. Most of them were empty. We found nothing. A group of soldiers moved on a house about fifty meters north of us. We had run out of houses where we were, so we thought to move up that way and see what was going on there. North and I went ahead while the first sergeant got the rest of our people together. By the time North and I reached the house it had been cleared. Some hajis were sitting on the living room floor. There were three young children, a boy and two girls, and a mother and a father. The television was on. Four paratroopers and an interpreter were in the room as well. And one of the paratroopers, a sergeant, an E-5, took an asp off his gear and flicked it out. He took the boy from off the floor and shoved him into a wall. He grabbed the boy by the back of his neck and he said, "I'm looking for some friends of mine."

He jabbed the boy three times hard in the ribs with the butt end of the asp. The boy's father, the mother, the two girls: not one of them so much as blinked.

He said, "Is there anything you want to tell me?"

He hit the boy some more. The boy took it quietly. His legs buckled but the sergeant had him by the neck. No one said anything. The sergeant hit the kid some more. He had his mind made up to hit the kid for a while, so he did. And it was meaningless because we were looking for some dead men. They'd died and gone to the Internet. That's where people go when they die these days. At least when they die like that.

I walked out of the house and I ran into Lieutenant Evans.

I said, "You probably shouldn't go in there, sir."

He said, "Why not?"

I said, "One of the Airborne guys is beating up a kid."

He said, "Oh."

CHAPTER THIRTY-FIVE

After we had been in Iraq awhile, it became apparent that they weren't about to piss-test any of us. Something decent they'd done for us, I imagine.

So you could get high.

But there was the question then of how.

You could get narcotics from the right interpreter. But then you might have a stroke or fall out of a fucking guard tower or something else infamous. And you didn't want that. So what you did was you'd have it sent in from the World. The mail people X-rayed the mail and they had drug dogs for it too. But it wasn't that serious. You could get a little weed in. You could get a little powder. Prescription drugs were wide open (within reason). If you could get somebody to mail it, and if they showed a little restraint, you were good.

Of course it wasn't every day you got such a care package. So what ended up happening was you'd form little cliques, three or four like-minded individuals getting weed or pills or liquor or whatever sent in from the World. Liquor usually came in mouthwash bottles. Little bits of weed came in all kinds of ways.

I'd left some money with Roy when I was home. Roy sent me an ounce baked into some brownies. He'd had his girlfriend do the baking. It was some care package: these brownies, plus Roy had thrown in a Johnny Cash poster, three packs of Winston Reds, and some Perc 10s in an Advil bottle for good measure. Real magnanimous of him. I said, Roy, you've done good.

He'd sent his girl to mail it at the post office and she did and then he found out she'd put his return address on the box. So he sent her to the post office to get the package back and she did. Then she took it back to Roy and Roy changed the address on it and they sent it again, fake address this time. That was Roy.

We had about got lynched out at the car bombing that afternoon. The car bomb did what car bombs do and four were dead in the market. It would have been more but the sheep took most of the blast. So you had flesh and blood and wool on the pavement. You had bloodstains on the pavement, little lakes of blood. And all the hajis were out there, like a macabre sort of block party. A teenage haji was punching a kid in the face. He shoved the kid down into the shins-deep garbage in the gutter. The kid came up with a splintered two-by-four, swinging it around and raving in boy-pitched Arabic that sounded like tears in his eyes. But then Teen Haji got the two-by-four away from him and beat him with it some. And the old hajis stood around and didn't do anything, lest they should be mistaken for men unaccustomed to brutality.

What was left of the car was there. Our patrol had been nearby when the battalion ordered us to keep the IPs from getting rid of what was left of the car before QRF could bring EOD out to look it over for indications of who had put the bomb together. So we were waiting for QRF. And more and more hajis closed in around us. There were only two dismounts in the street. I counted as one and the other guy, Lessing, was 30 meters up from where I was. The gunners and the drivers couldn't leave the trucks. The vehicle commanders could have left the trucks, but they didn't even though they should've. I was trying to watch all the rooftops and all the dark window spaces and all the corners all at once, looking for the haji who meant to shoot me in the face. It was early in the afternoon and the sky was clear so the sun had everything blinding. And all these hajis were getting out of control and I kind of wanted to just say fuck it and let them run riot all over the place so as to better illustrate for the VCs why some more help on the ground wouldn't have been amiss.

So Lessing and I were pissed off when we came back in, but then there was a package from Roy and there were these fucking brownies with an ounce of weed baked in them, and the fucking Winstons. . . . It was just what the doctor had ordered.

Lessing and I got high as shit. These were some fucking brownies. They tasted like straight weed: you could hardly taste anything else, just weed and a hint of chocolate. We got shitfaced on these fucking things. If we'd have had to deal with anybody but Borges or Burnes that afternoon we'd have been fucked. Anybody else probably would have sent us to fucking Leavenworth, or shot us on the spot, a summary execution, to make an example of us. It was that serious. We were so high.

Burnes and Borges rolled in around when I was getting into the Percs. I said to Lessing, "You want one of these."

He said, "No thanks."

I said, "C'mon, motherfucker. Don't disdain my favors. You always look out. What's mine is yours."

He said, "I used to be addicted to heroin."

"This isn't heroin."

"I robbed convenience stores."

"Suit yourself."

Burnes and Borges said they'd take some Percs since I was offering. I said, "Fuck that. Have some brownies."

And they did. And they too got retarded. I ended up keeping the pills for myself. I did give one to Borges because I kind of had to, but that was all; the rest I kept. Still they didn't hold me but a few days. When we didn't have any proper drugs, there was always computer duster to huff. It was summer and people were getting killed. People got killed more in summer. And we could be killed. And we had no way to know.

About Emily I guess I was deluding myself. Somewhat

knowingly. Or just knowingly. Or maybe I didn't know. I can't remember.

Often I used to come in in the mornings from IED ambushes, and I would go online and check my email. A lot of times she didn't email, and when she did it usually wasn't good. She'd say she was ashamed of what I was doing. But I didn't ever tell her what I was doing. She knew as much as she had before I left.

I'd bought a bootleg DVD from the haji shop. It was a movie about the lives of emperor penguins and what they endured so they could keep living in Antarctica and making babies and all that. I thought the world of these fucking penguins. I wrote to Emily and told her she ought to see the movie about the penguins. She didn't. Then I said, Of course she can't see it. She is in the fucking wilderness. So I ordered it for her on Amazon. Amazon sent the movie about the penguins to her in the wilderness. She emailed me and said the movie was stupid and the penguins were stupid. I thought, Why would she do that? Couldn't she just pretend for me? I would have pretended for her. But she had said the penguins were stupid. That was exactly what she had said. Stupid. I thought, She is good, so I have done something wrong.

After having my heart broken by email, typically what I'd do was drink coffee and smoke cigarettes. If there was a card game going, I'd play and I'd lose some money. Mostly I had bad luck at cards. But early in the morning there was often no card game. There was often nothing worth reading. No one awake. So what I'd do was I'd look at the IKEA catalog. I had copied and pasted a lot of shit about IKEA furniture into a Word document and I'd look through it and think about what kind of furniture Emily and I would buy when we went to live together. I thought if I did this shit in Iraq and I lived through it and I saved some money, it would be enough for me and Emily to start a life together. And we would have a savings and she would have a degree and I could go to school and it would be okay because it wouldn't be just something given to me. I'd need to be smart like Emily. And she would become something and I would become something, a librarian maybe, and we would have enough money and be middle-class and want for nothing and we would be independent of everyone and no old bastards who voted for wars could tell me anything because I'd done what they'd wanted. So I used to smoke Miamis and drink coffee and be tense after being out all night lying in the fields north of the FOB. I didn't actually watch much porn, you know. I mean I'd seen some, I'd seen a few Fuck Vans and all that, but mostly I didn't fuck with it. It felt like cheating. And when I'd jerk off in the porta-shitters, I didn't think of other girls. I'm not ashamed of this. I tried to be good.

CHAPTER THIRTY-SIX

One of my jobs was to get the pus out of the abscess on Sergeant Bautista's ass. He was a big guy and he had a big ass. He was from New York City. Neither one of us was wild about the arrangement but it couldn't be helped. I'd go see him in his room around 20:00. He'd be playing Madden, and he'd lie on his stomach with his pants down past his ass and I'd take yesterday's sterile gauze out of the abscess on his ass and clean the pus out of the abscess.

"It doesn't smell as bad as it did yesterday," I'd say.

"That's good," he'd say.

I'd say, "Yeah, that's a good sign."

Then I'd put some sterile gauze in the abscess, folding the strip of gauze triangularly and poking it down into the hole with tweezers.

I'd say, "Okay. See you tomorrow."

And I'd go and hand out the shit pills.

Also sometimes guys got crotch rot.

Mostly this was all I ever did.

I was not a hero.

A month before he was immolated on Route Polk, Sergeant Caves found a haji dog wandering around the company area. The haji dog was just a few weeks old. He could fit in the palm of your hand. He needed food and Caves gave him food and adopted him as his own and called him Sonny.

After Caves got killed, First Platoon took care of Sonny, and Sonny got to stick around. Sonny was well liked because he was a very good dog, courageous yet of a gentle nature. And when our company's dismount patrols left the wire in the daytime it wasn't out of the ordinary to see Sonny going along up and down the line.

Then one morning some POG from Foxtrot Company, name of Sergeant Teague, was out taking her walking exercise around the perimeter of the FOB and it took her past our company area. We'd just as soon as she didn't come around; she looked a lot like a fucking gargoyle. Anyway. Sonny barked at her and she got so traumatized from it that she went to the battalion TOC to complain about Sonny. And it followed that two heroes from HHC (officers) volunteered to come down to Echo Company and shoot Sonny. When they got there they found him resting on his favorite spot, beneath the shade trees by the horseshoe pit. They walked right up on him. Sonny didn't try and run because he wasn't afraid of soldiers. Maybe he thought they had come to give him something to eat, perhaps a cheeseburger. Instead they shot him in the snout. He got away and tried to hide himself under some boards. The two officers had to drop down into the prone to finish him off. They were wearing their ballistic eye protection so it was all on the level.

I don't remember exactly what I was doing when this happened. But I wasn't there. Probably I was kicking some doors in somewhere. Nothing dramatic or whatever. Just doors. I'd kicked a hundred doors in. More like two hundred doors. Nothing ever came of it. Not once. And I didn't get killed. The next day I was playing poker with the poker players. I'd been out on a patrol all the night before and I should have been sleeping but I wasn't because I could only sleep when I was on a patrol; that was the only time it appealed to me. So I didn't get much sleep and I was burned out and I was pissed about the dog when Arnold came in from radio guard to get me. He said, "Get your stuff. QRF just got called out."

I wasn't on QRF that day.

I could have gone anyway. But I didn't feel like it.

I said, "Sarr Garcia from HHC is on QRF. He's covering for Sarr Shoo while Shoo's on midtour leave. Sarr Garcia will be in the aid station. You can find him there."

"But—"

"Fuck you, Arnold! Fuck you, you goddamn motherfucker! You fucking bitch! You don't ever leave the goddamn wire. That's why you love this goddamn shit. Well fuck you, Arnold. I'm not on the fucking thing and I'm not going."

Arnold left and got Garcia. Garcia went out with QRF. I stayed at the FOB and played poker. That's how I missed the big battle, the one when the battalion sent forty hajis to the garden with the rivers underneath it. And I'm glad I missed the battle because it was probably bullshit and the Army just murdered your dog anyway.

CHAPTER THIRTY-SEVEN

Specialist Grace looked like Jean-Michel Basquiat and he was a Bradley gunner. His friend Carranza drove the Bradley. I hadn't seen much of either Grace or Carranza since Fort Hood. They were in Delta Company. We had different AOs. But sometimes I'd see them on the FOB, and when I'd see them I'd say hi and they'd say hi. They were good people.

This is what happened to them: they hit an IED up north of Checkpoint 9, during some big operation. I don't remember which big operation. There were so many. All the big operations had names. They had names so you knew they were big operations but then nothing ever happened. Just IEDs. Just kicking doors. More IEDs. More doors.

Grace and Carranza hit an IED. Carranza was wounded. He was in the driver's hatch and his face was fucked up and he was blind and the Bradley was on fire. Carranza's fucking face was gone, but still he thought to drop the ramp so that the guys in the troop compartment could get out fast. Grace pulled Carranza out of the driver's hatch. Grace had taken some shrapnel, but the shrapnel had hit one of the Kevlar wings that were Velcroed to the shoulders of his IBAS, so it hadn't hurt him.

The battalion had had to reiterate the order about wearing the Kevlar wings since we didn't want to wear them because they looked retarded. It was enough of a trick getting the hajis to take you seriously when you weren't wearing the wings; if you were wearing them you might as well forget about it. They were a fucking disaster: they made it so you couldn't shoulder your rifle right, they tangled with the straps of your assault pack. They made the days seem hotter than they would have seemed otherwise, and the days were hot enough already. But the lamest thing about the wings was they only stopped the kinds of bullshit that would send you home early and relatively unscathed. They were useless when it came to stopping the real shit. The only practical use I ever found for the wings was you could stack them on a Humvee seat and sit on them while you rode around because even trivial bits of shrapnel were crucial where your junk was concerned. But apart from that the wings were garbage. Most everybody would have been court-martialed rather than wear them. But Grace wore his wings. They'd told him to wear them and he did what he was told to do because he was pretty laid-back about shit. And he took the shrapnel on one of the wings. The shrapnel would have wounded him. Maybe he'd have gone to a hospital for a while and he'd have had a little rest and then been just fine. He might have even got to go home. But the shrapnel didn't wound him, because of the wings, and the pro-wing people made a big deal out of this.

The last time I saw Specialist Grace it was the day that all the enlisted on the FOB who weren't busy doing something real important got called down to the DFAC to see the Sergeant Major of the Army. He had come to pay us a visit. I got caught up in it, and I was standing in line, waiting to get into the DFAC. The battalion sergeant major was out there chopping it up with Grace, and he wanted all of us to hear him talking. He said to Grace, "You had a close call, huh?"

Grace said, "Yes, Sarr Major."

"It was a good thing that you were wearing all your body armor, wasn't it?"

"Yes, Sarr Major."

"What about these prima donnas who don't want to wear all their body armor because they like to style and profile?"

"I dunno, Sarr Major."

At no point did the battalion sergeant major mention that the IED that had caught Grace ineffectually on the wings had also gone through however many inches of Bradley hull armor or that PFC Carranza didn't have much in the way of his face anymore and his legs were fucked too.

When we were inside the DFAC, the Sergeant Major of the Army was introduced and he said a few words. The Sergeant Major of the Army was the highest ranking noncommissioned officer in the Army. So it was supposed to be a treat maybe. He was a real piece of shit. He thanked us all for our hard work, and then he told us about a change being made to the Army's pension plan for retirees. He said the Army was going to defer pension payments to retirees until said retirees were retirement age, meaning in their sixties. He said the changes would affect only future enlistees, but that didn't stop some of the old hands from giving the Sergeant Major of the Army a hard time.

One old hand stood up and said, "Now what exactly is going on here, Sarr Major?"

And the Sergeant Major of the Army said, "We looked at it and we saw that, since so many ex-military go on to be CEOs, that the pension payments could be deferred. But keep in mind that these changes don't pertain to anyone in this room. Next question."

"Are we going to get our pensions or not, Sarr Major?"

"Everybody will get his or her pension. This is guaranteed. We took a look at it and, since so many ex-military go on to be CEOs, these pension payments could be deferred."

After the big meeting Sergeant Koljo buttonholed the Sergeant Major of the Army outside the DFAC and said he had to do something because the Army wasn't letting us kill enough people.

"They're not letting us do our jobs, Sarr Major," he said.

You should have seen the look on the old motherfucker's face. It was beautiful.

And then Grace was killed on a dismount patrol two weeks later. Another IED. He was wearing his wings but they didn't do shit for him.

CHAPTER THIRTY-EIGHT

Some days you couldn't remember the last time it had rained. It was one of those days, but it came to be a very good day because there was a sandstorm. The sandstorms were wonderful; medevacs couldn't fly in them, so all patrols got canceled. This one was a good one. The wind blew and blew and you couldn't see shit.

Somebody said, "Look at this motherfucker go."

And somebody said, "Yeah, it's really going."

Then somebody said, "It's raining."

"Raining!"

We all ran outside and sure enough there were raindrops.

The raindrops felt good on your face. You couldn't remember the last time it had rained. You had come to want rain very much and here it was. You had it. Rain.

Everybody was coming out now.

"It's raining!"

"It's raining!"

"It's fucking raining!"

"I can't believe it!"

"I can't fucking believe it's fucking raining!"

Then somebody said, "It's not rain."

"It's not rain?"

They said:

"It's not rain!"

"It's not rain!"

"It's not rain?"

"No," he said. "All the fucking porta-shitters are knocked over."

"Fuck."

"It's not rain."

"It's the fucking porta-shitters."

"Fuck."

THEN CAME another hot bullshit day. The heat and the light made your brain skip when you tried to hold a thought. Thoughts wouldn't come in a straight line, and you saw translucent red stars. It was bullshit that I was on this patrol to begin with. I'd been out on an IED ambush all the night before and I was spent. Plus Koljo had shot a dog on our way back at dawn and I like dogs.

Shoo found me in the morning after I came in.

"Bad news," he said. "You've got to go out again in an hour."

I stared at him.

"I've been out ten times already this fucking week. What the fuck day is it? These motherfuckers are gonna work me to death, you know that?"

He suppressed a smile. "Sorry, dude. They put you on the patrol roster. I didn't even know till a minute ago. It'll be easy though. It's just a census patrol. I spoke with Lieutenant Evans already and he knows your situation. All you'll have to do is stay with the vehicles on the road."

I nodded to say I'd make it.

The census patrol left around nine. By noon the dismounts would be suffering. I was glad I wouldn't be with them. I'd be sleeping in one of the trucks instead. Then I'd come back. Maybe play a little cards. Maybe go to the haji shop and buy some bootleg DVDs, some Miamis. Maybe a little Wild Tiger. Go and get some dinner. The three-Humvee convoy went real slow up Route Martha; we were past OP2, the last OP on Martha, and there was no telling what might be on the road. The convoy stopped. The dismounts got out and assembled on the road. I stayed where I was in the back of Evans's truck and I kept quiet. I didn't want to draw any attention to myself.

I started to believe I'd really make it alright. Then Private Dallas knocked on the window: "The lieutenant wants you."

"Wants me?"

"Yeah. He says bring your stuff. We're moving out."

"No. I'm supposed to stay here with the vehicles."

"The lieutenant says you're going."

I had a special dislike for census patrols. Whenever we'd come to a house where there was somebody sick or ailing or in any way injured, the patrol leader would tell all the hajis that I was a doctor who had medicine. And he'd have me examine everyone. It didn't matter that I had no medicine, no antibiotics, no drugs except ibuprofen and the two kinds of shit pills and the morphine autoinjectors. It didn't matter that I wasn't a doctor. It didn't matter if the haji had a brain tumor. I was supposed to pretend to be some kind of great healer.

The first household of the day brought out an old haji who had some variety of advanced rheumatism, I think. I took a look at him. His knees were his chief complaint. He took a seat and gathered his man dress up high so that his testicles featured prominently.

Dallas said, "I think he wants you to suck his balls, doc."

I gave the old haji a three-day supply of ibuprofen and told him to go to a hospital.

The patrol continued.

Lieutenant Evans had the sort of intentions with which you can pave a road to hell. But I loathed him. And I loathed his patrol. The sun was blazing away on us, blazing away on the scenery. After some hours of getting our brains cooked and dragging all the stupid fucking gear around and knowing it was all useless, we were worn out. Some of the guys didn't look like they were up to it anymore.

I said, "Sir, it's really hot and these guys are beat and we're not accomplishing anything out here. We might want to think about heading back."

"No."

"Sir—"

"I said no."

"Okay . . . yeah, okay. You're right, sir. Let's keep going. Ask all these fucking hajis how many fuckin goats they fuckin own till one of your guys has a fuckin heatstroke out here."

The lieutenant was surprised.

I realized I had just done something insane. But I was already going, so I didn't stop. "How many fuckin times are you gonna ignore me when I try to tell you something you need to know? I don't tell you these things cuz I like to hear myself talk. I tell you these things cuz I want to help you. I'm trying to help you, Lieutenant. You remember when I told you not to drive in that shit cuz we were gonna get stuck? What happened? We got stuck, didn't we? And four guys got killed. You killed my friends."

This last part was a bit much. He hadn't killed them and they weren't my friends. They were more like acquaintances really. And then there was one other thing: if he hadn't got us stuck we'd have been the ones who got killed that day. But you didn't say these things.

I didn't hear what he was saying. I couldn't hear anything. I flipped him the bird and I said, "Fuck you and fuck your patrol."

I walked away. I went back to the road. When I got there I went to Evans's truck. Specialist Sullivan was up in the turret. He was monitoring the radio. He said, "The lieutenant says you need to come back."

"Tell him to get fucked."

"Really?"

"Tell Lieutenant Evans to get fucked."

Sullivan keyed the radio: "Um . . . he says he's not coming."

Evans said that would also be fine.

Ten minutes later the dismounts came back to the road. I'd calmed down some and I was ready for something bad to happen to me. Evans waved me over to him and I went over and we walked a ways down from everybody else. He said, "That wasn't a good thing you did."

I didn't want to look at him. I said, "I dunno, sir. It was fucked up of me. I apologize. I don't know what happened. I just kind of went crazy for a minute, you know?"

"You realize I could have you court-martialed for what you just did, right?"

"Yeah."

"I'm not going to do that, so don't worry."

I said, "Thanks."

"I'm not going to say anything to anybody about this when we get back. Nobody's going to say anything about it."

And he didn't say anything.

And no one else did.

And nothing happened to me.

I SENT a check to Roy with a note: more Percs, Oxys would be fine.

And goddamn if he didn't send me four 80s. Roy was paying $60 for 80s in those days. Not great.

Still, I was only snorting 20s then. A 20 would take me there. I'd get four good days out of an 80. But goddamn if the mail wasn't slow.

CHAPTER THIRTY-NINE

When Arnold got killed we had to pack him out. Arnold was dead as shit. Packing up his stuff was no good. He didn't need it. Who needed it?

There'd been seven of us in the room.

Now there were five.

Shoo had been on the patrol that Arnold got killed on. He told me what it had looked like. Said it was bad, just a complete mess. Like somebody'd run him through a juicer.

"That's bad luck," I said. "He hardly ever left the wire."

Shoo said yeah, "That was only the third time he'd gone out."

"Goddamn."

Then I had the day off. It was good. Burnes was hanging around as well, telling me some shit about something. He used to smoke weed when he worked at the airport in Boston and he hit an airplane with the fuel truck he was driving. I was high as shit. Burnes took a hit off his Miami and drank some of his coffee.

Then Shoo walked in. "Bad news, guys. You're going to have to stop smoking in here."

This was the worst news. Burnes and I each smoked about four packs of Miamis a day.

Burnes said, "You're kidding me. Why?"

I said, "Sarr, this is unreasonable."

"You've got a new guy moving in here, coming over from HHC. He's going to be one of Sergeant Drummond's joes. His name's Specialist Branson or some shit like that. He's moving in here today."

Burnes said, "C'mon, you're joking."

I said, "Sarr, we smoke. Lessing smokes. Cheetah smokes. We all smoke, except for Fuentes."

"And I don't mind," said Fuentes from over where he was in the corner. "It doesn't smell any worse in here than it would if they didn't smoke."

Shoo said, "Enough of this noise! I'm not asking you, I'm telling you. No more smoking."

Specialist Branson showed up an hour later. He came walking in the room like he owned the fucking place, the room we had lived in over eight months. He was a big motherfucker with a bald, pink head and a blond mustache. He didn't say hello.

Lessing had come back in the meantime. We'd told him what was being done to us. He said, "So this is the piece of shit?"

I nodded.

Burnes set his book down and looked at Branson. "What's your fucking problem, man? I'm serious, man. Who the fuck do you think you are?"

Branson looked around the room. He didn't seem to be worried about the way things were going. You could tell right away that he didn't waste a lot of time worrying about things.

I said, "We smoke in here, and you can get fucked."

Branson went over and looked at the wall above Lessing's bunk where Lessing had stapled fifty Maxim girls to the wall.

Lessing said, "Hey. Cocksucker. Do you mind?"

Branson left. He hadn't said anything, not one word.

Ten minutes later Sergeant Drummond walked in. "Lessing, you're gonna have to take those girls off your wall."

"Excuse me, Sarr?"

"You heard me, Lessing. Branson's a Christian, and those girls on your wall are offensive to him."

"Then tell him to go fuck himself."

"Oh come on, son. It ain't gonna hurt you none to take them old girls down off the wall. Just put em in a book so that way you can look at em whenever you want to. How's that sound?"

Lessing lit a Marlboro Red and looked at his boots. He was too upset to continue the conversation. Drummond was pleased. When he left he was laughing at us.

"Here comes old Branson," he said. "Make way for old Branson. Here he comes."

Shoo came back. "What's the fucking problem now?"

Lessing said, "Sarr Drummond said I have to take my pictures down because of the new guy, Sarr."

Shoo said, "You're kidding me."

He said no he wasn't kidding.

Burnes said, "This guy is a piece of shit. Please don't do this to us, Sergeant."

I said, "He's telling you the truth, Sarr. This guy Branson comes in, doesn't say shit to anybody, looks around, leaves, and then he's got Sarr Drummond in here two seconds later telling Lessing he's got to take all his pictures off his wall."

Shoo considered this; then he said, "No. No, that goes too far."

And he left and told Drummond to find somewhere else to put Branson.

And we smoked cigarettes as we were wont to do.

CHAPTER FORTY

By the time it was fall you could tell we were all a little off. In that state none of us could have passed in polite society; those of us who'd been kicking in doors and tearing houses up and shooting people, we were psychotic. And we were ready for it to end. There was nothing interesting about it anymore. There was nothing. We had wasted our time. We had lost.

People kept dying: in ones and twos, no heroes, no battles. Nothing. We were just the help, glorified scarecrows; just there to look busy, up the road and down the road, expensive as fuck, dumber than shit.

There were rumors of death: the occasional murders, the horrifying endings. Someone from Bravo Company: the medic quit, said he couldn't face going out anymore. One of EOD's people: there was a second IED under the first one. Gone. Etc. Etc. We set up a patrol base. Haji knocked it down with a car bomb. More women got shot to death: a woman holding a baby, a pregnant woman. At least it was fall. We had arrived in fall, so there was that point of reference. We were getting close. Really a year is nothing. It takes that long to learn to be any good in the field, and then once you know what you're doing, you're on your way out.

It'd been a while that I'd had the feeling that Staff Sergeant North hated my fucking guts. Maybe half the times I'd left the wire were with North. I think I was just about on every patrol North went on that year, over a hundred patrols probably with him. We'd been through some shit, got bored as hell together. Now the motherfucker didn't like me at all. That was fine. There was no danger in it. Just he'd talk shit, like I'd light up a Miami when we were somewhere in the daytime and he'd come up and get shitty about it and say, "This isn't fucking smoke break time."

And right in front of motherfuckers, like I was some fucking cherry.

For his own part he was kind of fucked. He'd start letting loose with his two-oh-three, lob some grenades around just for the shits of it, wouldn't even call in a test fire. That's when you knew he was in one of his moods. On a day like that he might walk the whole patrol into the river and we'd be bathing in shit and parasites. Still, that wasn't personal.

What was personal was North got to coming at me wrong all the time. It really started after I said all that greasy shit to Lieutenant Evans and walked off from that patrol. Now if North had something to say to me he'd either have someone else say it or he'd look off at something far away or he'd turn his back when he talked. It'd have made sense if North didn't also think that Evans was an asshole. And it'd have made sense if North was always about his discipline, but what with his sending two-oh-three rounds downrange for no fucking reason and talking shit about Evans when Evans wasn't around, it wasn't like North was completely all the way alright. So who the fuck knows.

Part of it was I wasn't as fucking wild about America as North was. That and the shit wasn't any fun for me. All it amounted to was some more people were dead and Emily was probably getting fucked by other guys. Probably every time I cleared a house some fucker was balls-deep in Emily. I was lovesick. And yeah it must have been nice to be North, to be tough, to believe in this, to be a killer. But I wasn't ever tough and I wasn't ever gonna be. If I was some kind of veteran now it was only on account of luck that I hadn't got my soft ass killed. Sometimes that's enough to have somebody fooled. But North knew I was a fake because he'd been there half the time and seen it. I'm sure there were some other people who knew, but no one hated me for it half as much as North did.

CORPORAL LOCKHART and Specialist Jeffries lived in a room across the way. They had lived there all year. It was a little room; you'd hardly notice it if you didn't know it was there. Specialist Haussmann also lived with them. None of them had left the wire much. Specialist Haussmann would have been alright, but he had a tendency to bitch all the time; he bitched more than he was worth, so he was set aside, and people had forgotten about him, and he was stuck.

Corporal Lockhart and Specialist Jeffries didn't bitch as much as Haussmann, but they were especially frail, and somebody had made them the company's arms room clerks. They listened to My Chemical Romance a lot, and they talked about what a fucking cunt Corporal Lockhart's wife was, and they had an idea to catch mice and make snuff films with the mice.

I saw one of the snuff films they made. A mouse in an empty ammo can. A small white hand (Lockhart's, I believe) descended into the frame. The hand held a can of Zippo fluid, and it squeezed the can. The mouse was soaked. The hand disappeared from the frame. The hand came back; it held a lighter now, ignited the mouse. The mouse ran back and forth, a little fireball; stopped dead in its tracks; tipped over like a ditched bicycle.

There was always a fuckload of mice running around the building, so they had plenty to work with, and they made I don't know how many of these mice snuff films. They thought they were clever, and they might tell you about how in one of them they drowned a mouse or how in another one they dismembered a mouse and cut the mouse's head off with a cigar cutter or how in another one, their masterpiece, they crucified a mouse on Popsicle sticks and disemboweled the crucified mouse while it was on the cross. Haussmann didn't know what to do. He kept trying to get moved to another room, but he couldn't get moved. "It isn't fair," he said.

Back in Killeen, Texas, Corporal Lockhart's wife had grown emotionally distant. In the time since he had gone off to Iraq, she had started partying a lot and working as a dancer and fucking a guy named Dale and spending all of Corporal Lockhart's money. She told him all about the shit in more detail than you'd have expected she would. It seemed a little overvindictive, but in her defense she was hot and Corporal Lockhart was the type of guy who went around crucifying mice.

CHAPTER FORTY-ONE

Haji hit Delta's patrol base. The road along the west bank of the river was the only way to get there and it was night and we were obviously going to get hit. Haji's thinking was he could throw a few clips and an RPG into the patrol base, and if he made some bodies there, great, and if not, he had left an IED on the only road in, and QRF was sure to hit it.

The first track missed the pressure plate. Our Humvee missed it too. And this was good for us in the Humvee, that we had missed it, because it was big enough to have fucked us up something tough.

The pressure plate was at a point in the road where the road was half-gone from old IEDs. The pressure plate spanned all that was left of the blacktop there. But at the same time the road was so torn up there that a driver might skip it altogether.

The third vehicle, Evans's track, set it off. The explosion was dull, like it had gone off underneath. Perez was up in the Humvee turret, yelling, "IED! IED!"

Sullivan let off the gas and the truck slowed to a stop. I slipped my aid bag onto one shoulder and opened the back driver-side door. I was half out when Sullivan hit the gas again. The Humvee bucked forward and I ate shit. Hueso-Santiago ran past as I was unfucking myself. He was the vehicle commander of the lead track. He had taken it upon himself to go see about the one that had been hit. And I was running that way too. I caught up with Hueso-Santiago. He was crawling all over the front of the disabled track. Everybody was fine but the driver, Private Miller, and he wasn't bad off. He had taken shrapnel on the inside of his left thigh. Hueso-Santiago pulled him out of the hatch.

The hole in Miller's thigh was big enough to put a thumb into it with room to spare. But he'd be alright. The shrapnel hadn't found the artery or anything. I packed the hole with gauze and put an Ace wrap around the thigh so as to keep pressure on the wound. I started an IV and gave him morphine. I'd told Hueso-Santiago to call the medevac in as urgent surgical because Shoo had once told me to always call our guys in as urgent surgicals even if they weren't.

This was an easy casualty. The casualty had a face. He wasn't burned up. He didn't bleed out internally. He'd be alright. He'd get a Purple Heart and the Purple Heart would get him laid a few more times than he would have otherwise and he didn't even have to get hurt that bad. The thing about Purple Hearts is you can't get hurt too bad. You get hurt too bad and girls won't fuck you no matter how many Purple Hearts you have.

QRF2 took a long time getting out to us with EOD and a wrecker. There was some shit going on at the FOB. People were saying, "The FOB's been overrun!"

This turned out to be an exaggeration. What really happened was a few of the battalion snipers had gone up in the scaffolds of the power plant and a guy out in front of the Delta Company TOC saw the snipers and mistook them for Haji. So he shot at them. The shots missed the snipers and came down on the Echo Company TOC. Echo thought the shots were coming from the scaffolds, having also seen the snipers up there. Echo started shooting. The shots missed the snipers and came down on the Delta Company TOC. Delta was now certain that the snipers were the Haj, and a lot of Delta guys opened up on the snipers. A firefight ensued between two American rifle companies with the battalion's snipers caught in the cross fire. In the midst of all the confusion an interpreter set up an IED in the battalion weight room. No one was seriously injured.

. . .

EMILY HAD left the state of Washington. She was back in Elba. She was going to school. She wasn't out in the fucking wilderness anymore and I could call her again. So I called her when I could call her, but there wasn't much to talk about. All I could say was I'd be back soon. I didn't recognize that this was something she maybe wasn't looking forward to, even though I knew, and I'd known the whole time. Still you hold with the lie.

I paid her tuition for fall semester.

She'd asked me for the money so I thought we were good.

CHAPTER FORTY-TWO

The worst possible outcome was to get killed at the end, after all the bullshit. If you weren't going to go home it was better to get killed early on. That was the logic. You didn't want to get killed at the end.

Two from our battalion were killed that morning. We were going out that night, a squad worth of guys from Third Platoon, led by Evans. It was supposed to be our last patrol of the tour, and the roster was a mix and match of shitbags and fat guys. I couldn't imagine us being effective. But we were just going out in Humvees and making a short trip up and down Route Martha. So it didn't matter.

We weren't out long when the company net said a Raptor was sending back video of four armed men. The armed men were east of us. Coordinates were given. Could Lieutenant Evans get there?

He looked at his map. "It's a kilometer, roughly."

I said, "Sir, this is a bad idea."

"Why is it a bad idea?"

"With all due respect, sir, they've got us out here with three of the most obese shitbags in the company, and those are your dismounts. Think about it. Do you think you can take those guys dismounted, off road, in the fucking dark, through all those shit canals for a klick? That's gonna make a lot of noise. Those hajis will hear us coming all the way. We might as well drag a fucking piano with us. I've seen those guys on dismount patrols before, sir. They're a fucking disaster. They fall all over themselves. Borges can shoot, but he can't walk for shit, and the rest of them are an out-and-out fucking liability. No upside. You can't expect to take those guys and one medic, not one NCO, and shoot it out with four armed men who will hear you coming from a mile away. I'm sorry, sir, but it's a real bad idea."

"... I don't know."

"Sir, with all due respect, it'd be different if we had any chance of succeeding. But look at what you've got to work with. It won't end well. Best-case scenario it'll be a waste of time. But do what you think is right and I'll go along."

He keyed the radio. "Echo mike, this is echo tree six actual. . . . It doesn't look like we can get there from where we are."

OUR LAST night on the FOB, some of us got together and passed around some cans of duster. We huffed duster till Sergeant Bautista lost touch with his central nervous system. He swayed back and forth like a blind piano player. A stream of drool ran from Bautista's lip and pooled in his lap.

We said, "Oh, shit. Look at that."

We asked was he alright.

After a minute he said he was alright.

Then we huffed one last can of duster.

And it was alright, like we were kids.

PART FOUR

HUMMINGBIRD

CHAPTER FORTY-THREE

The airliner touched down at Fort Hood around eleven on Tuesday morning. We were bused from the airfield to a parking lot on Battalion Avenue. We were told to line up on the sidewalk because we were supposed to go running into a gymnasium where a lot of guys' families were. A subwoofer was going in the gym, and you could hear the kick drum a hundred yards down the avenue. I was at the end of the line. We started moving up. Ahead guys were running into the gymnasium. The bass line was coming through along with the kick drum now. It was mostly joes towards the end of the line, mostly joes who hated shit like this. The dog and pony shows. I didn't feel like I'd done anything to go running into gymnasiums about.

There were smoke machines and we came in through the smoke. The DJ was playing the refrain from "Disco Inferno" on a loop:

Burn, baby, burn . . .
Burn, baby, burn . . .
Burn, baby, burn . . .

The families were in the bleachers, cheering and yelling guys' names out and waving and taking pictures and filming. The soldiers formed up in ranks. First Sergeant Hightower told us anybody who lived off-post was free to leave after they picked up their duffel bags. Anybody who was going to live in the barracks would report to the barracks and wait to be assigned a room. He said we were on pass till next Monday on account of that Thursday being Thanksgiving. He said we could fall out and we fell out. Guys looked for their people. Husbands embraced wives. Fathers embraced children. I had to get the fuck out of the gymnasium because I felt a panic attack coming on. Dry heaves and everything. And I guess I was ungrateful, given all the people in the gymnasium and the DJ. But they weren't my people and fuck the DJ. You do the best you can.

Things went faster than expected at the barracks. They had everything sorted out already since they'd been expecting us. We only needed to sign for our rooms. This is when I got separated from Echo Company and reassigned to HHC. Suddenly I wasn't a line medic anymore. My roommate was a random motherfucker I didn't know. He had come to the battalion midtour and had been in HHC the whole time. I don't remember his name. I remember he bought an Xbox 360 and he drank Pepsi and wore eyeglasses and had brown hair. He had a little headset so he could talk to his girlfriend in fucking Kansas or whatever while he played video games. That's all I remember about him.

I went to the mall in Killeen and I bought a cell phone at a kiosk. I got ripped off on the contract. People had started texting while I'd been away and I didn't know what texting was supposed to cost. I called my parents and told them I'd made it back okay. My mom said she and my dad were flying down to Texas because a friend of my dad's was about to die in Dallas. They'd arrive in Dallas on Thursday, and Dallas was only a few hours from Killeen so it would be easy enough for me to get up there and see them. I said I'd try and do that.

I took a cab to Walmart and bought some clothes and some bedding and a table lamp. I went back to post and drank heavily. There was a 24-hour PX gas station–liquor store on post near the main gate, so drinks weren't ever going to run out.

When I was drunk, I called Emily, and it didn't go well. I was hurt as fuck that she wasn't there. I wanted her there so bad. I said I knew she'd fucked around on me.

I said, "You broke my heart, you fucking cunt."

She said, "What are you talking about? Baby, you sound like a psycho."

I said, "Why would you do that? What the fuck did I ever do to you?"

She said she hadn't fucked around.

It was a bad time.

WEDNESDAY NIGHT I was over on the Echo Company side of the barracks, and Borges got in an argument with Haussmann. I don't know what it was about. But Borges tried to stab Haussmann and Haussmann got away and called 911.

The police came with North. North was CQ that night. The police weren't MPs, they were Killeen PD. I had already explained to Haussmann that he had fucked up and that he needed to unfuck things, and Lessing had done the same for Borges, and it seemed like we were all on the same page. The police split us up. One of them was over talking to Borges and Lessing and the other was talking to me and Haussmann, and I helped Haussmann tell the police there had been a misunderstanding. No one had actually tried to stab anybody. There had been some loose talk. That was all. Regrettable, yes. But really no big deal. We were sorry for the inconvenience.

"Loose talk?"

"Yessir. Loose talk."

He said we were full of shit. He said, "I think *you're* full of shit and I think *you're* full of shit."

He was pointing his finger in our faces and everything. I asked him why he was acting like that.

"I didn't fucking swear at you," I said. "Why the fuck are you swearing at me? I just got back yesterday, motherfucker. I guess that shit means yer fucking welcome, doesn't it."

North told me to calm down. And I heard something in his voice, like he wished he could be the one arresting me. I felt sick and I tried to ignore it.

Haussmann said, "Look, Officer. I'm sorry that you got called down here and that I've wasted your time. It was a misunderstanding. No one tried to stab me."

Borges was a ways down the hall with Lessing and the other policeman. Now he turned towards us and shouted, "DON'T LISTEN TO THEM, OFFICER. EVERYTHING THEY'RE SAYING IS LIES."

Somehow nobody went to jail. And everything was okay. There were no hard feelings. We all went to Bennigan's: Borges, Haussmann, Lessing, and I. The waitress was no less than a hundred months pregnant. She had the name Shawn tattooed in big script on the side of her neck. But it didn't discourage Borges from trying to seduce her. He was unsuccessful. And the waitress said she wasn't going to serve Borges any more Long Island iced teas.

Then Lessing said, "Is that motherfucking Lieutenant Nathan?"

And it *was* Lieutenant Nathan. We went over and said hello to him. Nathan was a good guy. Maybe he was a bit fucked up from the brainwashing. But who wasn't? And he was glad to see us. He said, "How ya doin, men?"

We said we were good.

He introduced us to his friend, another lieutenant. Nathan said the guy had been with the brigade's cav scout squadron.

"Oh," we said. "Okay."

Nathan went to take a piss.

We said to the cav scout lieutenant, "You guys had a tough time up there."

The cav scout lieutenant said, "So did you guys."

"Yeah. We did."

"But I think ours was a little worse," he said.

"But we lost more killed than you did."

"That's true," he said. "But we lost all ours in two months. Yours were more spread out."

Nobody took offense. That was how it was. The cav scout lieutenant told us about a staff sergeant of his who'd gone up in flames and jumped out of his track and run down the road on fire. He said in all the confusion they hadn't known where this man had run off to and they'd spent ten minutes looking for him before they found him in a bush in a ditch down the road, all burned to death.

Nathan came back from pissing, and he said, "Lemme buy all you men a round, okay? How about that?"

We said that would be great and thank you.

"What's yer poison?"

I said I liked Red Label scotch.

After he made sure we were all holding a double of Red Label he said he'd like to make a toast.

"To two smells," he said, "pussy and gunpowder. . . . Live for one. Die by the other. Llllove the smell of both."

We drank the drinks. Nathan went outside and threw up in a flower bed. Borges said he wanted to go to a strip club. We asked the lieutenants if they wanted to go, but they said no, they didn't. So we thanked Nathan again and we parted company.

Borges got thrown out of the strip club because he threw a Long Island iced tea at the DJ booth when the DJ wouldn't play any Cypress Hill. Lessing and Haussmann got thrown out for letting on that they knew Borges. I was away trying to get a drink at the bar, and I didn't know what had happened. After a while I figured out my friends were no longer with me. I didn't go looking for them though. Maybe I'd have tried calling them, but I'd left my phone at the barracks. So I said fuck it and I finished my drink and I had another.

It got to be closing time. A dancer had just finished painting herself red, white, and blue to the Toby Keith song in the evening's grand finale. I was at a table by myself, staring down at a gin and tonic I'd bought at last call.

Someone said, "Are you okay, honey?"

She was wearing plastic shoes. I said I was alright. I'd just got back with 4th ID and I was a little fucked up, but I was alright. She said some nice things and asked what I was doing for Thanksgiving. I said I wanted to go to Dallas to see my parents because they'd be there, but I didn't have a ride yet. She said she was driving up to Dallas to see her family and she could give me a ride if I wanted. I said thanks and that would be good. She gave me her number and told me to call her in the morning.

I met her at the mall. I gave her some gas money and we went on our way, north on 35. We were halfway to Dallas when she asked me if I wanted any Vicodin. I said I'd like some. I saw the scar on her arm. It ran from her elbow halfway down to her wrist. She told me about the car wreck she'd been in. She said she'd been driving her niece and they'd got into an accident on the freeway. Her niece had got hurt too. Firemen had had to cut both of them out of the car. She said her niece had been terrified and screaming because the girl was bleeding from the head and help couldn't get to her. She said she hated to remember that she had put her niece through that. I said it wasn't like she'd done it on purpose, things just happened.

My parents were staying at a hotel in Fort Worth. She dropped me off in the parking lot. I wished her luck. She said alright and she drove away. I had Thanksgiving dinner with my parents at the Houlihan's next door to the hotel. Then we went to the hospital to see the dying man.

His wife was 20 years younger than he was. She was his second wife. They used to work together.

My dad said, "This is our son. He's just back from Iraq."

The lady didn't give a shit, but she tried.

She said, "My brother's in the Army. He's some kind of mechanic or something. They go behind enemy lines."

We left it at that. My folks asked her how she was holding up. She said she was holding up okay even though his first wife and his first kids were giving her a hard time and she was all alone.

My dad said he wanted me to see his friend. We went into the room where he was laid up on a ventilator. There wasn't much left of him, and each breath was like it would break him in half. He may as well have been dead for all the good breathing did him.

They'd had a little girl and a house and a golden retriever. We went to the house after we left the hospital, and my parents talked to his wife some more for about an hour. They said for her to let them know if there was anything they could do. She said thanks and that they were very kind. But she was just saying things. They were all just talking. And everyone knew that nothing would be alright.

THAT NIGHT I talked to Emily on the phone. She told me what I already knew, and I slept on the bathroom floor. My parents drove me back to Killeen in the morning. It was taking a long time because traffic was backed up for miles on account of an accident that would take the whole day to clear off the road. Some more people had been killed. And my dad got to talking about his friend some, how they were before they'd got old.

CHAPTER FORTY-FOUR

A funny thing happened to me once: after we got married, Emily went and had electrolysis done, and then she took a series of lovers, and then there was the day that I found out I'd been something like the hundredth one to see her electrolysis. And this devastated me. But in all fairness: I *had* gone to Iraq. And in all fairness: our marriage *was* a lie. Maybe she'd thought I'd get killed and wouldn't ever find out.

My last three months in the Army, down in Texas, I was drinking two fifths of gin a night. I shit blood. I farted blood. I jerked off in bathroom stalls, not feeling so good.

I went home for Christmas and there was a girl; she said she was on her period so I titty-fucked her, while I was wanting to die. She said, "Do you mind not hitting me in the face with your cock?"

I went back to Texas, and it was a little better. People knew what it was like. And there were a lot of them losing their shit down in Texas, so Texas was good like that: you didn't feel like you were that fucked up as long as you were in Texas.

But then I was really getting out of the Army; my time was up. And you'd think that was all good, but it wasn't all good. I felt like I was abandoning my people. Really they didn't give a fuck if I was leaving or not, but at the time that was what it felt like to me, that I was abandoning my people. I thought, Maybe I ought to stay.

But I didn't stay. I left. The fuckers made me sign up for the National Guard before they'd let me go, but they let me go and I got the fuck out. I went back to Ohio. I stopped off in Elba on the way. Emily wanted a divorce. So we got divorced and then I went home. I had a little money and started getting fucked up on drugs. I felt that if I had a little money and I could get fucked up on drugs then I could make it and something good would happen eventually. What happened was I got coked up one night in March and called Emily in the middle of the night; and I said, "I forgive you. I need you so bad. Are you fucking anyone right now? I don't care what you did. I won't mention it. But I don't think I can do this without you."

She said, "What do you mean?"

"Do I have to fucking spell it out?"

I had rented an apartment on Coventry Road in Cleveland Heights, and Emily moved in the first week of that April and tried living with me. She'd just graduated from college with honors and she was beautiful and golden so whatever: I really fucking tried. I bought some stupid furniture. I thought, This is what people do when they settle down. I took Emily to the theater, and I bought her a dress to wear. She went and returned it for another dress and she put that one on and I put on the one suit that I had and we took some 1mg Xanaxes and went to the theater. It was a one-woman show about Ella Fitzgerald. I'd bought the tickets way in advance. Emily liked Ella Fitzgerald a lot. Anyway we got there and we were the only ones dressed up. It was a lot of middle-aged and older people from the suburbs there, and they were all wearing L.L.Bean and shit. Middle-aged people with money, couldn't wear a fucking sport coat or nothing. They deserved vomit. This was the life we fought for. The show was alright. Then Emily and I went home and took some more Xanax and blacked out and went to sleep and James Lightfoot tried to call me but I couldn't hear the phone ringing and that was the night he got arrested trying to break into my apartment building except it wasn't my apartment building; he'd tried to break into the wrong building. The cops found a knife on him. Drugs were involved.

. . .

MY FIRST Guard meeting wasn't a smash hit. Everybody thought I was a prick because I was bad at hiding that I thought everybody was an asshole. I showed up high on OxyContin, and I'd forgotten to wear an undershirt. I don't know, I just hated this fucking Guard unit because it wasn't Echo Company and half of them were off-duty sheriff's deputies and shit like that and the way they talked made me sick.

I was starting up going back to school again. I was going to a state school downtown, and I'd go to school and Emily would snort all my cocaine and leave a note in the drawer saying she wanted me to stop doing cocaine. She was a real first-class bitch; this is why I love her to death.

It didn't work out. It was 70% my fault. I'd been getting into the OxyContin pretty hard, and it made me feel a type of way so as I wasn't about taking any shit from her. Also I was pretty fucked in the head, and I was being a sad crazy fuck about some horrors I'd been through. It's true that you go through some horrors and it fucks you up. I don't care what violent motherfuckers say; if it doesn't fuck you up then it's only cuz you're just too fucking stupid. Still there's no use being a sad crazy fuck about it because you kill yourself like that. And I was seeing ghosts. And I was talking too goddamn much. And I was making her miserable. I guess I wanted her to feel like shit.

But what killed it was when I fell in love with an 18-year-old girl from Barcelona. Zoë. Technically she was 17 and 350 days. But I didn't do anything. I just took her out for pancakes. And Emily found out about it. Roy of all fucking people told Emily about how I'd taken Zoë out for pancakes. Plus he left most of the story out and made it sound like I'd been a real fuck about it. The thing was: I'd been drinking at Roy's and I had asked several people if they'd like to have pancakes with me at the Severance

IHOP, and all but one of them I asked were dudes. All but one of them weren't this girl Zoë.

I'd said, "Roy, you wanna go to IHOP?"

He'd said no.

I'd said, "Joe, you wanna go to IHOP?"

The same.

"What about you, James Lightfoot?"

They'd all said they were good on pancakes. Only Zoë had said she wanted to go. So I went with her and we were just going to have pancakes and maybe I was in love with Zoë but that had nothing to do with it. And maybe I was glad that it was just her who had gone, but I hadn't fixed it that way on purpose. Roy though, he didn't tell Emily anything like that. He made it sound like it had been some kind of clandestine pancakes date, and Emily got super fucking pissed at me. I came home and she threw a glass against the wall and said, "How'd you like your fucking pancakes?"

No shit. That was the end. A few days later Emily was gone. She took her stuff with her: the accent pillows, the Crock-Pot, all of it. I didn't try to stop her; she was better off the way she was going, and I was sick of her.

Zoë turned 18 but it didn't matter because I couldn't fuck for anything. I'd been gutted. I thought a lot about Emily and her lovers: the Puerto Rican with the Valiums, the wildlife photographer from France, Dave from the Giant Eagle. Those were just the ones I knew about. I wondered what they'd done with her, if they'd made her come. Had they cared about her or had they just fucked her? Had she done stuff for them that she wouldn't do with me? Had she talked about me? Had she told them I deserved it?

I more or less stopped going to school. School was too goddamn much. I felt like I knew too much already. I'd seen the end of the movie. The only thing school was good for was it got me out of two weeks of summer training with the National Guard. I'd said, I can't go. I'm signed up for school. I'm paying for it out of pocket. They'd said, We do this every summer. I'd said I hadn't known. They'd said, Everyone knows. I'd said, You should have said something. And goddamn if I hadn't known what I was doing but there was no way in hell I was going to hang out in the woods for two weeks and play soldiers with a lot of off-duty sheriff's deputies. I had more important things to do.

I'd stay up by myself in the early morning and snort cocaine and snort Oxy. A gram here. 40mg there. Another 40mg. I'd steal Wi-Fi from my neighbors and watch porn on the Internet. I'd write poetry. I'd drink vodka. Vodka was good because I could drink it all day and I didn't shit blood. I imagined all the porno girls were war widows and it made me sad. I'd get on the vodka and snort some powder at my little table and write five or six poems between three o'clock and nine in the morning—poems mainly about true love being impossible, poems mainly about what drugs I liked to do, poems mainly about barely legal girls getting down on some cocks, poems mainly about what a piece of shit death was. Then I'd go to bed. I sent a few poems to *The New Yorker*, but they didn't make it in. Then my laptop crashed and I lost my poems.

I HAD to take James Lightfoot to the police station in Linndale. James Lightfoot was a good guy but he was also fucked in the head. I don't know the details of exactly why or how he was fucked in the head or if there were any such exact details. Probably he was just born fucked in the head. And I guess I'd been born that way too and it was only a coincidence that I had been to a war and the war probably hadn't had much to do at all with my being fucked in the head. Anyway James Lightfoot wasn't a happy person because people treated him like shit because he was almost normal but then he wasn't and he had a lazy eye and he was real skinny like you knew he couldn't ever fight and what all he had was just the things that no one gave a fuck to take from him.

He had to pay off a warrant and I had to take the money in and pay it off because there were other warrants out for him and if he went into the police station they'd arrest him. I snorted some coke before I left my apartment and I picked up James Lightfoot and we drove to Linndale. I hadn't ever been to Linndale before. It was the first I'd heard of it. We got to the police station and James Lightfoot gave me the money to pay the warrant off with and I went inside. I told the policeman behind the glass that I was there to pay James Lightfoot's warrant off, and he said he needed to see my ID. So I gave him my ID and when he took it he went back somewhere in the office and I looked down at my hand and there was coke all over my hand from where I'd touched the driver's license. I was embarrassed and not a little worried but I stayed because if I left I was fucked anyway and then the policeman came back and he didn't even mention the coke on my driver's license. So I was alright and the warrant was paid off like that.

We drove back to the East Side, and James Lightfoot wanted to sign some of his paychecks over to me so I could give him the equivalent in cash for them since he couldn't have a bank account because he was in ChexSystems and his credit was totally fucked. We went to the bank and the teller wouldn't let me deposit the checks James Lightfoot had signed over to me, even though he was right there and he had his passport and I had enough money in my account to cover the checks. The bank people thought we were undesirables. So we got nothing and we left. I drove James Lightfoot to James Lightfoot's mom's house and I got on the phone and called the bank's eight-hundred number and told them that I was a war veteran and that the teller and the manager at the Warrensville branch had treated me like I was an undesirable and that I didn't know what I was going to do yet but it sure as fuck wasn't right the way they treated people. And I got off the phone. I was in the driveway and the summer burned my eyes and everything had changed and nothing had changed.

ZOË WOULD come around and spend time with me some days. We'd go to '80s night together every Sunday. I guess she liked me despite my being a lame fuck. That or she liked cocaine. Maybe it was a little of both. She really was good though. She played the cello and she'd gone to school for that. And she could speak all these different languages. She would speak French and I liked the way she did the *r*'s. I'd ask her to do the *r*'s and she would. Then I'd try but I couldn't do them for shit and she thought that was funny. I tried to snort a line of coke off her stomach, but there was no air-conditioning and her skin was dewing so it didn't work and I licked it off her.

We went to the lake. She drove. She had a little white Volkswagen. I couldn't drive it because it was a stick. She ran all the stop signs. This was some kind of matter of principle with her evidently; I don't know what specifically but she hardly ever stopped for them.

We got to the lakeshore and we were wearing our bathing suits. She looked real good in hers. She had the whole flawless complexion thing going for her. She was like a girl in a magazine. She looked good in the sunlight whereas I looked bad. I hadn't been getting out much in the daytime and I was very pale. You could see the marks all over from where the sand fleas had been at me the summer before, when I'd been out in the marshes and the shit canals and all that. I hadn't been eating much of late either, and I had the cocaine physique. And there were the cigarette burns too, as the tendency in those days was to burn myself with cigarettes whenever I got down in the dumps. All in all I was another stray dog with the mange.

Many dead fish were washed up on the lakeshore. They were all around us on the sand in their various phases of decomposing. But this was how it always was at the lakeshore. The lake smelled like gasoline. We went in the water and we swam around some. We kissed. After a while we drove back. And suddenly it was as if she didn't like me, as if she hadn't ever liked me at all. She'd do that from time to time; she'd just change her mind about me. It made me feel like shit; but then I'd say to myself, You totally deserve this.

She was supposed to fly back to Barcelona at the end of August. I'd always known that. That had been what was supposed to happen when I first met her. But I hadn't thought it was possible that I'd live to see it happen. Then it happened. Before she left she gave me a letter. The letter said: "Wait."

She waited two days.

I waited three days.

OTHER GIRLS. Some girls I didn't deserve. Some girls I deserved. One thing: I was always an asshole.

When I was gonna kill myself I went to the VA hospital. I waited in the waiting room. There were two other people there. Elderly. A man and woman. The man had an oxygen tank and one of those hats that tells you what battleship he was on. The woman—his wife, I imagine—looked like a potato that was about to whistle a tune. A happy tune. When it was my turn I told the hospital people that I was real close to doing it but I didn't believe in it and now I didn't know what to do. They said hang out here and they sent me back to the waiting room except to a different part that was boxed in with Plexiglas and they shut the door and I sat there for a while, away from the other people. Then a lady came and asked me if I wanted to be an inpatient and already I knew that'd be bad so I said I'd just leave. She said she'd make an appointment for me to see a psychiatrist in a few days. I said alright.

That Saturday the National Guard sent people to my apartment to come get me. I had my mind made up that I was through with the fake soldier bullshit. I followed them down to the armory and told the one guy I'd try from now on because I was on the spot and I had to say some shit like that even though I knew I wasn't gonna try and I didn't. After a while they lost interest, so I was free because I was more trouble than I was worth.

When I ran out of money that winter I had to go get a job. I worked at a restaurant again. Six nights a week and it paid shit. Girls left me alone for a little while.

And then it was spring again. And then it was summer again. Spring was like a foot in the grave. Summer was a fucking joke. I'd turned 23. James Lightfoot went to rehab. I moved to Belmar. Belmar was alright till the ceiling got wet and fell in. I called the landlord and said the ceiling had got wet and fallen in. He sent a guy who put in a drop ceiling. When the drop ceiling got wet and fell in I knew it was time for a change. I quit my job. I left everything. I left the furniture. Actually I threw it into the yard. I threw it off the porch from the second story. All I took when I moved was the bed and a rug I liked.

I was into heroin. I had sold my TV and injected it. I'd found a decent enough heroin guy: Three-Hundred. This was before Three-Hundred was a piece of shit. I moved into a one-bedroom above the sandwich shop at Coventry and Mayfield, next to the convenience store where they had wine. The sandwiches were excellent. Things were good. It was fall. I liked fall. I was completely fucking broke and the world's economy was in crisis. It looked like maybe the world would stop and then we'd be okay. No more pretending. I went to '80s night for the fuck of it. This is when I met Libby.

CHAPTER FORTY-FIVE

It was a lot of those little tea candles everywhere because the electric wasn't on yet, and Libby and I did some lines. We were drinking Gato Negro—the cheapest shit you could get for money—and she was talking softly because she wasn't sure of herself; she said she was wasting her time at community college:

"But my cousin lives in California. I'm going to move there and live with her. . . . She works for a movie studio in Hollywood. . . . She tells me lots of inside stuff about celebrities, stuff the public doesn't know about, like George Clooney's actually gay. . . . Yeah. But he doesn't come out because it'd be bad for business. . . . I'll probably live with my cousin at first. She says she can get me a job."

I said I'd miss her. She looked down into her cup. She wore lots of mascara. Her mother had died when she was in high school. I never asked how.

I said, "I don't think it'd be possible for you to be any hotter than you are. You're as hot as girls get. You're as hot as it's possible to be."

She said, "Thank you."

And when she was naked, she was on all fours, and I spit on her back.

She said, "Did you just spit on me?"

"Yeah."

"You do whatever you want, don't you?"

"Sometimes."

"I think it's a good thing."

. . .

NEXT NIGHT we went to a Halloween party across town in Tremont. She had brought two friends with her: Gilda and Megan. Megan was the only one wearing a costume. She had dressed up as a Nazi. I'd said I wasn't sure she'd be well received at the party if she went dressed up like that. But Gilda had said *she* was Jewish and Megan's costume didn't offend *her* so Megan would probably be okay. We did some lines and went to the party. Gilda met Roy there and Gilda left the party early with Roy. Then a girl named Jael got mad at Megan's costume. She said her grandparents had been in the camps. Megan took the swastika armband off her sleeve, but she still had the jackboots and the brown shirt on and nothing to change into. So we left. We went back to my apartment and there was no more coke and Megan wasn't feeling it. She said, "Take me home, Libby."

"Let's just stay a little while."

"I want to go home," she said. "I want to go home NOW, Libby!"

"*Jeez*. Okay. We'll go. Just give me one second, will ya?"

Libby asked when she could see me again.

I said as soon as she possibly could would be best for me.

She said tomorrow.

I said tomorrow.

LIBBY HAD angel wings done on her back. On some places on the angel wings were names written in small script. "They're the names of people I love," she said.

She'd lie on her back and with her head over the side of the bed. She said she liked this. She went: lucky lucky lucky lucky lucky . . .

She was 19.

These girls had grown up with the Internet.

I came in her face.

Libby wiped the come off her face and licked it off her fingers; and she said, "The monkeys are eating cawwits and the wabbits are eating *bananas*!"

And I was depressed again.

I HAD money on Friday so I bought some heroin and shot it with Libby and Gilda.

Gilda said, "Oh, my. This is nice."

Libby said, "Yeah, this is really great."

Roy came over and shot heroin too. We all drank Gato Negro. We smoked all the cigarettes.

Gilda looked like Tinker Bell when she was wasted.

I wanted to fuck Gilda.

She spilled half a bottle of Gato Negro on the rug.

She said, "How careless of me."

I said, "No worries, Gilda. You'll have that."

When we ran out of cigarettes Roy took Gilda home and Libby and I crashed but we couldn't sleep. So we got up and we went and took a shower. That's how I saw Libby without her makeup on. She looked so young it scared the shit out of me and I told her I loved her and she got real happy about it. She said she loved me too. This was the happiest that I would ever see her. And I already knew it would turn out bad because I was a fucking coward and my heart was rotten as shit.

CHAPTER FORTY-SIX

Gilda was fucking Roy. She was also fucking an Israeli guy named Ricky. Ricky wore a leather jacket but he wasn't shit. Libby told me about Ricky but I knew him from before and I knew he wasn't shit. He was one of these ones that everything he says is a lie and he goes around telling girls he's 27 when he's more like 40. And he wore a leather jacket. And he wasn't shit. One night Gilda and Roy and Libby and I went out to a bar and Ricky came around and it looked like there maybe was going to be some violence.

Ricky said to me, "Why does your boy keep looking at me like that? He needs to stop doing it. I'll hurt him, bro. I was in the Israeli army."

Roy was a fuck and I knew that. I'd seen him steal tramadols from a border collie with terminal cancer. But we went back a long way, and I was obliged to do whatever was necessary. There was that, plus Ricky was a bitch, and I didn't believe that shit he said about Israel.

I said to Ricky, "Don't take this the wrong way, but I'll beat the fuck out of you."

He said, "I'm not trying to start any shit with you, bro. I'm just saying that your boy should be more careful."

"Nobody wants you here."

"Fuck you, bro," he said. "Who the fuck are you? You're a fucking creep, bro. I know you're getting those girls strung out on *drugs*. You're scum!"

He had his mind made up that he wasn't going anywhere. Maybe he was the chaperone. Who can know what's in a man's heart. Anyway the rest of us said fuck it and we went back to my apartment and we were locked out so I kicked the door in and then we shot heroin and did stuff like that. It got late and Gilda spilled wine on the rug again.

She said, "I'm so clumsy."

I said, "Don't worry about it, Gilda. You're alright. But please be careful. I like this rug."

Roy said it was the party rug.

This was the night I said to Libby I thought we ought to get married. And she agreed that we ought to get married. So we were getting married. We told Gilda and Roy. Gilda said, "How lovely! I'll be the flower girl!"

Later I tried to fuck Libby but I couldn't get it up because I was on too much drugs.

CHAPTER FORTY-SEVEN

I had quit my job that past summer. The job had paid eight dollars an hour. It had cost me almost that much in parking tickets. It was a lot of fucks who worked there anyway. Actually everyone who worked there was a fuck. Except Joe. Joe worked there and he was alright. The rest of them were shit. They'd tell on you to the boss. They didn't do drugs. I think a lot of them were virgins. No one but Joe and I had ever had anything to do with murders or anything like that. The world meant something else to them than it did to me.

After he got back, Joe had had problems for a while. But he was getting better. He had stopped jumping out of moving cars every time he had a fight with his girlfriend when he was drunk and they were in a car. So that was progress. Soon he would be a decent human being again. We wouldn't be friends much longer.

I was back in school because I needed the money for drugs. Poetry class was twice a week and I was usually in bad shape if I made it at all. The lady who taught the class was named Dr. Archer. She acted bitter as fuck for a woman as young as she was, seeing as it wasn't like she was ugly or anything. She was real serious about poetry too. She came from England.

The class was doing "Ode on a Grecian Urn." Dr. Archer was asking us about the end. I was pretty wasted on some fucking skag so I missed most of what she was saying. But I caught the last part:

"'Beauty is truth,'" she said, "'truth beauty,—that is all Ye know on earth, and all ye need to know.' What do you think Keats meant?"

No one tried to answer.

I thought, Fuck it. I'll give it a shot. The line spoke to me, spoke to my heart, so how could it be that I should misunderstand it?

I raised my hand. Archer kept looking for someone else to call on. There was no one else. At last she had to say, "You."

"I dunno," I said. "Maybe he's saying that all things that are true are beautiful, you know? So beauty's the only thing worth living for."

All she said was no.

But the way she said it was as if I'd taken a dump on the floor and ruined the whole poetry class. Which I thought was a bit overmean on her part.

And her meanness made me wonder, Why this contempt? Why should this lady despise me?

And then I knew the answer:

There were two jackals fucking inside of her.

LIBBY AND Gilda had tried living together. They had signed a lease on an apartment some months back. I think I went over there twice. The only furniture aside from their beds was an inflatable sofa. And they had a little TV set with a DVD player built into the bottom of it. And they had maybe a hundred plastic martini glasses. I didn't like going to their apartment: too many dreams there that wouldn't ever come true.

They ended up breaking the lease. Some big fight or whatever; it doesn't matter. But they turned on each other.

Libby told me how Gilda kept fucking around on Roy with that bitch Ricky. Libby thought Ricky was a creeper. She'd seen Ricky make out with a 17-year-old girl!

At the same time Gilda was telling me Libby was a borderline retard and completely psycho and a slut who'd fuck more or less anybody and pretty much did.

"Don't you see it?" she said. "You have to. I know you do."

And it turned out Roy had been talking shit.

Libby said, "He talks shit about you."

I said that was okay.

"It doesn't bother you?"

"Why would it bother me? Nine times out of ten, you have a friend, he's gonna talk shit about you. That's just the cost of doing business."

"Does he know Gilda hooks up with other guys?"

"I imagine he presupposed it."

"Does he cheat on her?"

"What do you think?"

"Why? Did he tell you something?"

"No."

"And you don't care."

"That's right."

"And you don't care what he says about you."

"No. I don't."

"Because you don't give a fuck."

"Because I don't give a fuck."

LIBBY AND I went out on Sunday night. '80s night. Gilda went too. Roy didn't go because he said he was poor. Libby and Gilda danced together. I drank well vodka at the bar. Kamchatka. I was shit at dancing. The night ended. We went up the stairs and out onto the sidewalk. Libby and Gilda were excited.

"Two guys humped us while we were dancing!"

"We were dancing by ourselves and these two guys came up from behind and smooshed us between them and humped us!"

"Look! There they are!"

Libby pointed at two bros who were about to turn the corner. They were about to get away. I sensed Libby's expectation that I would do something. And I wasn't thrilled about it. But then I figured the bros weren't dangerous and there were two of them and one of me so she couldn't really expect I'd do much more than catch up with them and talk some shit and leave it at that. Which I about did, till I got carried away.

I said, "How much money you got on you?"

"What?"

I said, "Give me all your fucking money."

They raised an alarm.

It turned out these bros weren't alone. More bros appeared. And now there were six bros and it looked like I was about to get the fuck beaten out of me. I was lucky that two friends of Libby's happened to be out there. Two black guys. Gay ones. Two gay black guys in fur coats and diamond earrings. One of them a giant. They saved me. The bros didn't do shit. The bros were scared of the two gay black guys. Libby took my hand.

"I want you to meet my friends," she said.

The one, the giant, had to be six foot seven, and he was built like a fucking bull. I thanked him. He said, "So this is your boy, Libby? He's cute."

She said yeah.

Then a bro I hadn't seen yet came jumping up the street: "YOU BETTER POP OFF, SON. YOU BETTER POP OFF. POP OFF, SON. YOU BETTER POP OFF." And some more bros came and they took him away while he kept on: "POP OFF . . . POP OFF . . . YOU BETTER POP OFF . . . POP OFF . . . POP OFF . . . POP OFF, SON . . ."

He faded out.

The giant said, "Tell me, Libby. When are you two getting married?"

She said, "We're not sure yet."

He said to me, "If you ever hurt Libby, I'll kill you."

WHEN I told Libby I wasn't really gonna marry her she got upset. "Why are you doing this to me?" she said. "I love you."

I said, "I'm sorry but it isn't what you think. All this I-love-you-and-I-want-to-marry-you shit, it's fucking bullshit. I'm sorry but it's true. I know I said that shit. But there's no way I can really mean it. Not in real life."

"THAT'S NOT TRUE."

"But really that is the truth and I'm sorry. Please believe me. I wish things were different but they're not. It's just that it's no good and I may as well tell you now, right? It'd just be worse later, you know?"

"What are you saying?"

"I don't know what I'm saying. But it's how I fucking feel. I wouldn't do some shit like this to you for the fuck of it. I'm not trying to be a dick. I say I love you, right? I'd like it to be true. But it's fucking stupid and I should've known better than to do that."

"Are you saying you don't want to be with me?"

"No. I do. That's not the problem. The problem's just that I know it's no good and I don't believe in this shit."

"You don't trust me?"

"Honestly? . . . No, not especially. But—"

"WHAT DO YOU MEAN? WHAT HAVE I EVER DONE?"

"It's not anything you did. So don't worry. Really it's okay. But a motherfucker would have to be crazy to trust a girl this day and age. Nothing personal."

"Did somebody tell you something about me? Was it Gilda? She's LYING."

"Nobody said anything."

"FUCK YOU."

"AH, SHIT. Why the fuck are you mad at me? I'm trying to be fuckin honest with you."

"YOU SAID YOU LOVE ME. YOU SAID WE WERE GOING TO GET MARRIED. NOW YOU'RE SAYING YOU DON'T LOVE ME AND WE'RE NOT GETTING MARRIED AND I'M NOT SUPPOSED TO BE MAD AT YOU?"

"I do love you. Fuck! I mean I like you a lot. So much. I like you so much. You're really great. You know that. You're incredibly hot and you're much too nice to me. But I can't do this. Look around you. I've lived in this fucking apartment almost two months now and the lights aren't even turned on yet. Doesn't that tell you something? Ninety percent of the time I'm too high to fuck you and I know you like dick and I'm too high so that's lame. I understand why you fuck other guys."

"I don't fuck other guys."

"Yes, you do. And you don't need to lie about it. Who am I that you should need to justify yourself to me? You fuck other guys and you have my blessing. You like dick and there's nothing wrong with that. You're supposed to like dick and I don't doubt for a second that one of those pieces of shit is a better match for you than I am. You ought to marry that one."

"But I want to be with *you*!"

"How can you say that? You don't really know anything about me."

"Yes I do."

"What's my last name? . . . You see?"

"THAT'S NOT FAIR."

"Listen. I'd ruin your life. This is your lucky break. Trust me, you'll get over it."

"Are you breaking up with me?"

"I don't know."

Gilda had been out in the living room the whole time, and Libby and I were feeling dumb on account of Gilda's having heard us say a lot of crazy shit. And Gilda was bored. So we decided we would all feel much better if we did some heroin.

I called Three-Hundred. It was three in the morning but Three-Hundred picked up and I said I was sorry about calling so late. He said it was okay because he was always awake and I could come through. Libby and Gilda wanted to come along. So we all drove over to Buckeye and met Three-Hundred on one of the side streets over that way. He got in the front seat and looked back and said, "Good evening, ladies."

Three-Hundred invariably smelled like shit, and he was a fat fuck and he had breath like he ate shit for breakfast, lunch, and dinner.

I said, "Three-Hundred, this is Libby and Gilda. Libby, Gilda, this is Three-Hundred."

"Hi, Three-Hundred."

"We really like the heroin."

On the way back Libby asked me if Three-Hundred was his real name. I said it probably wasn't.

Gilda said, "He smelled like a zoo!"

Ten minutes later we were out of heroin but we were all high as fuck and Gilda flipped an ashtray over on the rug and said, "Darn."

I said, "Gilda, you're a fucking bitch."

Libby asked if we could call Three-Hundred again.

I said we didn't have any money.

She said, "Can we maybe get some and pay him back later?"

I said I didn't think he'd go for that. It was real late.

CHAPTER FORTY-EIGHT

December. Libby had been on me to go out to Chardon and meet her dad. I called her on the way because I got lost. I said, "I'm lost and I can't see a fucking thing. It's fucking dark out here."

She stayed on the phone and talked me all the way there, step by step. The house wasn't big.

"Okay. I'm here."

"Ooo-wee! I'm so excited!"

Her dad was in the living room. He said his name was Mark. I said hello to Mark. He was tall and very thin, soft-spoken, depressed, effeminate. Another man and a woman were on the sofa. I wasn't introduced so I just waved to them. They didn't wave back. The man had a silver crew cut. He looked like a sheriff's deputy. The woman looked like hell. Both of them were wearing turtlenecks. So was Mark. But what scared me the most was that they were all drinking pop.

Libby's kid brother came running down the stairs. He was 16 and half-naked. He was wearing silk boxers and a Santa hat, a plastic necklace that lit up. He said, "Come here, big boy."

He wrapped his arms around me and started dry-humping me really hard. He wouldn't let go. He was stronger than I was. I got the impression that he did lots of sit-ups. He kept humping me. I didn't know what to do. Then Libby took my hand.

"Come with me," she said. "I want to show you this."

She led me into a dining room, where there were stacks of old magazines on the table and on the floor, and against the wall was a china cabinet holding a number of framed photographs.

"This is my mom," she said.

She picked up one of the photographs and kissed it and handed it to me. Libby looked like her mother. The same eyes. The same mouth. The same smile. I handed the photograph back to her.

"She's beautiful."

"Thank you."

"You look like her."

"Thanks."

She put the photograph back in its place. Then she showed me another:

"That's me with my older brothers."

It was her and five guys with shaved heads. Any one of them looked like he could beat the fuck out of me.

I HEARD there was a party some days later. I didn't go. I hadn't been invited but I wouldn't have gone anyway. It was Ricky's party. Roy went. I didn't wonder at that.

Roy dropped by so he could meet this guy Pills And Coke at my apartment. It was a convenience thing since Pills And Coke was paying me rent to keep a safe in my kitchen. Roy was wearing a sweater with a reindeer on the front. He looked like a total asshole, and I was ashamed of him.

He said, "You're just chilling by yourself?"

I said I was.

He said, "That's cool. How's things with you and Libby."

"Fine."

"That Libby's a good girl."

"Yeah."

"I see why you like her so much. She's got that whole painted-whore thing going for her. . . . Say, man. You wouldn't happen to have any clean rigs around here, would you?"

I said no, but I had some slightly used ones and some bleach. He considered it and said it would have to do. I went and cleaned out a couple rigs. Pills And Coke came up and Roy bought an

80mg Oxy off him. If you didn't know any better you'd have thought Pills And Coke was Biff from *Back to the Future,* but he wasn't; he was Pills And Coke and it was almost 2009 and Pills And Coke wasn't old enough to have been in *Back to the Future.* I had decided that I had better get an 80 as well and I asked Pills And Coke to take it out of what he owed me in safe rent. He said I'd already run through all that. So I asked him to spot me one for a day or two. He said okay.

Pills And Coke left and Roy and I got to shooting our pills. Roy shot half his 80 and I shot the entirety of mine. Roy said, "I wish I could afford to shoot a whole eighty like that."

I said, "Work hard and save your money and you just might."

"Really?" he said. "So that's how you do it?"

"Something like that."

"Why aren't you at the party?" he said. "Libby's there."

CHAPTER FORTY-NINE

Zoë was back.

I said, "Zoë, what are you doing here?"

"Holiday," she said. "Visiting friends."

"Zoë, you live in Barcelona. How long have you been in America?"

"A month."

"Why didn't you tell me you were coming?"

"You don't check your email."

"Please come over."

Zoë had called. She wanted to see me. And I was dying in a good way about getting to see her.

She was fucking gorgeous and so cool.

I'd fucked her before. Maybe I could fuck her again.

Maybe that would save me.

One thing though: when I'd fucked her before, I'd fucked her all wrong. I'd been trying to make a big deal out of how much it meant to me to fuck her and I'd fucked her pretty lame. I hadn't understood that she wasn't trying to think about what this or that meant and she wasn't trying to be all sad about everything. Fucking the sad is like fucking the dead; it's not something healthy people want to do. And I'd been on coke and I'd been emotional. That's usually how I'd ruin things. And I think this is all very tragic.

Anyway. Zoë came over.

I said, "Zoë, I'm so glad you're back."

She said, "Yeah, it's cool."

Libby called. I didn't take her call. She called again. I ignored it. Then Libby was downstairs trying to get in. Then she was yelling up at the window, yelling like the world's most beautiful psycho.

Zoë said, "Is she your girlfriend?"

"No."

"I feel bad for her. I think I should go."

"Don't go. She'll give up. She'll get tired of it. Just give it a minute. She fucks lots of people."

"She must think I'm a witch."

"It's nothing. We'll just ignore her. It'll be fine."

And I'd thought still it'd be alright but then I ran into some bad luck. I'd taken a barr and drank a Gato Negro. I knew better than to do some shit like this; I'd always been a lightweight when it came to the benzodiazepines. But I was broke and the barrs were the only drugs I had and Zoë had wanted to do drugs and I hadn't wanted to disappoint her. And I don't believe in giving anyone anything I wouldn't take myself, so I took a barr; that's why I blacked out.

Such was life. I didn't understand it.

I came to on the floor.

And Zoë was gone.

Beautiful Zoë.

And there was Libby.

Beautiful Libby.

She kicked me in the side. "What is *wrong* with you?"

"Where did Zoë go?"

"She left."

"You've ruined everything."

"What did I ruin?"

"You don't fucking care. Leave me alone. I'm goddamn fucking miserable."

"Why are you so miserable? You always say you're so miserable. What do you have to be miserable about? You're a brat. Is *your* mother dead? You don't even have to work."

"What are you telling me about work for? You've never even had a job."

"THAT'S NOT TRUE."

"Babysitting doesn't count."

"SHUT UP."

"Well it fucking doesn't."

"Why are you always so mean to me?"

"I'm not mean to you. Now please get the fuck out of here."

"I love you."

"You know that's bullshit."

She kicked me again.

I said, "Shit! How the fuck is this cool?"

"I'm sorry."

She helped me up off the floor.

She took me to bed.

Try as I might, I couldn't fuck.

I said, "Hey, Libby."

"What?"

"I think the reason I'm so fucking miserable is I'm in the wrong place by mistake. Probably the wrong time too. I don't know. It's like I have nothing in common with this shit. A hundred years ago you could just buy some heroin at the fucking store and people'd leave you the fuck alone. But it doesn't work like that anymore. They want you to *agree* with them now."

"Why do you whine so much all the time?"

"I wish I could act like normal motherfuckers, you know? But when I try and fake it they can tell and they fucking judge me. How do they always know I'm against them? Shit. Fuck em but it's discouraging."

"This is boring."

"I want you to kill me."

"BORING."

"I'm serious."

"You're being stupid."

"No fucking shit I'm being stupid but I'm serious."

"I'm not going to kill you."

"Goddamnit, Libby. I'm asking you to do something for me. Can you please just shut the fuck up and do it."

"This is retarded."

"C'mon."

"No."

". . . Please."

"NO."

"You say you love me, don't you? If you really mean that then you'll do it."

"No."

"C'mon. Please."

". . . Right now?"

"Yeah. Right now. Why not?"

". . . Okay."

She straddled my stomach. Her crotch was cool and wet. She put her hands on my throat and leaned into it. She was trying to crush my trachea, I guess. It would have been better had she put the pressure on my carotid arteries. Then I'd have been out in a few seconds and she could have done what needed to be done. But the trachea hurt too much, especially slow like she was doing it. And there was the question of whether or not she could get it crushed all the way. I was surprised that she was really doing it. But I had no choice but to go along with it because it'd been my idea. So I just lay there. Her lip was shaky. We stared into one another's eyes. I couldn't breathe. Maybe she did love me. Maybe she was the best thing that ever happened to me. But I had to breathe. I grabbed her hips and threw her over my head. It took her farther than I'd have thought and she went headfirst into the radiator. I got up and she was laid out on the floor. A look of surprise.

She said, "What did you do that for? You told me to kill you."

I said, "It was a test. And you failed."

CHAPTER FIFTY

The rest of winter was graceless.

I dated Megan: she didn't pay for a bag of coke I'd got her so it turned into a date and suddenly we were dating and I'd met her sister and her mother.

Megan's mother looked like a bowler.

Megan's sister said she'd kill me if I ever hurt Megan.

I knew I had to get out. I got to panicking.

I tried about everything I could think of to get Megan to be the one to break up with me so as to spare her feelings. I acted batshit crazy; she liked it. I ignored her phone calls for days; she kept calling. I stopped paying for things; she paid for everything. I stuffed her socks in her mouth; she had an orgasm. Nothing worked.

So I had to tell Megan it was a mistake. This happened at her place. I had come over and gone right into it, hoping it'd be quick and painless. But Megan started crying. Her Chihuahua Tony was there. He saw everything. He was wearing his little Dracula cape, and Megan was on the sofa. You'd have thought somebody had died. She wanted me to feel shitty about not liking her more. I thought it was selfish. I said she was really overdoing it because my heart had already been murdered and so had everybody else's that I knew of so what was her excuse? We hadn't been seeing each other a month yet. This wasn't a big deal. But Megan wouldn't stop with her bullshit. She was doing a fuckload of crying, and Tony climbed up onto her shoulders and tried to lap up her tears and Megan said, "TONY, GO

AWAY," and she threw Tony on the rug and Tony climbed back up and tried lapping up her tears again.

"TONY, I'M SERIOUS."

She threw Tony on the rug again.

I said I was sure she was a fake because it was impossible that she could be so upset about this. I said girls did cold-blooded shit to me all the time and no one ever gave a fuck about that. Why wasn't it a big deal when a guy got shit on? I'd been shit on a thousand times and it was the twenty-first century and she was being rude.

Megan's sister didn't kill me.

No one has yet.

I HAD to take some kind of opiate or I couldn't go to school. I'd get panic attacks. It was all the people that did it to me. Either people terrified me or they made me feel like I was a fucking bastard in comparison. There was no in between.

When I had no choice I'd try and go to school without dope and I might lose my nerve in the parking lot and stay there in the car and smoke cigarettes and listen to the radio, maybe fall asleep. Then I'd go home. But this was stupid.

I MANAGED to piss Joe off.

He'd dropped in to see me on St. Patrick's Day. He wanted to maybe go and drink something and he caught me with my eyes cracked out of my head. So he got to making an intervention of it.

He said, "Maybe you should chill out on this stuff."

I said drug use was the only thing I didn't have a problem with.

He said, "I wish you could hear how fucking crazy you sound when you talk."

"Why are you bothering me with this?"

"You're my friend, man. I have to tell you if you're fucking up your life."

"I've kind of had it with friends."

"Alright. Good luck then."

"Yeah you too."

THAT NIGHT I broke into the coke safe and shot about 8 grams all told probably. The night stilled. I began to hallucinate. A car was parked somewhere beyond the light. It was watching me and my eye trembled. I heard a radio. Men were on the stairs. There was a shadow in the hall. Somebody was kicking my door in. I flushed an ounce of coke down the toilet. I threw a shoe box full of used syringes out the kitchen window. The shoe box landed on the roof of the convenience store next door and the syringes scattered all over the roof. I surrendered to a phantom SWAT team.

I said, "Let's do this nice and peaceful."

I opened the door.

No one was there.

The sun was rising and the cars were coming out when I climbed up to the roof of the convenience store with a broom and gathered up the syringes. I was dressed up like I worked. I tried to act like I belonged up there.

CHAPTER FIFTY-ONE

I picked Emily up at the Greyhound station. She was on her way to Elba. She had been living with her dad down in Florida and she'd started shooting dope there.

I'd had no idea.

It was a three-hour layover.

Emily said she wanted to get high.

I took her with me to meet up with Three-Hundred and she paid for the heroin.

We went to Walgreens for rigs.

I said to her, "Can you go in and get the rigs? You look more respectable than I do. And I've kind of burned this place up."

She said okay.

She went in and came out with rigs for us.

She was an angel.

We didn't shoot up till we were back in my apartment. I cleaned some spoons off real good. We had saline wound wash from the Walgreens. I'd given her extra money for it. It was a special day.

She shot up like she knew what she was doing.

When it hit her she said, "Fuck."

And it hit me and I was right as rain. If you know, then you know what I mean. If you don't, then don't ever find out.

I kissed Emily.

She kissed me back.

I said, "I've been a real fucking bastard since you left. I'm no good."

She said, "I've missed you too."

She'd been fucking with some guy down in Florida. She shot dope with him. She was working at her dad's dental practice. She was the receptionist. She said she'd been bored as shit. But she met this guy and he was alright and he got her shooting dope. And there was a time she'd shot too much heroin. Not all at once, but over the course of an hour or two. Lover was there. This was at his place. She couldn't breathe too good. She'd been worried she was going to die. She rode it out though. Lover had kept an eye on her.

"He said I'd turned blue," she said.

"Goddamn that's terrible. That scares the shit out of me."

And I'd get tore up thinking about it before long, after I'd dropped her off at the station. I'd be thinking about this guy and him watching her turn all blue and what else, watching her gasp for air. I pictured her lying on the floor in some piece-of-shit tract house down in Florida. Wall-to-wall carpet and all that godlessness.

I still loved her.

She wouldn't fuck me though.

She said I had to get an HIV test before she came back.

And I said alright. And she said she'd be back.

THE FREE clinic did the HIV test with fake names. The name I got was Deon Valentine.

"Deon Valentine . . ."

"Deon Valentine . . ."

"Deon Valentine . . ."

The lady asked how many partners I'd had since the last time I was tested.

"Does it count if I tried but I couldn't . . . ?"

"Was there genital-to-genital contact? . . . Then yes."

"Is that a lot?"

"No. Not really. Have you used intravenous drugs? . . . Have you had sex with any intravenous drug users? . . . Have you shared needles with anyone?"

PART FIVE

THE GREAT
DOPE FIEND
ROMANCE

CHAPTER FIFTY-TWO

There was nothing better than to be young and on heroin. Emily and I were living together. The days were bright. You didn't worry about jobs because there weren't any. But you could go to school so you could get FAFSA, you could get student loans and Pell Grants. And if you were getting G.I. Bill, that'd cover your tuition; then you didn't need your FAFSA for school and you could go and buy dope with it instead. Which was all you really wanted. You could kill yourself real slow and feel like a million dollars. You could grow high-class weed in your basement and pay the rent like that. Of course the future looked bad—you went into debt, you got sick all the time, you couldn't shit, everyone you met was a fucker, your new friends would eat the eyes out of your head for a spoon or twenty dollars, your old friends stayed away—but you could do more heroin and that would usually serve to settle you down, when you were going on 25, back when you could still fake it, and there was nothing better than to be young and on heroin.

CHAPTER FIFTY-THREE

Around ten at night Ari had called back. This was where Ari had said to go. I got off the freeway at Fleet Avenue and made a few turns and parked in the street. The house smelled like cat piss. Ari looked like Justin Bieber. He said Gary was on his way. This wasn't Ari's house; this was Gary's house. I didn't know Gary; I knew Ari. Ari was from Shaker. Really I didn't know Ari either. He used to go to '80s night. I was just hoping he could get me some heroin. I was in need of a dope boy. I was getting Oxys pretty cheap—about 50¢/mg—and those were fine, but what I wanted was the real thing. And this was where I was.

Ari and I were waiting in the living room. A retarded woman was watching TV. The living room carpet was red. The retarded woman had a blond mullet that went halfway down her back. Ari called her Shelley. Shelley was watching *CSI*. She didn't want to change the channel. She had a husky voice and her consonants were kind of fucked but you could understand what she said and you could hear the desperation in it. Shelley was desperately retarded.

Gary showed up with the heroin. I was surprised because Gary had achondroplasia. Ari hadn't told me Gary had achondroplasia. Ari hated me. Gary took the heroin out of a little metal box with a magnet on it. He said, "Check this out."

There wasn't a lot of heroin. Just two grams. Gary said, "This shit's supposed to be fire. That's what my dude told me."

I gave Gary $140 for a gram. The price was real shitty. I only wanted to pay $100. But Gary had said what he said and I'd allow for quality. We shot up around the kitchen sink: Gary, Ari, and I. The kitchen was trashed. Shelley watched us shoot up.

"You ted I can have tum, Gary."

"I'll get you in a second," he said.

"You ted I can have tum."

"Would you shut up, you retarded fucking bitch?"

The heroin was alright. Not worth the money. But we all felt it. I had 0.7 grams left. I'd take that home. Gary said, "You like Dilaudid?'

I said I'd take all the Dilaudid I could get.

He said cool.

"You ted I can have tum, Gary."

"Go watch TV."

Gary sold me ten 4mg Dilaudids at $7 each and I was glad and I got the fuck out of there. The night was very cold and the cold was good. The cold was familiar. I called Emily and I drove home.

Emily was in the kitchen. She said, "Happy Valentine's Day."

I wouldn't ever get tired of coming home to her. We shot dope and watched late-night TV. Maybe we should have fucked on account of it was Valentine's Day and all, but we didn't give a fuck about Valentine's Day. We only gave a fuck about one thing. So that's how we were together.

CHAPTER FIFTY-FOUR

When Ari's folks kicked him out he came to live down Gary's way and Gary put him up in an abandoned house. And it was fucking freezing. But Gary had cracked the gas line so the stove would run. A sofa was next to the stove. All four burners on the stove were going. From the waist up the kitchen was an inferno, but if you sat down too long you could have frozen to death. We were waiting on Gary. I gave Ari cigarettes. Ari was getting sick. He was feeling bad. This was Ari in poverty. Ari's poverty was based on his belief that he shouldn't ever have to pay for anything or do anything to make himself useful to anyone. Now he was getting sick and he was wearing his sleeping bag like a cape and things weren't going especially well for him.

I wasn't doing much better. Emily and I had each shot a 20mg of Oxy earlier in the morning, but that'd only keep us well for a few hours. A 20 could take you there if you had no real habit but it counted for next to nothing when you were as accustomed to things as Emily and I were. That was how dope had worked on us. It had got so we were wasting our time if we weren't putting at least $45 in our veins, and even then it was just a little moment till we were sick all over again.

So yeah. Emily was over at school and soon she'd be fucked and she was counting on me to come through for her. I wasn't having any luck yet, but I had a couple irons in the fire: this shit with Gary, plus I was waiting to hear back from Big about some Oxys. I'd skipped class. I always skipped class to go look for dope.

It was more important that Emily go to class since she was the smart one. She was a grad assistant, and it would have looked worse if she missed. People would have said, Where's the grad assistant?

GARY SHOWED up. He didn't have any dope. He'd said he did but he didn't. He had lied. Gary was a real full-of-shit motherfucker and I'd already known that.

Gary had a $20 crack rock.

Ari said, "What about the dope?"

Gary said, "I'm still waiting on Old Boy to call me back."

Ari's nose was runny. He was making sad faces.

I lit a cigarette.

Gary said, "You got any glass?"

I had a bowl in the car but that wasn't what he meant.

"Fuck!" he said. "If I could just get a Brillo pad we'd be alright."

I said I'd take him to the store. We had some time to kill and we'd do just as well to smoke some crack while we waited. So we drove to the store. Gary said if I spotted him the money for the Brillo pad he'd let me and Ari smoke the crack rock with him. I spotted him the money. Gary got out and went into the store. He took forever. He came back. He had bought a box of Brillo pads and a tall boy of Mickey's. I said nothing about the Mickey's. Gary tore off a piece of Brillo pad and put it in the bowl and he had the crack rock in there too. He took a big rip of crack smoke. Then he exploded. Spit went everywhere. Gary opened the door and puked so bad he fell out of the car. He had got some puke on his clothes. The puke smelled like Big Mac sauce. It was my turn to smoke some crack but there was no more crack left to smoke. Gary had got the whole rock, one hit.

Ari's phone rang. Gary picked it up. It was Old Boy. We were good. Twenty minutes later we were back at the abandoned house, shooting up in the inferno. The heroin was super-stepped-on. I said, "No offense, Gary, but this shit is kind of some garbage."

Gary said, "I don't normally go through that guy. I only called him cuz you said you needed something quick. But my other dude, he told me he's got some fire. I just won't be able to get up with him till later."

We agreed we would do that. I was sure Gary was fucked but I'd give him another try. In the meantime I had to run. I texted Emily when I was on the freeway. I got downtown and made a left off of Chester and waited for her to come down. We drove around to the parking lot.

"How is it?" she asked.

"It's so-so."

"As long as it gets me well, man."

"It will. It isn't that bad. It's just the dope's expensive for what it is and Gary and Ari depress the shit out of me."

"Hmm."

"What do you think?"

"I do feel better."

"How's your day been?"

"Totally fucked. The Writing Lab is a fucking joke. I have this one student. He's on the basketball team. He doesn't do anything. He expects me to write his assignments for him. I'm pretty sure he's illiterate."

"Well the basketball coach probably promised him that you'd do his homework for him. That was probably their understanding."

"Fuck their understanding."

"Yes, I know."

"Ugh. I don't want to go back up there."

"Then don't."

"Sure," she said. "That's a great idea. Maybe I can join the fucking circus."

"Just saying."

My phone buzzed. I had a text. It was from Big. He said he was about to be on the East Side if I wanted to meet up with him.

I called him. Everything was good.

I said to Emily, "Big's gonna meet me at Rock-and-Roll McDonald's."

"Why there?"

"It'll be alright."

"How many are you going to get?"

"We've got enough for a lot of them."

"Then do it up. This heroin is shit."

"You wanna come?"

"Sheesh. I dunno."

"C'mon. We'll buy these fucking pills, come back over here, shoot the fucking pills. It'll be great. Romance, you know."

"Fuck it. I have an hour and a half till I have to be back."

"You'll make it."

Rock-and-Roll McDonald's was just over on Carnegie. A lot of drugs got bought and sold there. Of course the police knew about it and there was usually an undercover cop or two at Rock-and-Roll McDonald's. Still you had to go and do some dirt there every now and then because if you didn't you were fucking nothing. I had even seen the mayor of Cleveland there before. He had cut me and about five other cars in the drive-thru line. Cleveland was a small town.

We arrived before Big.

I had an idea.

I said, "Let's go inside."

"Really? You want to go inside?"

"I'm tired of waiting in the car all the time. And we've got money today."

"Whatever you want."

"Don't order a fucking salad either."

"I'm going to order a salad."

"Okay. But you have to get a milk shake."

"Deal."

We went in and ordered—burgers and shakes, French fries, the whole shit. Emily got a salad. We sat down where we could see the cars turning in. Big would be along in a minute. He wasn't the type to keep you waiting. He was good like that. He may have shot some people to death at one time but that was nothing to do with us and he had paid his debt to society so there was nothing more to say about it but thanks for the dope. I only wished he sold heroin. He didn't. He only sold OxyContin. He had his own script on account of his fibromyalgia and he could ride around with pills all day with no problems.

I saw him turn in. He was driving a white Chevy Blazer.

I said to Emily, "I'll be right back."

I went outside and got in Big's truck.

He said, "I fucked a pink toe last night."

Big was a corpulent man, in his 60s.

"She had a nice ass for a white girl," he said.

"That's good. Let me get twenty of them."

He said no problem.

I had the money. It was Pell Grant money. I counted it out. Big counted out the pills. Big always had a fuckload of pills on him. He was an LPN and he bought pills from old people. Once I asked him how he knew which old people would sell him their pills. He said it was simple—you asked the poor ones.

I said, "Thanks a lot, Big. I'll be calling you."

He said, "Alright now."

I went back inside Rock-and-Roll McDonald's. I had just spent $900 I couldn't afford to spend. But I had a lot of OxyContin in my pocket and it'd last Emily and me through to Monday, so I felt alright about everything. Then I became aware of the man who had followed me when I came inside. He sat at the table just past my right shoulder. He was middle-aged, pale as a ghost, wore a turquoise jacket and faded jeans, showed male pattern baldness. He had no food in front of him. Emily saw him too. She looked at me and I winked and she gave no sign and I was proud of her. She was too cool. She was like a cross between Mary Poppins and Billie Holiday.

I said, "How's the salad?"

She said, "It's alright."

"That's good," I said. "So what's this shit with this illiterate motherfucker again?"

"It's not fair. He's so fucking arrogant but he's completely stupid. I don't see how he can be so arrogant when he's that stupid."

We were talking real loud so the police could hear us. And we kept on talking real loud. We talked about school real loud, talked real loud about the illiterate basketball player and what she was going to write her thesis on and what so-and-so had said about so-and-so. We talked about a girl she worked with who was a piece of shit. Things like that. Whatever else. We acted like we were just good people out having some lunch.

CHAPTER FIFTY-FIVE

I was looking for something cheap but good. I thought if I could find that then it would be alright and we'd manage.

That night Gary got out on me for $180. It was a loss but not a total disaster. Emily and I had the Oxys we picked up earlier from Big. So we had time. As far as the money, I thought $180 was fair to never have to see motherfucking Gary again.

I left Ari at the abandoned house. I had said I'd look out for him when Gary came through. That was off now. But I figured he'd be alright. I got home. Emily had made me something to eat. She asked me how it had gone with the heroin and I told her.

"Fucking goddamn!" she said. "A hundred and eighty dollars?"

I said it wasn't like I'd done it on purpose.

"I know but, baby, you have to see why I'm upset. I've been here working, taking care of the plants, making your cocksucking dinner, and I need to write a paper while you're out playing the big shot and losing our goddamn money!"

"Did you say 'big shot'? What the fuck is this? Are you a fucking idiot? Is this nineteen fucking seventy? You think I like this shit? You think I like dragging my fucking dead ass all over town and dealing with these fucks?"

"Baby, I'm serious. We're spending over a thousand dollars on dope, every week. We can't do that. It's unsustainable. It's insane."

"Okay. So file that under No Fucking Shit. What am I supposed to do about it? Can I just quit? What about you? Do you think you can quit? If you can, let me know, and we'll quit right now. Won't that be nice? Let's quit right now."

"You fucking asshole."

She started to cry.

"Goddamnit. You're crying."

"Fuck you, you motherfucking asshole. This is serious and all you are is a motherfucking asshole."

"Goddamn fucking shit. . . . Would you please calm down. . . . Look. . . . Shit. . . . Please stop crying. I love you."

"Don't you understand that we're completely fucked?"

"I understand. Believe me, I understand. I really do. And you're right. And I'm sorry. I feel it too. It's just we're so fucked and I don't know how we're gonna get out from under this thing so all I can do is try and hold things together the way they are. We have so much to do all the time and it's like when can we get sick for a month, you know? When will we have time to do that? It's a fucking trap, you know?"

"But we have to."

"I know. But just not right now. We will though. We can hang in a little longer. Then we'll get off it."

"You don't mean that."

"No. I do mean it. I'd like nothing more. Truly. This can't go on forever. That's fucking obvious. So something's gonna make us change. We just have to stay together. That's what's important. Please come here."

I held her.

". . . It'll be alright. Don't worry about it."

". . . You're full of shit."

"Goddamnit."

"I'm sorry, but it's true."

"I feel fucking horrible."

"Me too. I fucking hate this shit."

We felt so fucking horrible that we had to shoot some more

pills. We each did an 80. Then we felt better. It had only cost us $90, and we could make it through the night. Tomorrow it would only cost another $90 to get us out of bed.

We watched TV again. We went to bed late. We heard a plane flying low over the house. There was a plane that flew low over our house sometimes at night.

Emily pressed against me. "Hmm . . . how come you never fuck me anymore?" she said.

"I love you too much."

"You can fuck me in the ass if you want."

"I'd like that," I said. "But my heart's totally broken."

"So's mine."

"I know it is."

CHAPTER FIFTY-SIX

Ari called Saturday evening and said he was sick. He said, "Do you have anything?"

I said, "Man, what the fuck?"

He said, "Please. I'm fucked up."

I said, "Alright. I'm on my way."

I drove to the abandoned house and Ari really was sick and it was cold as fuck in that house. Ari looked bad as shit going around wrapped in his sleeping bag like he was, guts all inside out, nose running all over him. I knew what he was going through. I went through it all the time. About every week it would happen to me. That's why I hated seeing other people sick; it reminded me of how fucked I was.

I said, "What happened to your boy? Shouldn't he be looking out for you?"

"I'm sorry about the other day," he said. "I didn't know."

"Here's an eighty," I said. "It's for you. You can have it and it's yours and you won't owe me shit, but you have to put me on with somebody, somebody who's not a fuck. You give me another motherfucker like Gary and I'm gonna come back and burn this fucking house down with you in it. Please believe me. And I deal with him directly. I don't deal with you. Make sure he understands that."

"Okay, whatever," he said. "Sure. Thank you."

Ari shot up 40mg and was saved. Then he called Manny and Manny said I should come through. He was out in Painesville. I wasn't thrilled about Painesville but I'd go see him.

I met him at a gas station off Route 2. I called him from the parking lot. He said go inside. He was standing in the chips aisle, acting paranoid as all get-out. He was on meth and he'd been picking holes in his face. He had his hat pulled down and his collar up. He was talking in a whisper and I couldn't hear him. I got frustrated.

I said, "Look, man. I got this money."

"Not here. Go over there and leave it by the Doritos."

"Uh . . ."

"The Doritos."

"Man, I'm not gonna leave the money by the Doritos."

"Would you keep yer fucking voice down. Everybody can hear you."

I rolled up my sleeve and showed him my left arm. My left arm was fucked. My right arm was fucked too, but I only showed my left arm.

I said, "Look, man. I'm not fucking around. I'm on the level."

"Yer not hearing me."

When I got home with the dope, Emily asked me what had taken so long. I said I'd bought a gram from a new dope boy. She asked if he was alright. I said he was alright enough. She was happy about that. We shot some of the dope and it was good. It was cheap for how good it was. Emily and I were very happy. That night we danced in the living room. We danced for something like a half hour straight. We danced like in third-class ballrooms. We just made it up.

Let's sing another song, boys, this one has grown old and bitter.

It was a good night. It just happened.

CHAPTER FIFTY-SEVEN

The good thing about Manny was he was a serious dope fiend and he was up against it just as bad as you were, so he didn't make you wait. He'd even drive you with him to get the dope if need be. There were a lot of people in Painesville who wanted Manny dead. So he had to move to the city. And that was good too because I'd hated going all the way out to fucking Painesville.

He had a room at the Euclid Lodge. He was staying there with his boyfriend, an ice monster named Chauncey. Chauncey was ten years older than Manny and he said he was from Florida. Manny said Chauncey's dad had been a congressman or something like that. Manny said his own family bred horses. "I come from a very wealthy family," he said. "But I'm cut off."

I didn't care. Yet it was important to Manny that I believe him and when he was out in Painesville he had driven me past a horse farm and said it was the horse farm his grandfather owned. It was dark and I didn't see any horses.

Manny definitely was a police informant and a lot of people went to jail. Like Ari. Manny sold him a scale with dope all over it. He said he'd sell Ari the scale for $10. That was a good deal so Ari bought it and five minutes later he was getting arrested for paraphernalia and possession with intent to distribute. This was a shitty thing that Manny did to Ari.

Sometimes when Manny needed to get somebody fucked off, the police would raid his room at the Euclid Lodge and strip-search everybody and take one or two kids to jail. But Manny and Chauncey didn't ever go to jail.

The police had a room directly across the hall from Manny.

One time I had parked and I was walking up to go in and a policeman called down to me from the second floor.

"Hey. You left your window open," he said.

I turned around and looked and saw that I had, and I waved to the policeman and said, "Thanks."

He said, "You're welcome."

The worst thing about Manny being a police informant was he would get on with some good heroin and then it wasn't long before he'd have to give up the source. Like there were these two guys who had this tar that smelled like rotting fish and got you higher than fuck's sake for $100/gm. Your ears would ring like a motherfucker. But we weren't getting it two weeks when Manny had to turn those guys in.

And I said to myself, You really ought to get away from this shit while you still can.

And I said to myself, Duly noted.

THE PROBLEM with Emily and me was we were killing one another. Apart we probably could have managed, but the two of us together was a form of suicide. It took teamwork to get your life fucked up so bad. But we couldn't let go.

Emily had been giving me a hard time for a few days then. She was real pissed at me because I'd got ripped off for $600. It was something Manny had put me onto and I should have known better; I should have known there was no such thing as a $600 ounce of cocaine. But I was a greedy fucker and I thought my ship had come in: I could have flipped those ounces for $900 all day, and people would have loved me for it. Then I figured out what it really was and the money was gone and there was nothing to be done. It was touching how Manny kept on like he hadn't known; he had even cried real tears. But I was still out the $600.

Emily said, "You're *killing* us, baby."

I said, "Goddamn would you shut the fuck up?"

It was a terrible mistake to say this. She got to screaming at me then. She'd scream like a great bird sometimes. She'd grow wings and fly around the house screaming like that. She'd be up around the ceiling, screaming. It was really awful. It was like arguing with a pterodactyl. You could do nothing.

I said, "Jesus. Please."

But it wasn't ever over quick once she got going. She kept on. She blamed me for everything. She had a point. But it wasn't like I ever saw her quitting dope.

Say we tried to quit. Say we'd had enough of spending all our money and having a lot of shitty motherfuckers try and get over on us. Say we'd said fuck it and the weekend came and we had time to get sick. We might go a little while, maybe make it to Sunday night, make it with all the fever and the puke and the wishes we were dead. Then one of us was sure to say to the other, "You know, we're doing pretty good. I think we deserve a little break from this."

And the other was sure to say, "Yeah, that's what I was just thinking. Plus we have to take care of the plants."

"That's right. The plants. I'm gonna call Big."

"Yeah, do that. But only get two."

"Okay. I'll ask him for four though. We have to go to school tomorrow."

"You're right. Better get four."

We'd be throwing up when we said all this. But already we would be feeling better. There was a hopeful urgency in those moments and life was beautiful.

BIG SAID come on. We drove across town in our pajamas. It was raining. We had enough for five—$225—and we parked somewhere off of Fulton. Big was on time. He pulled up in the white Blazer. Big always came through in the clutch and he didn't treat us like fiends. Most of the time they do.

I got in his truck: "How do you do, Big?"

He said, "What's good?"

I gave him the cellophane from my cigarettes. "You got five of those?" I said.

He counted five. "Haven't been seeing you as much as I usually do," he said.

"Yeah, I guess not."

He handed me the cellophane back. I folded it and put it in my pocket.

He said, "You've been fuckin with that heroin."

"Yeah, that's sort of what it looks like."

"Uh-huh. You know I don't mess with that shit. I just fuck with the pills because I know what I'm getting, I know what I'm selling. No problems. No riding dirty. No scales or any of that bullshit. Nobody running a game on me."

"I see what you mean."

"Alright. I'll catch you later."

"Alright."

Big drove off and I walked back to the car. Emily had the kit laid out on the center console—the spoons, the needles, everything—and we shot up and we were right as the rain. We went home.

IT WAS the middle of the night. Emily and I were in the basement and she'd filled the garbage can with water. I said, "How long have the plants been flowering?"

She said, "Five weeks."

I looked at the instructions that had come with the nutrients kit. I'd always thought the nutrients kit was a scam.

I said, "We should just use fucking Miracle-Gro."

"That's what I've been saying," she said.

We were in the room we called the laundry room. That was where the sink was, next to the washer and dryer. The dryer had been broken for a while. We couldn't get the dryer fixed because of the grow room. We used a clothesline instead to dry our clothes, and our laundry doing had suffered.

There was a 600W high-pressure sodium light hooked up in the corner. That was for the cuttings and for the mother. The mother had been cut all to pieces. We'd taken a hundred cuttings off her. We kept a mound of leftover potting soil in the opposite corner. We mixed our own potting soil. We had such millipedes in the house you wouldn't believe.

Emily checked the pH. We needed acidity. I turned to get it.

She said, "Not that one."

I said I know. I took the other one. "How much do you think we need?"

She said, "Here. I'll do it."

She did and she checked the parts per million too. She told me what they were. And they were alright. But I didn't know what they meant. We picked up the garbage can and carried it into the next room. It was a finished room, carpeted and drywalled and all that shit. It had a big stupid fucking tent in it. Inside the tent was Mylar or something else that was like Mylar. I didn't care if it was Mylar or if it wasn't, just I didn't know and it bothered me sometimes that I didn't know things I should probably know. I knew that I'd glued the Mylar to the walls in the corner of the laundry room and I thought it was probably different stuff but I wasn't sure. It was a fancy tent. The only thing that made the tent not completely fucking stupid was it was easy to hang the lights off the frame. It wasn't my idea to buy the tent. All I did was set the thing up. It was Roy who'd said we needed the tent. He'd been our partner in the grow room when we started. Then he stole from us and he wasn't our partner anymore and we thought he was a real piece of shit. Still I had this fucking tent and I didn't know how I was ever going to be rid of it.

We only had two 1000W lights—there had been three but we'd had to give one to Roy when we wanted him gone. We were getting a pound per light and we averaged $4500/lb selling it off in QPs and ounces. It took about three months to grow the shit—one month to get the plants up to the right size, two months for the flowering cycle. The lights were on 24/7 in the first month and 12-on/12-off the last two months. This used a lot of electricity and we had to run the lights off ballasts that ran off a subpanel. We had made the subpanel and wired it to the breaker box. We'd had to disconnect the doorbell to make space for it. We had bought all the wire and the conduit and the panel and everything at the Severance Home Depot. I'd been trying to figure out what kind of wire we were supposed to buy, and we were all three of us fucked up on heroin and Roy was being a prick. I'd try and say something and he'd have his fancy little smirk like he always had on his face and he kept looking at Emily and rolling his eyes and she was rolling her eyes. She had taken his side. I couldn't believe her. She had taken the side of this bitch. And it was one of those situations where you wanted to kill a guy but you couldn't because you were at Home Depot and there was a law against it and you needed money for heroin and your money was in this thing and it didn't matter because she'd done what she'd done already and everything was fucked forever and there'd be no changing that. I thought, She's a horrible cunt whom I love.

And later, when Roy had stolen from us, Emily was real bent out of shape about it.

She'd said, "Why's he doing this? He's such a fucking asshole."

And I heard something in her voice then.

And I didn't wonder at that.

CHAPTER FIFTY-EIGHT

Manny owed Cookie $600 for the dope Cookie'd fronted him. But Manny didn't have any $600 and he wasn't going to have it. What Manny usually did in these situations was get the dope boy fucked off. But he waited too long.

Sunday morning I got a call from Manny. He said he had to talk to me about something important and he said we needed to talk in person. He didn't sound right. I was thinking maybe he was setting me up to get me fucked off, but I needed to buy some heroin and Manny had said it was real important. So I said okay. After all I liked Manny. Manny was a human being. He was a fuck but he was a human being.

I said to Emily, "You'd better stay here. I might go to jail."

She said, "What's going on?"

I said I didn't know, probably nothing.

When I got to Richmond Mall I called Manny. He said to stay where I was parked. He came around in a blue Ford Explorer I hadn't seen him in before. There was another guy driving. Manny was in the passenger seat.

They parked in the spot next to me and I got in with them. Manny was wearing a Yankees cap pulled down real low, but I could see his face was lumped up pretty well and that was too bad for Manny because the driver looked like Muhammad Ali circa the Cassius Clay era. Manny said, "This is Cookie."

Cookie said I could buy dope from him now.

I said okay.

I had enough for a gram—$120—so I bought one gram and took it home and shot it with Emily. It was decent, not great.

My phone rang. It was Cookie.

He said, "How was it?"

I said it was decent.

MANNY GOT Cookie fucked off two weeks later. Cookie tried to get away and he took the police on a chase. It wouldn't have been a big deal except that Cookie still had Manny in the car with him. That made it kidnapping.

I got a call from Cookie's brother Pistol. He said he would sell me heroin. So I was alright. Then Pistol got himself fucked off shooting at Manny and I got a call from Black. Then Pistol was out on house arrest and I was supposed to go through him again. All this didn't take two months to happen.

THE HOUSE was in the suburbs, on a street not far from mine. It was a nice street, plenty of big trees—oaks, I think. And Pistol would have cars full of dope fiends waiting out there, cars full of dope fiends like Emily and me. Often he would take hours before he was ready to serve us some dope; and we'd say, "This guy's such a fucking asshole it's amazing."

And we'd all be sick and making sad faces until he called us one by one and had us pull up into the driveway. He'd serve us from the side door of the house so as to not set his ankle bracelet off.

I didn't like going over there, especially after the surveillance truck appeared. It was parked a few driveways up from Pistol's. You might even see the police in it, see them getting in and out or see them doing whatever. They definitely didn't give a fuck if you saw them. And they saw me. They saw my plates. All of that. But it couldn't be helped. I had to go where the heroin was.

One morning the police raided the house and took Pistol back to jail. The whole family—the mom, the little kids, everyone who wasn't in jail—had been there when it happened. They were upset. I didn't know what all had happened when I got a call from Black that afternoon. He said for me to meet him over on Belmar. He was standing out there on the sidewalk, waiting with his other brother Raul. I recognized Raul because I'd seen him before and he was a big smiling type of motherfucker and he had a big shiny watch so he was easy to recognize. Raul looked five years older than he was; he was only 23. Anyway. I thought I was just driving out there to buy some heroin and I didn't know why they were standing out there waiting; usually when we met up that way we did transactions car to car, and they weren't ever on time.

I parked at the curb and got out and walked over to where they were. I asked Black how he was doing and Black told me what had happened that morning.

I said, "Shit. That's too bad. Your brother's a good dude. I hope he's alright."

Black looked at Raul. Black was making sad faces, being all dramatic about things. He was just a kid. I think he was 20. He said, "What I want to know is why they were saying your name."

Raul was standing behind me.

I said to Black, "What are you talking about?"

"They said a white boy who drives a black Ford."

"Dude, what's that mean? Of course they're gonna know that shit. There's been a surveillance truck parked outside your house for the last two weeks. I told you that. Probably everybody else did too. So you've got a surveillance truck parked outside your house and you're running it like a trap house in the middle of the fucking suburbs and when the police kick your door in you want to say it's my fault? What are you, nuts?"

"They said your name."

"They could get that off the plates."

"They didn't say your government name."

Then it occurred to me.

"Oh," I said.

"Oh what?"

"You know the Dale-Junior-looking motherfucker? Short? Red hair? Freckles? Calls himself K-Mart. Buys dope off you? He came up to my car and talked to me the other day when I was out on your street, waiting on your brother. He knocked on my window and started talking to me about dope and everything else and how he'd been a mule running dope out of New York and some bullshit. He wouldn't shut the fuck up. He tried to get my phone number and I told him I didn't have a phone. I got a bad feeling from the guy. He was real fucking nosy, you know? And I didn't really say shit to him but he did get my name. I imagine he's the one who told it to the police. Apart from that I don't know shit about what happened this morning."

Black looked at Raul.

Raul said, "I believe him."

Black said, "You don't know how much sense you just made."

"I need some heroin."

"I have to get it out of the car."

"I've got enough for two."

"I'll put you together."

I drove home. It wasn't quite three in the afternoon. Emily was watching *Springer*. We split the heroin up and I told her what all had happened.

The heroin was okay. The two grams were light.

Emily said, "Why would the police do that to you? You could have been hurt."

I said, "This may come as a surprise to you, but the police think we deserve to die."

I called Black.

I said, "This was light."

He said, "Really?"

"Yeah, by four."

He said, "I got you later."

. . .

I WENT back out to meet up with Black and I was waiting in the car again, outside his house. I was glad the surveillance truck was gone. Raul came out and he walked up to the car and I rolled the window down. I thought he was going to drop the heroin off. But he didn't. He said no, Black would bring it out in a second.

I said alright.

He said, "Hey, you know somebody I can get an ounce of coke from?"

I said I might know somebody but I had to call and check.

"Yeah, do that," he said.

I got on the phone and called Mike, a.k.a. Pills And Coke. I told him what was up.

Mike said, "Who is this guy?"

I said it was a guy who sells heroin.

"Is he black?"

"Yeah."

"Shit. I don't know."

"Well, he's right here. What do you want me to tell him."

"Is he alright?"

"Has been so far, yeah."

"He said a zone?"

"Uh-huh."

"Can I talk to him?"

"I can give you his number."

"Okay."

"I'll text it to you."

I got off the phone and said to Raul, "He's gonna call you. Let me get your number. I'm gonna text it to him."

He said alright.

Black came out to the car. He gave Raul a look like, What are you doing?

Raul smiled and said, "What?"

Black didn't smile and he shook his head. We traded the money and the heroin. I had a scale and I weighed out what he'd given me to see that it was right. I asked Black if he still wanted to buy a QP. I said I was still holding one for him if he wanted it. He said to bring it by next time and he'd take a look at it. I could tell by the way he said it that he wasn't about to buy shit. But I said I'd bring it anyway.

I felt like I'd accomplished something. I had another number I could call now if and when I ever got hard up to find some dope. And I'd done Mike a good turn. Mike had been fucked up for a minute. I'd paid him back in full for the contents of his safe, so it wasn't like it was my fault. Mike's problem was he had got himself fucked up on the pills and coke he was supposed to be selling and had got to be a dope fiend almost as bad as I was. He was even getting his pills from me now. He didn't let it go to his head though; he was still arrogant as fuck.

SO OF course the heroin didn't last us very long at all. It was all gone a little after we woke up the next day, and in the afternoon we were back waiting again outside the house on the nice street with the big oak trees and there was Raul again and Raul came up to the car.

I said, "Emily, this is Raul. Raul, this is Emily."

Emily said hi.

Raul said hi.

I asked Raul how it had gone with Mike.

He said it had gone well. The coke was good. He said he would hit Mike up for some more. "You know how when you're cooking it up with the baking soda and it sizzles?" he said.

I didn't know. But I played along.

"Did you bring some of that loud with you?"

I said yeah.

He said, "Let me see it."

I gave him a bud to look at.

"Oh that's nice."

"It's called Grapefruit," I said. "It's got a really good taste to it."

"I might have to buy some of this."

Black came up to the car and looked at Raul again with the same look as from the day before, and Raul smiled again and went back inside. Emily said to Black, "Your brother's nice."

He said, "Raul's some shit."

I said, "You want to look at this QP?"

He said he'd have a look. I handed him the bag and he opened it up. He said, "So this is that gas, huh?"

Emily said, "Yeah. It's gas."

He said it looked real good but he couldn't buy any just this minute. Maybe later.

CHAPTER FIFTY-NINE

The story of being a dope fiend is people will lie to your face and you can't call them on it lest they not give you what you need when they get around to it. Saturday was no different. Emily and I woke and shot up the last of our dope and the day began. A day didn't begin until we had run out of dope and it was time to get some more.

"How much money do we have?"

She said, "Nine hundred dollars."

"That's not bad."

I called Black but he didn't pick up. I sent him a text. He texted back saying he wasn't together yet.

Emily said, "We could call Big."

"Yeah, maybe we should do that."

It was tricky having a little money. You might think you could buy a quarter ounce of heroin to last you a few days, but that would be a mistake. If you bought three grams of heroin you might get one gram of heroin and two grams of cut. If you bought seven grams of heroin you might get one gram of heroin and six grams of cut. So when you had some money the best thing to do was hold off. You couldn't go wrong buying pills though. Pills didn't get stepped on. And Big wasn't a fuck.

We went to see Big and we bought ten pills and came home, by which time it was just around two in the afternoon and the day looked like it would be alright when all was said and done. Then my phone rang. It was Mike.

I said, "Hey, Mike."

He said, "Do you have a gun?"

I said, "No."

He said, "FUCK."

I said, "What's up?"

"You don't have a gun?"

"No. Why?"

"I just got robbed."

"You just got robbed?"

"Yeah. Yer boy set me up."

"Just now."

"Yes."

"Shit, man."

"I need to get my car. I left my car there. You don't have a gun?"

"No. But I've got a bulletproof vest if you want that."

"I'm on my way over."

"I thought you didn't have a car."

"I'm driving Rachel's car."

"Oh. Okay. Yeah, I'll be here."

Rachel was Mike's girlfriend. They lived together. They slept in separate rooms though. Which I thought was odd. Rachel was the type of girl you wanted to sleep with. Maybe one of them had sleep apnea. I don't know. But I felt bad about Mike. Mike was getting the treatment. The world was treating Mike like a fucking loser. And he was new to it so it was harder on him, harder on him than it was for the likes of . . . me. And I felt bad. I was the one who had put him on with Raul, and now Raul had robbed him. Raul was black and Mike didn't like dealing with black guys. He didn't like dealing with black guys because he thought that you couldn't trust them; namely he thought that they would rob you. I said to Emily, "Mike's coming over. He says he just got robbed. He's got to get his car. I'm going to take him."

"What?"

"Mike got robbed."

"By who?"

"By Raul, I think."

"What a piece of shit!"

"I'm not sure, but I think that's what happened. Mike's on his way. We'll find out from him."

"He's coming here right now?"

"Yeah. Like he'll be here in a couple seconds."

I went and got the bulletproof vest. It was in the closet on the stairs. An IBAS, ACU pattern. It had once belonged to the Ohio National Guard but it didn't anymore. There was also a Kevlar helmet in the closet, but I thought that was probably a bit much.

Mike was outside. Emily let him in. I said, "Mike, you alright?"

He said, "Fuck no."

"What happened?"

"I got fuckin robbed."

"I know. But what happened?"

"Raul told me his boy wanted to buy an ounce of coke. I drove out to meet him and the motherfucker pulled a gun on me."

"Was Raul there?"

"No. Just his boy."

"I'm sorry, man. That's fucking bullshit."

"My car's still up there. I have to go get it."

"Yeah, I got you. I'll take you up there right now."

"Alright. You think I should wear that vest?"

"I don't know. Wear it if you want to. Let's shoot up first before we go. Hey, Emily."

"Yeah."

"I'm gonna spot Mike an eighty. Don't be mad at me."

"That's fine."

Mike said, "Thanks. I appreciate it."

And we shot up, all three of us did. We had to because Mike had just got robbed. He had got robbed for an ounce of coke and that was about an $800–$1000 loss. The least we could do was we could all get high. So we did. And I drove Mike over to where his car was. His car was parked outside some apartments. A blue Mercury. All the doors were open. This was just north of Mayfield on Coventry, a little short of East Cleveland. It was a pretty lame place to have to say you got robbed. This wasn't exactly the Terrordome. Two young girls were jumping rope. Mike got out and hurried over to his car and we got out of there. Mike had the bulletproof vest on. We looked like some dorks. When we got back I fronted Mike another pill and he went home. I called Black and he answered. He said he had picked up something and I could meet him if I wanted. So I said I was on my way. I bought a gram. I didn't bother calling Raul. I asked Black and Black said he hadn't known anything about it. I didn't believe him but it didn't matter.

CHAPTER SIXTY

In these years I didn't sleep and when I slept I dreamt of violence. I dreamt of Iraq. I dreamt of movies I had seen. I would die in my dreams and not wake up. I'd be dead in my dreams and then die some more, and when I woke up I was tired. No matter what else, I was unhappy.

Days came like dead moths on the bathroom counter. I got a letter from some people who said I'd fucked up school so bad that I had to give all the money back for the last semester. They said I had to give the money back right away. So I had no choice and went and saw my parents about it. They gave me money. Still I didn't ever have money. I could get more money when school started up again, but I'd have to be real careful and I didn't think I could be careful because there was always so much to do and I couldn't get it all done and be careful.

Emily said we should get a dog and we did. We went to the animal shelter in Brook Park and got a dog for $60. It was a girl dog; Emily named her Livinia. Livinia was a mix of some kinds of hounds and she had a brown-grey coat that shone and she was very timid so we felt for her. And we said, We will protect her and she will be fine from now on forever. Emily said we had to quit dope and I said I would quit dope and she said she would too.

I went to the doctor, a psychiatrist. I told him I was fucked up. I had been to see a psychiatrist before. That had been at the VA, years ago, after Zoë left. I had seen this psychiatrist a couple months until one day I'd had to take Roy to the Bureau of

Motor Vehicles all the way on the West Side because Roy was living on the West Side and I had forgot about an appointment I had till about half an hour before. I called the VA and they didn't answer the phone so I left a message and said I had to cancel the appointment. When I called back to reschedule they didn't ever answer the phone so I left messages for a while. It was three years. They still hadn't returned my calls and Roy and I weren't even friends anymore.

Now I went to see this other doctor, Dr. Kaufmann. I could see him for free because the government was giving him money to study on people like me. He was over at the college hospital and he didn't want me to say anything but tell him numbers and go home and write numbers down, one through ten, all hours of the day and night, write these numbers down and keep track of them like they meant something and I didn't write the numbers down like I was supposed to and I felt like a goddamn criminal.

When Emily went to detox I was supposed to not do heroin. I was supposed to stay home and get sick. Emily had signed up for the detox. James Lightfoot had told her about it. He had told Emily that there was a detox at a hospital downtown that was free the first time you went; the state of Ohio paid for it. So she went to the detox and I stayed home that weekend with the dog and the dog hadn't been fixed yet and she was going around in a diaper and making sad faces because she missed Emily. And I think I meant to get sick. But I fucked up and shot dope all that weekend. James Lightfoot came over and we shot dope. James Lightfoot was still a friend of mine. He bought most all the weed that Emily and I grew and he'd track it out and sell it. Actually he was a lot of help to us sometimes; he was good at keeping up with things when he wasn't too fucking strung out. But he was still undeniably fucked in the head with the sadness and had the death wish bad enough that it was a mistake to have him around when you were trying not to shoot dope. So what happened was

James Lightfoot and I shot some dope and I didn't get sick like I was supposed to have. This was more fucking up.

I went Monday and got Emily from the detox. We stopped on the way back and bought some heroin. Things went pretty much back to normal and Emily was pissed at me because we were still on heroin and she said it was my fault.

One morning the landlord called and said he was coming over with an inspector from the city to inspect the house. Emily asked him when he was coming over. He said two hours. She said okay. The problem was the grow room. The plants were just beginning to flower. We had to tear them down. We had to take everything apart. There was nowhere to take the plants and they were too big and too many to hide, so I had to hack them into pieces and stuff them into garbage bags and put all the soil in garbage bags and stuff the garbage bags wherever they'd fit in the car while Emily was taking apart all the hardware. Then we took down the tent and scraped off the Mylar that was glued to the walls. It was a motherfucking disaster and it made it so we were even more fucked, but the landlord was none the wiser so there was that at least.

Black went to jail. I was coming out of the psychiatrist's office one evening when it was raining and I got a call from Raul. He told me. He said it was nothing major and Black'd probably get out on bail in a few days or maybe a week or two, but he said he'd sell me heroin till then if I wanted some heroin and I said I'd like to meet up with him right away. He had me meet him off of St. Clair. He was a while getting there. When he finally showed up it was almost ten o'clock. He said that he was sorry but he had been riding with his uncle and his uncle had got pulled over and the police had given them a hard time. I gave him some money and he gave me a bag of dope. The bag of dope was wrapped in a piece of white plastic torn off a shopping bag it looked like. I drove home.

Emily and I were going to split the heroin up. I caught a smell off the bag of heroin and I told Emily and she smelled it too and we agreed that it smelled like Raul ate a lot of fruit snacks. After we shot the dope I called Raul. He asked what I thought of the heroin. I said the heroin was fine and I asked him if he always was going to stick the heroin up his ass before he sold it to me. He laughed.

Dr. Kaufmann had made an appointment for me with a drug counselor at the hospital. So I went to that but the drug counselor's office wasn't well marked at all. So I couldn't find it and I walked around the hospital in circles looking for it. When I found it I was 15 minutes late but it wasn't my fault. They kept me waiting. Over an hour. Then I went through the whole thing with the nurse and she took my blood and asked me questions and she was very nice but the doctor, the drug counselor or whatever, was a dyed-in-the-wool motherfucker. I told him I didn't have any confidence in Suboxones on account of they didn't ever work on me at all. I tried them all the time. I'd get sick and I'd take a lot of them so as to not be sick and I could take four or even five, dissolving them under my tongue one after the other, and they wouldn't help me for shit. I was telling the truth but he said I was a liar. He asked me what I was seeing Dr. Kaufmann for. I said I thought I was seeing Dr. Kaufmann for PTSD and he asked what could I have PTSD from and I said I'd been in Iraq. He asked me when. I said I'd got there in '05 and left in '06. He said the war had been over by then. So I left because I couldn't stay there. And I remembered how when I was in Iraq I used to get chest pains. How I'd leave the wire all the fucking time and I started getting chest pains that would drop me to the floor like a heart attack and I couldn't breathe, and then Shoo took me to see the PA at the battalion aid station, Captain I've-Forgot-His-Fucking-Name. And the PA—not a doctor, mind you, but he acted enough like one—wouldn't see me and he told Shoo to tell me to come back at sick call the next morning. But I didn't. I just had the chest pains instead. Normally I wasn't around when they did sick call. Normally I was outside the wire maybe getting fucked up by a bomb or shot or something. I was nothing then and I'm still nothing.

CHAPTER SIXTY-ONE

What ended up happening was Emily and I were fighting a lot. She was blaming me for everything that was wrong with her and I wanted her to shut up sometimes. We were both doing as much dope as we could get our hands on, and we would be high as shit and I'd nod out in my chair a little and drop lit cigarettes in my lap. Then she'd come downstairs with her video camera and start chasing me around the house going, Look at you! Yer so fucking high it's disgusting! And I'd say what the fuck and she was high too and what did she mean.

One thing really fucking us up was the Oxys were running out. Soon we wouldn't be able to get them anymore. It wasn't Big's fault. Big would always get Oxys as long as they were making them. The problem was they weren't making them like they used to. They had started making them so they were like hard rubber and you couldn't crush them up, and if you did somehow, they'd gel up when you put water on them and it made it so you couldn't shoot them. There were still some old ones going around but they were running out fast. Emily and I couldn't do shit with anything we couldn't shoot. Soon we were going to be stuck with just heroin, and Big didn't sell heroin and we would be at the mercy of some dope boys, whom you couldn't count on for shit, and we would get sick a lot more.

School started in fall and I would go to class as much as I could because I had to and I had some luck with that. Emily always had to stay at school all day because she taught a remedial writing class for the undergraduates in addition to going to her own classes and her last class didn't get over with until eight at night on Tuesday and Thursday. So I spent much of the days at home alone and not doing the things I was supposed to be doing. I'd get so depressed I couldn't move. Emily would get to telling me I was a worthless fuck. And she was a cunt for that; but she had her reasons, I guess. All the same I didn't like it and it didn't help me.

There was a girl in one of my classes and we had talked before and I knew some about her. I knew that she had a kid and that things were tough for her. She wanted me to help her get some heroin. It seemed like the worst thing you could do, to give some kid's mom heroin. But she asked me a few times so I brought her back from school one day and we got some heroin and we shot up in the kitchen and she said that she liked me and I said that I liked her too and that I hoped she'd find somebody who'd love her like she deserved to be loved. Then she kissed me. I'd been hoping she wouldn't but I liked it. It was good to be kissed by her. It was good to be kissed by someone else. Her tits were hard and she pressed against me and grabbed my cock. I tried to take her pants off but she stopped me and said she was on the rag. I said fuck. She said, Let me lick it. I didn't want that because I hadn't taken a shower in almost three days and I hadn't cut my pubic hair in a long time. I tried to take her pants off again and she said again that she was on the rag and she kept saying, Let me lick it. Then she got on her knees in front of me and started fucking with my belt. There was nothing I could do so I put my cock in her mouth. I could smell my cock and I knew it must have tasted real bad but what was done was done and I came and it came out real hard and some of it bounced off her teeth and went up her nose. She wiped the come off and said she had come up her nose and I felt good about that and bad about that at the same time. We didn't say much after this and I drove her back to school. It was the last time we saw each other outside of school and when we saw each other at school after that we didn't look at one another. And I felt bad about this and about how life was just slow death and getting your stupid cock sucked at random when you weren't ready and how it was regrets and forgetting everything you ever had believed in.

PART SIX

A COMEDOWN

CHAPTER SIXTY-TWO

How do you get to be a scumbag?

I got to be a scumbag because I needed money and because I was hanging around dope boys too much.

The night wasn't especially good. We drove around all night, Raul and Rider and I. We were looking for a certain car. We were going to rob the guy who owned the car. But we didn't ever find him. We went to his house.

Rider said, "He's not here."

Raul said, "Are you sure this is his house?"

Rider said, "I'm positive."

But he said it like he wasn't positive.

Rider had a scar, a crescent that traced the left side of his face. It wasn't from an accident; someone had cut him. I bought heroin from Rider when there was nothing else. Rider was bad news. He had asked me if I could kill somebody for him. He needed me to kill somebody because he owed a lot of money and it was the best way to clear his debt. Rider was in trouble. He didn't tell me that part. He just said I'd make 10 racks if I killed this guy. Anyway I'd said no.

Rider was full of shit. He was the type who'd lie to you about what time of day it was and for no reason. He was the type to get people into fucked-up situations and hope that they'd perform miracles for him. Rider didn't ever carry his own weight. But he was Raul's boy. And Raul would believe him, like he'd believed him about this car.

Eventually I got tired of it.

I said to Raul, "This probably isn't happening."

Raul said, "This is some bullshit."

Rider said, "Man, this nigga's got at least a hundred racks."

But we were done listening to Rider.

We dropped Rider off. I was burned out and I felt like shit. I hated the way I felt.

I said to Raul, "What about the other thing? I can definitely do that."

He said, "Yeah. Let's do that."

I said, "All you have to do is drive. I'll do all the work."

He said okay.

It was a quarter to six in the morning and I was about to be sick. I had no heroin and I had no money and I owed Raul $600. He didn't want to front me anymore.

I said, "You know I can't do shit if I'm sick."

He had me take him to a trap house. He came out with a gram. He said that was it though. I dropped him off at his girl's house. I said I'd call him in the afternoon. Then I went home. It was a quarter to seven. Snow was on the ground. It was old snow, dirty and iced over. Sometimes I'd forget what month it was.

Emily and Livinia were in bed. I woke them. It was warm upstairs. My heart ached. It was good. Emily got up. Livinia went back under the covers; she liked it there; she liked to sleep in the morning.

Emily and I shot up and got ready to go. I dropped Emily off. She said she wouldn't mind taking the bus home. I'd said I had to go to my parents' house for something. She was fine with that: maybe my mom would give me some groceries to bring home; maybe my dad would give me some folding money.

I parked and I went to class. I wanted to feel as normal as I could feel for a few hours. I wanted to pretend I was polite society. I wasn't supposed to meet up with Raul till three o'clock. I got home at half past noon and I let Livinia out. I had been by the Wendy's and I'd bought her a cheeseburger. She wolfed the cheeseburger down in about two seconds and then she looked at me like, Where can we get another one of those?

She reminded me of myself, insatiable.

I shot the last of my dope. I smoked a cigarette.

IT HAD been about twenty hours since Black had called.

He'd said I was some shit.

I'd said, "Huh?"

He said, "You some shit."

"Hello? Black?"

"You gonna make me put my black mask on."

"What?"

"You gonna make me put my black mask on."

"I can't hear what you're saying."

"I'm gonna put my black mask on."

"What did I do?"

"Pay me, motherfucker."

Emily was watching TV. She said, "Who was that?"

I said, "It was Black."

"What did he say?"

I lit a cigarette and sat down.

"What did he say?"

"He said he's gonna put his black mask on."

"What?"

"That's what *I* said."

She kicked the end table. "Suck my dick, dude!"

"Shit! I dunno. That's what he said. He said he was gonna put his black mask on."

"What does that mean?"

"It doesn't mean anything. He's a fucking bitch."

RAUL CALLED at half past three. I was ready and I went out. I felt good. I was nervous, but not nervous in a bad way. I felt alive, that was all.

We met up a little after four. Raul had borrowed his cousin's car. A nondescript car, a few years old. Something grey and Japanese. Temp plates. It was perfect.

Raul was driving. We passed the bank I was supposed to rob. From the street you could see inside through the front window. The location didn't seem too bad, but when we went past the bank I saw something I didn't like.

I said, "This one's no good."

Raul said he thought it was a good bank to rob.

I said, "The tellers are behind bulletproof glass. It won't work."

"Grab one of the customers," he said.

"How about I grab your fucking grandmother? Let's find a different one."

We drove around and looked for something better. Then the banks were closing.

I said, "Fuck."

Raul said he knew a bank that stayed open late. "It doesn't close till seven," he said.

I said alright.

The bank was in a shopping center. It was an older shopping center and I thought that was good because the bank probably didn't have shit for security. The doors were old; the cameras were probably shitty.

I said, "This one's good. Let's wait till there's no people."

We waited. I was ready to go as soon as it was empty. I didn't want people in the way. I was wearing a hoodie and a knit hat. Raul had brought them for me. I had a can of bear spray. The bear spray was Emily's; she had it from when she'd been out in the woods in Washington State. I'd borrowed it without asking. I hadn't ever robbed a bank before. I didn't know what to expect. But I was fine with it. Just I didn't want people in the way.

I don't imagine that anyone goes in for robbery if they are not in some kind of desperation. Good or bad people has nothing to do with it; plenty of purely wicked motherfuckers won't ever rob shit. With robbery it's a matter of abasement. Are you abased? Careful then. You might rob something.

I owed some dope boys some money. I didn't give a fuck. Fuck Black and his fucking money. He could get it how he lived. I was only ever afraid of one thing in my life, that I wouldn't be able to get heroin. I wasn't ever more than twelve hours from total collapse. And there was the desperation. I was compromised.

RAUL WENT to take a piss. He went around the side of the building and pissed and he came back. "It's twenty to seven," he said.

"You're right," I said. "I'm gonna do it now. Fuck it."

There were three people working in the bank and there was one customer. The customer was a woman. There were two tellers who were young women and a manager who was an older man, and he was fat and just looked like shit, like a 60-something-years-old baby. Suspenders. You name it. He sat at a desk in an office. One wall of the office was glass and the manager watched me and I could feel he was sure of why I was there. I had the hoodie up and I was wearing my hat real low. But he didn't want to be sure. It was snowing outside. Maybe I was just cold. I went to the desk where they had the pens and the deposit slips. I took a deposit slip and wrote on it. I wrote the word *fuck* about ten times. Slowly. I was waiting for the customer to leave. She was a small woman, mid- to late 40s, a black wool coat; she had shoulder-length black hair with grey in it and was someone's mother.

She left.

I walked up to the counter and gave the note to the teller on the left. She didn't need to read the note. She got the money out. And the other teller was looking at me like, Aren't you going to rob me too?

I probably should have on account of I'd made this much trouble already.

But I didn't.

I didn't really want to rob anyone.

I just wanted some heroin.

I wanted it to be over.

I walked fast out the door and got in the car and lay down in the backseat.

I said, "I did it. Go."

Raul took off. Sirens were coming on but we had blended into the traffic and we'd already got away. I put the temp plate back in the window. The street was a river of light.

We split the money. He dropped me off at my car.

I said, "I need some dope."

He said he didn't have any.

"I'll call you in a minute," he said.

He called ten minutes later. "Call Black," he said.

I bought three grams from Black and paid him the money I owed and drove home. Emily was back at home already. I showed her the heroin and the money.

I said, "I robbed a bank."

She said, "I thought you were acting strange this morning."

I said I'd felt funny all day.

CHAPTER SIXTY-THREE

Emily was in the other room, on the mattress on the floor beneath the window, with the blankets twisted and disheveled. We couldn't be next to one another on account of our kicking and sweating and our throwing up into little plastic trash cans. I had to get up and do something. My legs were damp.

I stood in front of the kitchen sink for forty-five minutes, drinking water so I'd have something in my stomach apart from bile and snot, and down went the water and up came the water—part bile, part snot now—and didn't let go of my lip and hung down to the drain. It had been more than twenty-four hours since our last shots. All our credit was used up. We needed money. We were fucked.

When she moaned—though it hurt me and I could have cried and it would have cost me nothing—the moan was beautiful, and I felt an urge to run to her when she moaned and said "fuck" like she did. Her bottom lip was perfectly shaped. The beads of sweat were perfect. Her eyes closed and her shirt off. Her pajamas stuck to her. Her scent that was all of her. The strand of hair against her cheek to the corner of her mouth. We came in seconds. When you were sick that was all it took. I had to figure out what I was going to wear.

I left the house in some grey slacks and an oxford shirt that were from the thrift store, in a baseball hat my mom had given me and some phony eyeglasses and a peacoat. I brought a little green plastic trash can with me to throw up in. I was feeling melancholy, but it was a calming melancholy. Life was fucked but I was good. This was what I knew. And fate was fate. My heart was full and life was precious.

We had had a break from the snow and you could see the dormant grass. The day was cold but it was forgiving. It was time to commit a robbery. I drove by the bank. There was a police car parked across the street but the police car was empty. I turned onto the side street that was past the bank, and I threw up in the little green trash can. I took the side street down and turned left onto North Park, made the first left, and went halfway down and parked.

No plans. No stopwatch. No ski mask. No gun. Because I didn't like shit like this I didn't give a fuck about doing it the proper way. Emily was sick and all it was I had to rob the bank or go to jail and I could say I had tried. I figured the best thing would be to just go ahead and do it so I could find out what was going to happen. I got out of the car and started moving that way, stopping once to vomit on a tree lawn. When I got to the bank I took a look around for the policeman who belonged to the police car, and I saw the policeman walking half a block up and he turned to go into a bar.

Now would be fine.

The bank was busy but there were many tellers and the line moved quickly. I took an envelope out of my pocket and examined its contents. I had to puke. I unbuttoned the top button on my shirt and kind of pulled my peacoat over and threw up down my shirt. The lady behind me asked me if I was alright.

I said, "Yeah. Just a sneeze."

I threw up again.

"I think you're really sick."

"No, no, I'm fine," I said. "Man, I keep sneezing."

I was called to the counter. I took a piece of paper out of the envelope and unfolded it and handed it to the teller: "I received this in the mail yesterday."

The teller read the note; then she put some money on the counter. I took the money and the note, and I left. Once I was in the street I started running. I turned the car around and threw up all over myself and drove to North Park. If I made a right I'd be in Cleveland proper in about twenty seconds. If I made a left I'd be where rich people lived. I took a left and drove through Cleveland Heights. I laughed when I got away. When I passed Lee Road I knew I was home free. It was as if nothing had happened. I got home and Emily and the dog were on the couch. Emily had her eyes closed. I walked into the living room and got all the money out of my pockets.

"We need to get some dope. Right now."

She said, "You're such a badass."

I called Raul and said I'd like to meet up with him immediately. He said he'd meet me at the Subway at Mayfield and Warrensville. I got changed and Emily and I hit the road. Raul was actually on time for a change. Emily got in the backseat. I was so glad that I wasn't in jail and that we had lots of money. I bought all the heroin that he had in his pockets. Seven grams. Raul got out and Emily and I got off in the car. Big motherfucking shots we did. And our hearts were beating their wings slowly. We were saved. We felt like angels must feel like.

Seeing as we were both hungry we went to Subway and ordered some sandwiches. We ordered big. We even bought some of those cookies they have by the register. I tipped the sandwich artist $20. He said he liked my T-shirt.

Emily and I shot a fuckload of dope that night. We weren't worried; we knew we'd have it all next week and the week after and maybe the week after that.

I got a call from Joe. I hadn't heard from Joe in over a year. I said, "Joe, how the fuck are you doing? It's so fucking good to hear from you."

"Did you—uh—rob a bank today?"

"... No. Why?"

"They've got a picture of a guy who looks a lot like you on the news, and he robbed a bank."

"... Oh. Man, that's weird—No—Yeah, that definitely wasn't me. Strange. Huh ... Hey, man, I've got to go, alright? Okay, yeah. Listen, I'm gonna call you though. . . . Okay, later."

The news was over, so I went online. One of the stories on the home page of the local news channel was about the bank robbery. I clicked on the story and saw a surveillance photo of me that was pretty clear. I may as well have sat for an oil painting.

"I'm going to jail," I said.

Emily looked at the picture: "Holy shit."

"I'm fucked," I said. "Shit ... Fuck ... Fuck ... But who the fuck watches the Saturday local news broadcast? Nobody, right? No. . . . No. I'm alright. Look. It says they're looking for a guy who's six three. I'm five eleven. Fuck. Look at the fucking picture though. But you can't really tell it's me, can you?"

I shot half a gram of heroin to calm myself down.

I looked at the picture again.

"No," I said. "We're alright."

Getting rid of the money wasn't going to be a problem. Our rent was past due and we owed eleven hundred dollars. Eleven plus the seventeen hundred. Plus the five hundred I owed Pistol and the five hundred I owed Black. That was thirty-eight right there. That left just thirty-five and that would be gone in three weeks.

I slept well for the first time since I couldn't remember.

SUNDAY. I woke up and did a nice-size shot of heroin. I rolled out of bed and went down to the kitchen, cooked up the shot, and put it in a vein on top of my left foot. It itched some.

The actual getting high part of heroin was fine so long as you had a tolerance. It was more or less safe as milk like that. The first twenty seconds were quite fine, especially when you were getting off first thing in the morning. The only thing better than the first shot in the morning was the first shot after you'd been sick for a day or two. In those instances the 180-degree turn from abased wretchedness to resplendent consolation was something like a miracle.

The dope came up from my foot, the rush came on, and my blood sang nicely with it. My brain humming away. I sat in my blue chair and smoked a Pall Mall and thought about my problems.

I called Raul and told him I wanted to buy half an ounce of heroin. He said he was in Akron but he could do it when he got back and he'd call me as soon as he did. I took a shower and put on my cleanest clothes and drove out to visit my parents. My dad was in a good mood that day for some reason I couldn't have guessed at and my mom was trying to be cheerful and fussed over me and I felt bad. I was uncomfortable in comfortable places. Nice people looked so nice when you were on heroin.

"How's school?" my mom asked.

"It's okay," I said. "Most of my professors are alright. One of them's a prick, but the other three are good."

"Well, I'm glad that things are looking up," she said.

I said I was doing good as far as my GPA, better than I'd done in a while.

"How much more do you have to do?" my dad asked.

"I can get done in three semesters. I might have a credit hour or two left after that. But not much."

My mom asked if I was staying for dinner.

I said I was.

My dad cut up some leftover roast beef for their dogs. My mom did the dishes. I didn't ever have to do the dishes since I got back from Iraq. My mom thought I was a hero. I wasn't. But then I didn't try to correct her. Not that I wanted to lie by omission about being a hero. I just didn't want to have to explain anything.

It was dark when I drove home. I shot the last of my heroin. Emily and I had done three and a half grams apiece in a little over thirty hours. Seven hundred dollars.

Raul didn't get back from Akron until ten o'clock. He called me from his girl's apartment and said he had what I'd asked him for. I got the money together and I went out to see him. I called him when I got there. He came down. He got in on the passenger side. "Any of your people watch the local news?" I asked.

"No. Why?"

"They had a picture of me on there last night. It was very clearly me."

"I didn't watch it."

"Yeah. It's just got me worried."

"I robbed a guy at an ATM machine once," he said. "They had a picture of me on the news but they never caught me."

That was comforting.

I said, "I figured it's probably not a big deal. If I don't hear about it in the next couple days I'll never hear about it. I can't be doing this shit though. The shit's just too fucking dumb. You got that half?"

"Yeah, I got it," he said. "This shit's supposed to be pure fire. Be careful with it. I bought it down in Akron today. That's what I was doing. It's double-bagged because it stinks like straight heroin when you open it up."

I didn't check the bag. I had done right by him. We had robbed some shit together. I had bought a lot of grams from him. I figured if he was going to rip me off he'd have done it already. When I got home I found out I'd paid Raul thirteen hundred dollars for half an ounce of instant mashed potatoes. I called him. I said, "Raul, you know this is instant mashed potatoes, don't you?"

"I'll make it up to you," he said.

And he hung up.

Emily said, "What are you going to do?"

"Realistically there's nothing."

"You're going to let him get away with that shit?"

"Yeah pretty much."

"Those guys don't respect you."

"No, I don't imagine they do. Still you'd think just on principles of human decency he'd have had better manners than that."

"You should fucking kill that motherfucker."

"Eh."

I had a theory. My theory was that I was a piece of shit and deserved it when bad things happened to me.

Was I bitter?

A little, of course.

But a loss was a loss. You didn't ever get it back. Even if you recouped the money, the injury was still done. What was best was to write it off. So long as you didn't give a fuck you had them beat. Only a thirsty no-account fucking loser would resort to such tricks as selling a half ounce of instant mashed potatoes. So why countenance it. Countenancing it wasn't about to put dope in our veins. Morning would come soon. On its heels would ride the sickness. Moves had to be made. It was almost midnight.

I called Black. No answer.

I called Pistol. He picked up.

"Sorry to be calling so late," I said, "but if you could come through I'd take four right now for your trouble."

He said he couldn't do it. "It's been dead out here all day."

"Shit. Well hit me up whenever you get things together tomorrow. I'll take four for sure."

"Alright."

Rider's phone went straight to voice mail.

Nobody got on again until Tuesday and we were sick sick sick.

CHAPTER SIXTY-FOUR

Raul had said he was going to give me back some of the money he'd ripped me off for. He was going to pay me back in heroin. Which was fine because if he gave me cash I'd have just spent it on heroin anyway. Six of one, half dozen of the other.

It was night. He called and said his kid was in the hospital and he was going to be running a little late. And he was either on the way to or from the hospital when he was pulled over. He called me again. It was hard to hear him. "I'm about to get arrested," he said. "They're searching my car right now. Go to my mom's house and tell her I got locked up."

The line went dead. I put my coat on and left. I was at Raul's mom's house ten minutes later. I knocked on the side door. Nobody answered so I kept knocking. Eventually she opened the door.

I said, "Sorry to bother you, ma'am. But Raul called me a few minutes ago and said he was getting arrested. He asked me to come and tell you."

". . . Okay."

"When I talked to him he said the police were searching his car and they were going to find some heroin."

"Okay."

"Let me know if there's anything I can do."

"Sure. Thanks."

She closed the door lightly and then locked it. Pistol pulled into the driveway. I walked up to his car. He opened the driver door.

"What are you doing here?"

I told him what happened to Raul.

Pistol didn't say anything.

I said, "Do you have one you could spot me until tomorrow? I left in a hurry and I didn't bring any money with me. I'll definitely have you tomorrow though."

He didn't say anything.

He weighed out a gram.

I said thanks and I walked to the curb where I was parked and I got in my car and drove away. I thought about my theory again. *Let me know if there's anything I can do.* I was a real asshole. I'd been at those people's house trying to act like I was worried about Raul when the truth was I couldn't give so much of a fuck about a guy who wouldn't have pissed on me if I were on fire. And they knew that. I thought, Was I just being polite? And the answer was no, I was just being full of shit. What a fucking ghoul I was. And then I didn't know what their fucking problem was either, how they'd both acted like it was my fault. And that's how it is. The very same who bleed you dry and fuck you are as bitter toward you as if you were getting over on them. And they're half-right, and they're half-wrong. This is what we do to each other.

CHAPTER SIXTY-FIVE

Rider said he knew a bank in Bath, Ohio, that would be perfect to rob. This was more of Rider's bullshit. Like I'd forget he wanted me to kill a guy in Bath for him. He really thought we were going to drive out to Bath and I'd say, Okay, Rider, where's the bank? and he'd say, Change of plans, we're gonna go murder this nigga instead.

Rider was a piece of shit like that.

I told Rider he could drive if he wanted but I was going to rob a bank downtown. I went to pick him up in the morning. He was with Pistol. Pistol had brought a pistol for me, and he spotted me two grams of heroin. I said I'd bring him some money in the afternoon.

It was a school day and Emily was over at the school and I wanted to make sure she got her share of the heroin in case I went to jail. So we stopped there first. She came out of the main classroom building and met us in the parking lot across the street. I asked Rider to let her have the front seat, and he did.

"Is it good?" she asked.

"I haven't done any yet," I said. "Pistol calls it Gunsmoke."

"Gunsmoke?"

"That's what he calls it."

Emily and I shot up. The heroin was tremendous. It was black in the syringe. "Well," I said. "That's . . . really . . . fuckin nice. He must have made a mistake."

"Mmm . . ." Emily sighed. "This is some good shit."

I lit a cigarette and said I should be going. "I'll pick you up tonight."

"Okay," she said. "Be careful."

"I will, my love. Have a good afternoon."

Rider said we were the coolest white people he had ever met. Emily went back to school, and Rider asked to borrow my phone real quick. I gave my phone to him. Somebody picked up and Rider said, "Hello . . . Yeah. Right now. Yeah, I'm about to do it right now."

He was trying to sound like he was fine with it, even happy about it, but you could tell he was scared as shit. When he got done with the phone I asked him if he was sure he was good and he said he was. I dug around in the backseat looking for something to wear. Rider got in the driver seat. I lit another cigarette and told him I was ready. I had put on some Adidas track pants and a black fleece jacket and a balaclava.

He said, "You look mentally ill."

I said, "I am. Let's go."

The bank was only a few blocks west. We parked across the street out front and down a ways, facing east. "Keep the doors unlocked," I said. "I'll be back in less than two minutes."

I crossed the street. The pistol was in my waistband and neither of the two pairs of pants I was wearing was having an easy time staying up. So I only had one free hand. I went into the bank and moved to the counter. The bank was empty except for one teller—a woman—and two men—the manager and a client. I ignored the two men. They ignored me. They were talking business. I gave the note to the teller. She tossed some ones banded to a fifty onto the counter. I looked at her. She had a fat face and she glared at me with little red pig eyes. Her name tag said Sheina. I said, "Sheina, don't be ridiculous. You're better than that."

She cleared out the cash drawers and I was feeling an ocean of sympathy for her. There were oceans inside of me. It wasn't her fault she had little pig eyes. I knew that. You get the eyes you get. You don't have any say in it.

We were on the freeway, and Rider wanted to see the money. I started going through it and counting the bands and fanning out the loose bills and handing him half as I went along. He kept saying, "Gimme more. Gimme more. Gimme more."

There was a lot of traffic. We were as good as gone. Things were going well. Then Rider changed into the exit lane.

"Stay on the freeway," I said. "Take it to two seventy-one."

But he wasn't hearing me.

"Stay on the freeway, Rider. What the fuck are you doing, man? Don't get off here."

He ignored me.

"Stay on the fucking freeway, man."

He got off the freeway. Three exits down from where we had got on. And there was a police car rolling up at the bottom of the ramp. Rider started screaming: "OH, FUCK. OH, FUCK. NNNO. NNNO."

I said, "Goddamn stay cool, man. Just go slow. We have nothing to hide. We're just minding our own business. He won't chase us if we don't run on him. Look. We're cool. He's just sitting there. We're cool. Just go slow. Don't run on him."

The police car stood still. Rider was hyperventilating. We drove through the intersection. Then he veered onto a residential street that ran off of Superior. Three quarters of the way down he threw the car into park.

"What's up?" I asked.

Rider's eyes were coming out of his head. He started screaming again: "NO. NNNO. NNNO. FUCK THIS. I'M GONE. I'M GONE."

He got out of the car and walked away. I thought he had acted strangely. I didn't see what his fucking problem was.

I thought the best thing to do would be to get back on the freeway. So I did. I rode 90 east to 271. I smoked Pall Malls and set fire to the little bands from the money and dropped them in the ashtray. It was an okay time. The Gunsmoke still had me good. I wasn't worried about anything.

I got off the freeway at Chagrin and I got some burgers at the Wendy's there and I went home and took Livinia out and fed her. I called Pistol and said I had his money together. He told me to go ahead and come around.

"Do you have three and a half I could get?"

He said no problem.

When I met up with him I didn't say anything about Rider being a pussy. I didn't want to embarrass Rider. Plus I thought he might shoot me if I told anybody about how he'd acted. It wasn't the sort of thing he'd want people to know. I paid Pistol the money I owed him for the three and a half grams and gave him the clothes I'd worn during the robbery and asked him to get rid of them for me. I gave him back the pistol. I gave him $500 for his trouble.

CHAPTER SIXTY-SIX

I'd get sad as fuck when I thought about Emily and how I wasn't going to be there for her because I was going to jail soon. I wondered what would happen to her and what she would do. And we were sad when she found the abscess in her arm. Her forearms were swollen. There was all this shit in her right arm. She was pushing it out and she said, Look. It was like dirt. We cleaned it out and treated it with alcohol many times and the abscess got better but she was frightened and ashamed and it was terrible.

I thought, My poor angel.

I don't know. I could have still not gone to jail. It was mid-March and I had robbed something like seven or eight or nine banks and hadn't yet been arrested.

I don't think anybody cared. The police, I mean. This was just kid stuff, what I was doing. All it took was that you realized there was nothing stopping you and then you wet your beak.

Still you knew the police were fucking dangerous.

I think maybe I was about to give up.

RIDER SAID, "The nigga's some shit. My dude's baby's mom and his son live with that nigga and he beats the shit out of them."

Rider was trying to appeal to my sense of white-boy chivalry so I'd go kill the Bath guy for him. Going on five months he'd been trying to talk me into killing this guy.

I said, "Why doesn't your dude call the police or child protective services or something?"

"Cuz the nigga's got control of that bitch. She won't say anything against him. She's a fiend. He's got her on that shit."

"You mean heroin?"

Rider looked out the passenger window.

"Why doesn't your dude just do it himself?" I asked. "It would save him some money."

"Because they'll *know* he did it. That's why we need you. You don't know the nigga from Adam, so they won't be able to link you to him."

The baby started yelling in the backseat. Rider turned around and told the baby to shut up.

"Shut up, lil nigga," he said.

Rider had brought the baby with him. The baby wasn't two years old. It couldn't even talk. It wasn't Rider's baby. Rider said the baby belonged to a bitch he was fucking.

Rider hadn't said anything about a baby. I'd called him looking for heroin and he'd said he had some, so I'd gone to meet him. I'd parked out front of some apartments and called him and he'd come out with this baby and got in the car and he didn't have any heroin. I was crushed.

He said, "I have to go to Varsity Blue real fast."

Varsity Blue was a clothing store where they sold jerseys and sneakers and tracksuits. They didn't sell heroin at Varsity Blue. But it was wasn't far, just down Superior. I parked and Rider went into the store. He left me with the baby and the baby was crawling all over the place. The baby grabbed my lighter out of the cup holder and tried to chew on it. I took the lighter back and said, "You probably don't want to do that. You don't know where it's been."

The baby made a real serious face and thought about this.

Rider was in the store almost an hour and he didn't buy anything. He came out of the store looking pissed off. He was pissed off because he was a fucking loser. I was a fucking loser but Rider was worse.

He got in and I drove across the street to the McDonald's and bought the baby some French fries. Rider tried to call some people but nobody picked up.

I said, "Now what?"

He said, "Drive over to Clair."

I did. We went up a ways and he told me to park in front of a convenience store. He went inside for an hour and came out and told me it was dead.

Then I got a text from Pistol: "Where are you."

"Clair."

"What did u want 2 do?"

"3."

"Belmar n 20."

This was good. Rider's mom lived on Belmar. I could leave him and the baby there. Meanwhile Rider was talking and I wasn't listening and he was saying he wanted me to take him over to the West Side and he could get me some heroin over there.

"Can't do it," I said. "I've got to run up to Belmar."

"But I just talked to my partner over there. He says he's got that fire."

"You just said it was dead."

"I meant it's dead on the East Side."

"I'm meeting Pistol over on Belmar."

"Drive me to the West Side first."

"No. Can't do it. Sorry."

"It won't take long."

"It'll take hours. Everything you do takes hours. You do nothing and it takes you hours."

"What about the three hundred dollars you owe me?"

"I paid you that shit already."

"You didn't pay me."

"I don't have time for this."

"WHY WOULD I LIE ABOUT THREE HUNDRED PETTY-

ASS DOLLARS?" he said. "I SPEND THAT SHIT ON LUNCH, NIGGA. I SPEND THAT SHIT ON LUNCH."

I put the car in gear. Rider grabbed my arm.

"What? You want to have a fistfight with a fucking baby in the car? What are you, fucking nuts?"

Rider didn't move.

I said, "I've got four hundred dollars on me. I have to give three hundred and sixty to Pistol. I don't know what to tell you. You can fuck that up, or I can drop you and the baby off on your street. You're making me late. I'm about to be in a bad way. Emily is about to be in a bad way. I've got to get this heroin fast and I've got to take it over to her at school. That's what I've got to do right now. I've looked out for you before and you know that. But I can't right at this moment. So I'm asking you as nicely as I know how, please spare me this bullshit today. I've got a lot on my mind. But call me when you get this other thing together tonight. We'll do that for sure. My dude's got the money for you as soon as you get it together."

He calmed down some: "He just wants one zone?"

"Yeah, I think so. But if it's right he'll get more."

WHEN I saw Pistol he said Raul might be getting out soon. I said that was good and I got well and I went up to the school and Emily got well. That evening Rider called and said he had picked up. I went to see him and he had four ounces of coke on him. I tried some of it and it was right. I said if he gave me the one ounce I'd run it up to my dude and bring him back nine hundred dollars. But he said no.

"It'll save me a trip," I said. "It's the same dude as last time. He's good for it."

Rider said he couldn't front me that much. He needed the cash up front. I knew he was just saying that because he wanted to step on the coke before we met up again. But there was nothing I could do. I needed money. If I didn't get money I got sick.

Time was working against me. Motherfuckers knew that. That's how they get over on you.

I said I'd get the money.

I called James Lightfoot. He told me to come through. I did and he gave me a thousand dollars. Then Rider wasn't picking up his phone. Two hours later he called me back. I met up with him and he gave me the coke. I took the coke to James's house. The coke was fucked now. Rider hadn't just stepped on it, he'd murdered it. That was Rider.

I was thinking James thought I had ripped him off.

"Who the fuck is this guy?" he asked.

"He's a piece of shit," I said.

"Then why do you fuck with him?"

That was a good question. I didn't have a ready answer for it. All I could say was I felt like shit about it. Anyway, James took it easy on me. He didn't give me a hard time about the loss he took even though it was my fault. He already knew I was a fuckup. He knew that I'd fuck up but I wouldn't rip him off. As it stood, James and I needed money and I knew one way of getting it.

CHAPTER SIXTY-SEVEN

James was in the driver seat. I was in the passenger seat. I was well. I was wearing an Indians hat and eating an apple. James said, "There might be cameras on the light poles."

I said, "I've been looking and I haven't seen any."

"Are you sure?"

"Pretty sure. I don't think they get many robberies out this way. It should be alright."

We were parked in front of the Whole Foods. I had a good view of the bank. I had a gun. It wasn't my gun. I forget who had given it to me. Funny thing about guns. If you're known to rob things people will just give you guns. It's kind of like sponsoring missionaries.

I discarded the apple; I said, "You ready?"

James said he was ready.

"Alright. When you see me come out, start driving toward the exit over there. I'll walk through those two rows of cars and I'll get in and we'll go. Too easy."

"Okay," he said. "Just remember that the back driver-side door is broken."

"Okay."

I fixed the hat so it was low over my eyes, and I got out of the car and walked into the bank. It was the first warm day of the year and the door of the bank was open so I went in and went about robbing it. But this didn't go well. I got the first drawer but then the teller got to being obstinate and the manager wouldn't shut the fuck up. He kept telling me to take my hat off, calling me sir the whole goddamn time, and when I didn't take my hat off he hit a button. I didn't know what the button was about. I figured it was a silent alarm. Then I looked behind me and saw the door was closing on its own. Hydraulics, I guess. The bank was full of people. This motherfucker was trying to lock me in with them. The people were all looking at me now, looking at me trying to rob this bank. I could see they were thinking, Is this all there is to it? I didn't want to disappoint them. I pulled the gun and put three shots into the ceiling: BAM BAM BAM.

"I DON'T EVEN WANT YOUR FUCKING MONEY."

BAM BAM—two more in the roof.

I walked to the counter and pointed the gun at the manager. He either had pissed or was in the act of pissing. I said to him, "Open the fucking door, you bitch, or the next one goes in your face."

"Just go," he said.

The door was free. I walked out. I walked off the curb and through the two rows of cars in the parking lot. James was pulling around. I grabbed the handle of the back driver-side door and pulled it but the door wouldn't open. I kept pulling. I knocked on the window. I said, "Unlock the shit."

James said, "IT'S. FUCKING. BROKEN."

Right. I scrambled around the back of the car and got in on the front passenger side. James hit the gas and we were gone.

"What the fuck happened? Did you shoot somebody?"

"Fuck no."

I was counting the money.

"Fuck . . . Fuck . . . Fuck . . . I didn't do so good, James. Those people were very fucking rude in there. They tried to lock me in the fucking bank. That's never happened before."

"How much did you get?" he asked.

". . . Two thousandish."

"Shit."

"I know, man. I'm sorry. It was no good. The fucking manager was yelling at me. This old cunt didn't give a shit if everybody died. It was fucking bad. Not at all how they're supposed to act. Really reckless of them. Over pieces of paper."

I gave James half the money.

"I'm sorry, man."

"It's alright," he said. "At least we got away."

"Yeah. Fuck. I've got to break this gun down and get rid of it."

THAT AFTERNOON Emily and I went to the dog park with Livinia. The weather had been lovely all day. It seemed it was a good day to go to a dog park, and it would have been if it weren't for the other dogs. The other dogs fucked with Livinia, they ganged up on her and chased her around and got on her back and drooled on her and nipped her.

"I don't like this shit at all," Emily said.

A chow was in the act of dominating Livinia.

"I think she's alright," I said. "I dunno. I think it's how they play, but I can't tell. Does she not like it? I get so worried. Fuck fuck fuck."

"Well I don't fucking like it," Emily said. "I think we should stop bringing her here. I think it scares her."

"But she gets so excited when we bring her here. It's not bad when there's no other dogs. I like it when it's just the three of us out here."

Livinia got up and broke free and she was off and running. She was always the fastest dog at the dog park and she was hard to catch, but the ground there was deep with ugly pea gravel and it inevitably tripped her up and the other dogs would catch her; there were just too many dogs and they'd corner her.

Another couple came over to us.

"Nice dog," said the woman. "She's pretty and so fast."

"Thanks," said Emily. "Which one's your dog?"

"The chow."

"Oh. He's a frisky little guy."

"Do you live around here?"

"We live in University Heights," Emily answered.

"What do you do?"

I didn't like that. I disliked what-do-you-do people. What kind of people were these?

"We go to CSU," Emily said, blushing. "I'm a graduate assistant there."

"Do you go to CSU too?" she asked me.

I knew what she was thinking; you look a little old for that.

"Yeah," I said. "I got started late. G.I. Bill."

"You were in the military?" the man asked.

"Yeah."

"What branch?"

"Army."

"You go overseas?"

"Iraq."

"Jeff's a cop," said the woman.

"Cleveland Heights Police Department," he said.

"Come here, Livinia!" Emily called. "Come here, girl! Come here!"

"How do you like it?"

"It's a job," he said.

"Yeah. A job's pretty hard to come by these days. You're lucky."

Livinia came running and she stood between Emily's legs. Emily asked her who was a good girl.

I lit a cigarette: "It was a nice day today, wasn't it?"

The woman agreed that it had been a nice day.

"What do you guys think of this dog park?" I asked. "Do you think it's sanitary having all these dogs shit and piss all over this pea gravel? It seems like, you know, with grass or something, it would absorb it, process it all. But with this gravel . . . where's it all go? It just gets churned up in the gravel, I imagine. I know you pick up the shit when they shit, but there's still the residue.

It can't be healthy, can it? It has to build up over time. Do you think there's such a thing as cholera for dogs?"

It was dusk. The air was cold all of a sudden. Jeff went to pick up some dogshit from the chow.

"We have to be going," said Emily. "I have a paper I've got to finish. It was nice meeting you."

CHAPTER SIXTY-EIGHT

was in a cold sweat. I was driving; Raul and Emily were in the car with me. Raul had got sentenced for the heroin. The hearing had been that Monday. It was Tuesday. Raul said the judge had let him out because it was his birthday that week. He'd ordered Raul to turn himself in on Friday so he could go to prison. Raul would be gone for a year and a half. Possession with intent to distribute. It seemed like a long time to me but I didn't know anything.

Emily and I needed to find some heroin. We had been sick for two days. Raul was having no luck helping us. He was calling everyone he knew. No one was picking up. Probably because he was going to prison he was making people nervous.

I was throwing up in the little green trash can. I was always careful to keep an eye on the road when I did this. Emily said, "Hang in there, baby. Something's got to come through soon. It's been too long."

"I'm right as rain," I said and wiped the vomit off my chin with the back of my hand, "close enough for rock and roll."

Raul didn't give any sign that he minded my vomiting in the little green trash can while I was driving. He just sat there, calm as if nothing foul were transpiring. It was polite of him.

"Hold on," he said. "Here we go."

A silver Mitsubishi Galant pulled out in front of us.

"Pull up beside that car," he said.

I did and Raul rolled the window down and waved at the Galant. "He's about to turn," he said. "Get behind him and follow him."

The Galant turned off St. Clair and onto a side street and pulled over. The passenger got out and came up to Raul's window. I held up seven $20 bills and said, "I got one forty on a gram if you can help me out. I'm kind of desperate right now, you know."

After saying this I realized I might have fucked up Raul's percentage. But then I needed to get this done, so fuck it. If Raul wanted a cut he could get it from them. Plus it wasn't like he didn't owe me money and it wasn't like I was ever going to see a dime of that shit.

The passenger said alright. He said to follow. He got back in the Galant and it went on. We followed it around a few streets. Raul's phone rang. He picked up and said alright; and he turned to me and said, "Pull over. Park here."

The Galant went up a little farther ahead and stopped. The passenger got out again and walked down the middle of the street with his hands cupped over his mouth. Then a kid came out from around the back of a house and went out into the street to talk to the passenger. They talked and the kid went back and the passenger turned and waved to Raul.

Raul said, "Give me the money."

He got out of the car and walked up to the Galant and got in the backseat.

"That was so cool," Emily said. "Did that guy do a little birdcall?"

I agreed it was cool. "These guys don't fuck around," I said. "I wish they were our dope boys."

It wasn't two minutes and the kid was back with the heroin. He dropped it off in the Galant and went on his way. Raul got out and brought it to us. The Galant drove off. I took the scale out of the armrest and put a card on the scale and zeroed it. I put the heroin on the card.

I said to Emily, "It's one over."

"Beautiful," she said.

"It smells like fire too."

And we got off. The heroin was good. Very good. Not stepped-all-over like the dope we were accustomed to buying, the dope we were accustomed to selling our souls for.

I said, "Holy fuck."

It was hitting me hard like it used to.

Emily said, "Hot damn."

It was hitting her hard too.

I said to Raul, "I don't suppose you'll give me these dudes' number."

"They told me not to," he said.

I didn't believe him, but whatever.

CHAPTER SIXTY-NINE

It was Raul's idea to rob the bank at Warrensville and Mayfield. He wanted to put some money up before he went to prison. We were headed to the bank: Raul, Rider, James, and I. I was hoping that with three inside we'd take a lot more money and somebody could mind the doors, which would be a must as we were unarmed. I had asked James if he wanted to drive. I thought it was going to turn out better than it did.

I wasn't worried about what James would do. I wasn't worried about Raul either. I was mostly just worried about what Rider would do. Rider didn't handle pressure well. But he was Raul's boy and I was hoping Raul's presence would give him courage.

There were bad signs from the start. We were driving around the bank and checking things out and I wanted to see it from the other side of the street.

"Let's just do it," Raul said.

"No," I said. "Let's take another look."

We crossed Mayfield on Warrensville. We were heading south and I could see the parking lot behind the buildings that were across the street from the bank and four police cars parked in the lot. They were all of them facing the same way, ready to roll out.

"Look at that shit," I said. "You see? We'd have been fucked."

"What am I doing?" James asked.

I said, "Just keep driving straight."

We ended up driving over to Belmar and we tried to rally there. James traded Rider an ounce of loud for a few grams of heroin. I took Raul aside.

I said, "What about this shit Rider's always talking about in Bath? That's a lot of money."

"What do you mean?"

"You know. Killing that guy."

He said, "That's some bullshit."

"Figures."

"That dude out in Bath is a state's witness."

"Huh."

"Yeah. He's a witness in a case against a nigga Rider owes fourteen racks to."

"Man, that Rider's no good."

"So what's up?" James asked when we got back to the car. "Are we doing anything or what?"

Rider said he needed to go to Severance. I said I thought we could rob a bank on Chagrin Boulevard. James said that would be fine. Those of us who were junkies shot some heroin. We headed out and dropped Rider off. I was glad to be rid of him. We got to Chagrin and looked at two different banks and decided on the one that was in a shopping center. It was a newer bank, and I was sure that it would have man-trap doors. I said to Raul, "When we're leaving it's important that we hold the doors open. If we get caught between the doors going out they'll lock us in and we'll go to jail and it will be a terrible thing. So I'm gonna hold the inside door open while you get the door to the outside. Then you hold that one open and we go out together. This is very important."

"I got you," he said.

I said to James, "Let us out on the sidewalk. We'll walk there and you pull into the parking lot without us. That way nobody will notice you till it's over."

We drove up and down the street once more so as to have time to smoke a last cigarette. Then James pulled around and let us out at the curb. It was in the mid-40s outside, nowhere near cold enough to warrant all the winter shit that Raul and I were wearing. I had on James's frock coat and his Shaker High School ski cap and his neck warmer. Raul was wearing a parka and a balaclava that covered his whole face like he was a ninja. We were halfway across the parking lot.

"You good?"

I heard a muffled affirmative.

We got to the door and I had pulled the neck warmer up so it covered the lower half of my face. I went in saying, "ATTICA. ATTICA. ATTICA ATTICA."

Raul wasn't saying shit. I looked over my shoulder, looked over the other shoulder. Raul wasn't there. I looked back at the bank employees. They looked at me. I said not to tell anyone. I turned around and walked out. Raul was in the backseat of the car. James had waited for me.

I said, "Let's go."

We got out onto Chagrin.

I said, "Raul, what the fuck are you doing to me? That was fucking embarrassing."

James said, "Fuck!"

I turned around and saw police cars a little ways off in the oncoming lane.

I said, "Pull over."

"What?"

"Pull over to the side of the road. Just do it. Raul, lie down."

James pulled off to the side of the road.

The police came on and they went by.

James said, "Shit."

I said, "That's what they always do. But seriously, Raul, what the fuck? How could you do that. That was fucking infamous."

Raul said he was sorry.

I said, "Forget it. I know another bank we can rob."

James said, "You want to try this shit again?"

I said I did.

I said, "Raul, do you still want to rob a bank today?"

He said he did.

"Are you sure though?"

He said he was sure.

I said, "Alright. Let's go."

James said, "Fuck it."

We parked on Van Aken. We were up at Shaker Square. I said, "Raul, you go in first and I'll follow ten seconds after you. James, when we go in you go around the curb to the right and we'll get in around the corner. Raul, are you ready?"

"Give me a minute," he said.

James said, "Are you gonna do this fucking shit or not?"

Raul said, "You want to do this?"

James called him a pussy: "Fuckin pussy."

"Everybody calm the fuck down," I said. "Let's not argue."

So James and Raul made peace. And James let Raul have his sunglasses to better hide his eyes. We drove up alongside the bank.

"Alright," I said. "Raul, you go ahead. I'll be right after you. Count on it."

Raul got out and walked into the bank. I counted to five and said, "Well, here I go."

I went in the bank and Raul was standing with his back against the back wall. He was standing across from the counter. There was only one teller. It was a small bank. The teller was looking at Raul and she looked scared because he was dressed up like a ninja in a parka and it was 40 degrees outside.

Then Raul ran. He ran past me and out of the bank. I was so goddamn depressed. The teller's drawer was open and I leaned over the counter and cleared the money out of it. On my way out I passed a man coming in and he pretended that he didn't notice me. Out on the sidewalk I went the wrong way at first; then I remembered what I'd told James to do and I went around the corner. Raul wasn't in the car.

"Where's Raul?" I asked.

James said, "Fuck. I don't know."

"Shit."

James started to drive away. I took a breath.

"We can't leave him. We have to look for him."

James shook his head no and said, "Okay."

He turned the car around and we looked for Raul. We were going at parade speed and it was a fuckload of people around so this wasn't good. But James kept his cool. We were out there forever but he didn't panic. And Raul came running from behind us and got in the backseat and said, "GO GO GO."

We drove away.

"How much did you get?"

"I dunno," I said. "Count it."

I gave the money to Raul. He counted it.

"Thirteen hundred."

"You didn't get anything?"

He said, "No."

I DIDN'T care about what happened to the money. I think Raul kept all of it. I didn't ask. I was tired of everything. This had nearly been curtains for me and I felt like a fucking purse snatcher. James called later and said Raul had tossed his sunglasses away when he was running from the bank. James said he had paid three hundred dollars for those sunglasses. I went over to his place and gave him three hundred dollars. I had lost three hundred dollars on the bank robbery. And with his sunglasses money, James had broke even, minus the gas and a balaclava, which he had written off as negligible.

CHAPTER SEVENTY

It was Sunday morning. Emily and Livinia were asleep in the bed and I listened to them breathing, their little clicks and drafts, and the light glowed through the drawn shade. It would be a fine day, and I knew it just as well as anyone did.

When you have been afraid for a long time, you see how fear will come and go. How fear will overtake you. How fear will subside. How fear guts you for a moment. How hope puts you back together, till the fear comes back. Then the hope. Then the fear. I was only ever afraid of one thing in my life, and that was heroin.

There'd been a dozen witnesses the other day. Somebody had to have got the plates off James's car what with all the running around and the frock coats and the parkas and the bank being robbed.

Raul had left his fucking mask outside the bank.

We were fucked.

Yet I was still free.

I went downstairs and I called Black.

I lit a cigarette.

Black said to come on.

I drove to the Walgreens over on Monticello. I was thinking about PFC Arnold, a kid I knew in Iraq, how the old boys used to say he was a shitbag. Then he got killed and they said he was a good guy, and his name was in with the good names, the names of our war dead, and if a shitbag talked bad about the name when the old boys were around he risked a punch in the mouth.

Honestly I didn't know much about him; I can't say we were

friends. They put us in the same room and he lived in the room eight months till he was killed. I helped pack out his things. We spoke now and then and I'd had nothing against him. He cut my hair a few times. I'd thought he was alright, but not all the time.

He'd been a handsome enough motherfucker, 20 when he was killed, born and raised in Oklahoma, didn't know his dad. His mom had raised him on her own. She was a hooker. He'd tell you that. But he didn't say it like it was a bad thing. He liked his mom. And he was polite, always polite, so polite that when people talked shit to him they got away with it. Somebody might say, "Arnold, you're a retarded shitbag."

And he'd blush and look all around himself as if to say, Yes, I know. And isn't it wonderful?

His wife was a few years older than he was. They knew each other from Oklahoma and had five kids together. Only it was maybe that two of them were his. His wife fucked around on him a lot. But then he fucked around on his wife a lot too and it didn't seem to be a deal breaker for either one that the other was fucking around. They were Wiccans. So was his mom. They were all Wiccans.

His mom had come down to Fort Hood before we left for Iraq. It was Halloween. She was dressed up as a cat, with the black tights and the little furry ears on. It was nighttime and her hair was black. I met her by the stairs in the barracks. She was smoking a cigarette. She asked if she could use my phone. She was a while on the phone and I smoked two cigarettes. She said she was sorry she'd taken so long. I said I hadn't noticed she was a cat. She said cats were her familiars. I didn't know what that meant. She said it was a Wiccan thing. I still didn't know what it meant. Did they help her do magic? No. It wasn't really like that. It was more like she had a special connection with cats, especially black cats. It was hard to explain. She asked me for a cigarette and I gave her one.

She asked if I had a girlfriend.

I said I was getting married in two weeks.

She said, "I know a lot of guys still mess around though. I don't judge. I get it. I understand why you guys want to have sex before you go over there."

I said I wasn't trying to fuck around on my girl. "Sorry."

She asked if I knew Arnold. I said he was in my company. She said she was his mom.

She couldn't have been much older than thirty.

"I was a child when I had him," she said.

"Doesn't Arnold live off-post?"

She said yeah. She had hooked up with some guys though and she was partying with them, but they were lame-os. She asked if she could use my phone again.

When she was on the phone there was a guy I knew but didn't know; he was wearing JNCOs and a wifebeater and a cowboy hat and was skinny. He came outside.

She said, "I'm on the phone."

He lingered, but only a minute. She gave me the phone back.

"That was one of the lame-os," she said. "Ugh."

Her people took forever to come get her. We went to my room so she wouldn't have to wait outside. She asked if she could smoke. We smoked cigarettes and talked about what kind of music she liked. She liked alternative rock.

She borrowed my phone again. Eventually her people came and got her. I waited half an hour; then I jerked off.

A few days later Arnold asked me if I'd had sex with his mom. "She said you're really nice," he said.

I said I hadn't had sex with his mom but I thought she was a really nice lady.

Arnold liked that. He was good.

It was three guys from Second Platoon who had fucked his mom, three guys from Second Platoon who had run a train on her. People talked shit to him about that. But Arnold was alright. "She made them wear condoms," he said.

Then we went over to Iraq. And then some other shit happened and whatever. Soon it was July. And Arnold got killed in July. It wasn't long after he had come back from midtour leave. I remember because he had chlamydia and gonorrhea at the time. He had caught the chlamydia off a girl at Camp Liberty when he'd been on his way home, and he'd given it to his wife when he had got there, and his wife had given him the gonorrhea, or it was the other way around. Anyway. He was driving a Bradley out on Route Martha one night and he ran over an anti-tank mine, which killed him instantly. I wasn't there. I had been across the way on Route Polk then. But Shoo had been there and he told me how it had been fucked up because Arnold was a mess. Shoo said he'd looked down into the driver hatch and it was so bad he couldn't make heads or tails of it.

Thus Arnold was a great guy and everybody said as much. Which was odd since there had been a lot of people wanting to beat the fuck out of him, and I'll tell you why: Arnold wanted to be a computer genius. He used to say he was going to bring down Bill Gates. Those were his exact words: *bring down Bill Gates*. That's what he used to say he was going to do. And he came up with a computer virus, for practice, I guess. This was when there was an insatiable demand for fuck videos, and Arnold put together a massive file of that shit—gang bangs, barely legal, cum shots, anal, ass to mouth, lesbians, bukkake, MILFs, humiliation—and he got his virus on there one way or another and went around talking up this big porno file he had and he got some guys to download it off him and those guys shared it with other guys and soon all the computers began to crash and the computers were forever worthless after that. Nothing could be done for the computers. So a lot of people wanted to beat the fuck out of Arnold. But nobody did. Then he got killed and they said he was good. And maybe if I had got killed I'd have always been good.

But I'm forgetting . . .

. . .

I WAS waiting in the parking lot at the Walgreens. Black drove up and he parked and he got into my car. He fronted me 2 grams.

He was wearing a new tracksuit.

Adidas.

Yellow on purple.

I said to him, "Cool tracksuit."

He said, "It is, right?"

He was happy about his tracksuit and it was an alright tracksuit and we pretended like we were friends. But we weren't friends. I was just a dope fiend as far as he cared. And for my part, if I ever knew a better way to get heroin, I'd just as soon not see him again.

I said, "You hear from Raul yet?"

He said he had.

"How is he?"

"He's good."

"Tell him what's up for me, will you."

"I will."

"This makes it six, right?"

"Yeah."

"What about that other thing we were talking about? You still want to do that?"

"Yeah."

"Okay. What about tomorrow?"

"Tomorrow's good."

"Alright. I'll call you."

I took Warrensville back. I went into the house quietly and went upstairs quietly and sat down on the edge of the bed, beside Emily. She stirred and murmured. I leaned over and kissed her ear.

"Guess what."

"What."

"I just saw Black."

"Yeah?"

"Guess what else."

"What else."

"He's bought himself a new tracksuit."

"So?"

"So it's purple with yellow stripes and he really likes it a lot."

She rolled over and I pressed the bag of heroin into the palm of her hand.

"Care to weigh it out?"

"Mm-mm."

"You don't have to do it now on my account," I said. "We can wait till later if you want to go back to sleep."

"No," she said. "You go ahead and weigh it out. I'll be down in a second. I have to pee."

"I love you."

"Mmm. I love you too."

I went downstairs and split up the dope. It was three light. Never mind. I'd get it back. I put a shot together. There was hope for me yet. Life was good when you were cooking up a shot of dope; in those moments every dope boy in the world was your friend and you didn't think about the things you'd done wrong and fucked up, the years you'd wasted. I put the needle in my arm. The needle was dull so it pushed the vein away when it was going in. But the vein couldn't run forever. I felt a little pop and my blood flashed in the rig. I sent it home.

ACKNOWLEDGMENTS

It was fall of 2013. I was twenty-eight years old and I'd been locked up about two and a half years by then. I got a letter from Matthew Johnson. He had read an article about me being a criminal and he wanted to introduce himself and he sent me a five-dollar money order and asked me to write him back. So I wrote him back and said thanks for the five dollars and yeah it sucks being in prison but I'll be alright. He sent me some books to read. One of the books was a collection of Barry Hannah stories. He asked me to call him and I did and he asked what I thought of the books and I said I liked the Barry Hannah book the best. Looking back now, I think this thing with the Barry Hannah book was a test, and I'd passed. And Matthew sent me some more books and one of them was *Hill William* by Scott McClanahan, and I said that I liked that one the best and Matthew said maybe I ought to try and write a book. He said he and his friend Gian were publishers. They were called Tyrant Books. And I said I really appreciated all the books but I didn't think I'd be able to write a whole book. A little story, a poem maybe I could handle, but a long-ass book . . .

Anyway he talked me into it. I started working on the fucker that February. I sent Matthew some pages. He said they were good and send some more. I did. He said keep going. Then I sent him some more pages and he said, Alright, everything you've sent up to now was horrible but these last pages aren't so bad and maybe we can do this.

Two and a half years went by. The book wasn't done yet. We had about two-thirds of a manuscript. I didn't know how the fuck I was gonna finish it. Things had got so bad I could tell that Matthew couldn't think about the fucking manuscript without getting depressed real bad.

Enter Josh Polikov.

Josh was working for Matthew and Matthew said to him, Yer gonna help me with this.

So he and Josh were going through it and Josh found some old pages I'd written that actually weren't terrible and he showed them to Matthew and Matthew agreed that they weren't actually terrible and Matthew sent them to me and said, Do something with these.

And that's how I finished the manuscript.

We still weren't done, not even close.

The manuscript wasn't so much a manuscript as it was a plastic bin full of paper. Every page had been rewritten one hundred times over. There was no Word file. It had all been done on a typewriter. Any given page, sometimes the first version was the best, sometimes the seventy-ninth; and Gian DiTrapano was supposed to edit this shit and turn it into an actual coherent thing. Which somehow he did. And he did such a good fucking job of it that Tim O'Connell from Knopf thought it'd be a good idea to buy the publishing rights to the manuscript from Tyrant. This was in February 2017, about exactly three years since we started.

We still weren't fucking done.

Tim O'Connell said he liked the manuscript a lot but I needed to get a little better at writing before he'd print the thing and he said I'd need to rewrite it again. So I about died. But then I got to rewriting it again. And I was looking at Tim's edits. And there were some big changes. And I was like, Tim, what about these changes? I dunno. He said, The changes are good. I said, Yeah, well . . . And it was kind of a thing. And then we all talked on the phone, Matthew and Tim and this lady (Adeline Manson) and I. And they said to the lady, Tell Nico what you told us. And she said, When I read your version I thought the main character was an asshole, and when I read Tim's version I thought the main character was an asshole but I kind of liked him.

So that settled it. And we finished writing the book after that. And if you've read this book and you thought the main character was an asshole but you kind of liked him, that was all because of Tim O'Connell.

Tim and his brilliant assistant, Anna Kaufman, really did work absurdly hard getting this manuscript into shape, and if they hadn't helped me out so much then you'd have never read this book, and I am very much indebted to them and also to Daniel Novack, who gave me good advice that I was all too glad to take, and to Susan M. S. Brown, who did copyedits for this book and saved me from more than a few errors that would have caused me no end of embarrassment. Any mistakes in the text are mine and I insisted on their being in there.

I was very lucky. I've had a lot of help. I should not forget to mention Rosemary Carroll. Rosemary looked over all our contracts and watched out for us whenever we needed watching out for. And in our dark days she assured Matthew that he wasn't wasting his time on me.